MW00893052

off
SIDES
ANDI JAXON

Cover Image: Katie Cadwallader Photography
Cover Model: Austin & Lance
Cover Design: Y'all That Graphic
Editing: Rumi Khan
Proofing: BSS
Formatting: Andi Jaxon

BLURB

The captain of the hockey team has a lot of responsibilities but when it's just us, all he wants is to be my *good boy*.

Senior year should have been the same as the previous years: football, hook ups, and homework.
But after the season ended, somehow, Joey Carpenter happened.
He's weaseled his way under my skin. Into my heart.
The strong, intimidating, hockey player melts so beautifully for me and I'm addicted.
He pretends like he doesn't need anyone, but I see him.
See what he really needs.
The longing to be cared for is there in his eyes.
I desperately want to give it to him.
If I'm being honest with myself, I need to matter.
I need to save him.
Save him from himself.
Save him from his family.

Will I be able to convince him that he deserves to be loved without conditions or will they leave him ragged and broken?

Off Sides is a one night stand to lovers, hockey, romance with daddy vibes and angst.

Dear reader,

While I tried to keep to the timeline laid out in *Hidden Scars* and *Blurred Lines*, these two were not having it. They had a mission of their own and said to hell with my timeline. So if you notice some discrepancies, I beg you to ignore them. Nick and Joey sure did.

Please skip the next page to avoid spoilers if you don't want the content warning.

CONTENT WARNING

Death of parent (cancer) - off page, emotional abandonment of a parent, disappearance of a high school girlfriend, substance abuse by a sibling, knife fight (sibling not main character), degradation, mental health rep (anxiety, lack of self worth, panic, and one character gets triggered into a panic attack), slap on the face by a parent.

For all the oldest children who were forced to take on too much responsibility, I see you. For the kids who needed their parents but weren't the priority, I see you too.

PROLOGUE

joey

Banging on my bedroom door wakes me, just like it does every morning for the last few years. Since Dad died of cancer when I was fourteen and Mom had to start working overtime to make ends meet, I've had to take on the responsibility of raising my siblings.

"I'm up!" I yell and sit up when the banging starts again. Charlotte, my little sister, huffs and runs down the hallway. The floorboard outside her door squeaks as she hurries to get dressed.

I drag my ass out of bed, pull on the jeans I dropped on the floor last night, and grab a hoodie before heading downstairs to make sure Charlotte and Mathew eat before getting on the bus.

I grab some bread to pop in the toaster and scramble some eggs. Matt wants cheese on his; Char wants salt but no pepper.

I get them plated up and on the table, when a cloud of perfume comes down the hallway.

"Charlie! Stop spraying that!" Matt yells from his room.

"Fuck off, Matty!" she screeches back using the nickname he hates.

"Both of you, come eat. You're running out of time." I pinch the bridge of my nose and sigh. I'm so tired.

Char drops down in her seat and eats the eggs but eyes the bread like she's afraid it's going to bite her.

"What's your deal?" I lean against the counter and watch her push the toast off her plate.

"I can't eat carbs, they make you fat." She looks at me like I'm an idiot and it makes me want to punch something. I'm so tired of all these fad diets and social media telling everyone that you have to be a specific size and shape to be attractive. She's sixteen, for fuck's sake.

"No, they don't. Carbs are fuel for your body. Eat things like bread and pasta in moderation and you'll be fine." Being an athlete means I know a lot about nutrition. Over the years, we've been taught how to fuel and condition our bodies for optimal performance, even as teenagers. I'm seventeen and I've been paying attention to how I fuel my body for years already.

Matt scarfs down his food so fast I don't know how he doesn't choke on it, then we're grabbing backpacks and hoodies, and I snag the uneaten toast, before running out the door to catch the bus.

This is the last year we'll all be in the same school since I graduate in June. Char is a sophomore and Matt is a freshman so I can keep an eye on both of them. Matt is a shithead but he's my little brother and I have to try to keep him out of trouble. Every year it gets harder.

When I'm not at school, I'm at hockey practice. I don't have time to raise my siblings but I still do it because I'm the oldest.

We make it to school and Matt disappears with a group of kids that are trouble. Great. I shake my head and sigh, knowing I'll have to deal with it, but I don't have the energy today.

"You know he's getting into a fight at lunch, right?" Charlotte stops next to me, but her face is in her phone.

Exhaustion has my shoulders dropping.

"Who's he fighting?"

"That kid with green hair and a spiked choker." She clicks the gum in her mouth. "Hangs out with Darius and Mark."

"Awesome." I let out a breath and run my hand through my hair. "Get to class, I'll see you later."

"Yup." She walks off toward her group of friends and I head to my first period, dreading what my day is going to bring.

I barely stayed awake through my first-period English class, was late to second-period history, and my stomach was growling loud enough to be a distraction through Algebra II, but I've finally made it to lunch. I have no idea where this fucking fight is supposed to happen, Char didn't know, so I'm on the lookout for the group of dumbasses.

I'm so hungry, though. Hustling to the cafeteria, I grab a tray, not caring what's on it as long as it makes the hunger pains stop.

I've barely sat down next to my best friend, Josh, when I hear it.

"Fight! Fight! Fight!" being chanted.

"Fuck's sake!" I throw my tray across the floor in my frustration and take off toward the noise with Josh on my heels. I'm so tired of dealing with my brother's bullshit. We're all struggling since Dad died but he's the only one making it everyone else's problem.

A crowd has formed around my dumbass little brother and Evan, the green haired kid with black eyeliner, a punk style, and a fuck-you attitude. Honestly, the two are pretty evenly matched and I'm not sure who would win but I'm not going to find out either.

Josh and I push our way through the students, all chanting and itching to watch the show. I'm almost to Matt when Evan pulls a switchblade out of his pocket and flicks it open.

What the fuck!

My heart starts to race as fear for my brother floods my system. He can't get hurt. Mom will kill me. It's my responsibility to keep him safe.

I've failed.

"Shit," Josh mutters under his breath. "You grab Matt, I'll get Evan."

"You're a fucking pussy!" Matt yells at Evan. "You're so scared of getting your ass beat you brought a knife!"

Shut the fuck up!

If we make it out of this without getting stabbed, I'm going to beat his ass myself.

I'm to the front of the crowd and Josh is almost in position, but I can see the next movement before it happens. Evan's body tenses and he lunges for Matt. I yell "No" and dive for my brother, shoving him out of the way, but I'm not fast enough.

Evan's blade arcs through the air, slicing Matt's arm open. Girls in the crowd scream, and there's a wrestling sound behind me that I'm hoping is Josh getting the knife from Evan because I'm too focused on my stupid brother to check.

Blood trails down his arm, dripping onto the floor. Matt's face is a mixture of fear and adrenaline. The pain hasn't hit him yet, but it will.

I grab his arm and force him down the hallway away from everyone before turning to look at him.

"Oh my God!" Charlotte yells when she catches up to us and sees the blood. "Is he okay? What the fuck, Matt?!"

She smacks his other arm and I lift the bleeding one up to get a better look. It's pretty deep.

"You might need stitches," I sigh. That means Mom is definitely going to find out about this. We're so fucked.

"No, just wrap it up. I'm fine." His face pales at the idea of going to the hospital and since I've been playing hockey most of my life, none of us are shy about blood or wounds. We know how to take care of cuts and nose bleeds.

"You're not fine." I shove him into the boys' bathroom so I can clean it up and get a better look. Charlotte apparently gives no fucks and follows after us.

"You can't be in here." Matt glares at her but all she does is lift an eyebrow at him.

"You're an idiot," she scoffs and pulls a first aid kit from her backpack.

I look at her, confused as to why she carries that around with her. It must show on my face because she rolls her eyes at me.

"Between hockey and this ass running his mouth, I never know who's going to be bleeding or when." She hands me the case and I set it on the sink, clicking the lid open. She has a point.

I get the cut cleaned up, listening to the teachers in the hallway yelling at students to break it up and hauling Evan and Josh to the office. A few people are loud enough for me to hear them say Evan was fighting Matt while Josh was trying to be helpful. It's only a matter of time before they notice the blood on the floor and follow it in here. Matt is going to be suspended at best, expelled at worst. What the hell am I supposed to do if he's suspended? I can't miss that much school just to sit with his ass at home.

The cut is on Matt's inner, upper arm and the edges don't want to stay together.

"I don't have butterflies, you need stitches," I tell him, again.

"Please, Joey. I don't want Mom to know." He sounds like a little kid and it breaks my heart a little.

Glancing up at him, I see the tears welling in his eyes and the slight tremble of his lip. Charlotte puts a hand on his shoulder and looks at me for answers I don't have.

"There's no way we can hide this from her." I find some antibacterial ointment and slather it on some gauze then wrap it as best I can, but it doesn't take long for blood to seep through. "I'm sorry, man, you have to go. I can't fix this."

A sob escapes him and he covers his face with his good hand. I pull him into my chest and wrap my arms around him in a hug. Charlotte wipes a tear from her eye and I pull her into me too. For just a second, we stand there and the weight of the world is heavy on my shoulders. None of us want to burden Mom. She works so hard to keep us afloat, but she still has Dad's medical bills on top of everything else. Cancer is not a cheap disease. It takes everything from you then demands more.

The door opens and Mr. Phillips stops in the doorway.

"Miss Carpenter, what are you doing in here?" he asks quietly.

She sniffs and straightens her spine, refusing to let anyone but me see her crumble. She wipes her face, turns to face him, and pops her hip.

"Making sure my brother was okay?" she sasses him and Matt snorts a laugh into my chest before standing up and wiping his own face.

"Go to class."

She grabs her stuff and with one more glance at Matt, she leaves.

"Come on, Matt, we have to call your mom." Mr. Phillips doesn't sound any more excited about this than we are.

"He needs stitches."

Mr. Phillips stops and looks between us, concern pulling his eyebrows together.

"Stitches?"

"Evan cut him." I lift the arm in question and the gauze I put on is already starting to leak.

"Oh!" The teacher rushes forward and grabs Matt, rushing him to the office and the school nurse more than likely. I follow behind them. Evan is nowhere to be seen and Josh is sitting on a chair.

"You okay, man?" he asks Matt, then gets up and follows us when he sees the blood dripping down his arm.

Guilt churns my stomach until I'm ready to throw up but there's nothing to come out. I want to punch something, pace, scream, but I can't. I have to hold it together because that's my job. Everyone is allowed to break but me. Never me.

Being the oldest means I have to keep it together when I want to fall apart. Char and Matt look to me to stand strong during the hard times but no one is ever there when I need it.

The nurse forces me and Josh out of the room and the vice principal, Mr. Clouse, calls me into his office to call my mom.

I tell Mr. Clouse the number to her cellphone and wait while he dials and puts her on speakerphone.

"Hello?" Mom sounds tired when she answers. She's almost done with her shift and this is day five in a row of twelve-hour shifts.

"Mrs. Carpenter, this is Mr. Clouse from Hillsbury High School."

She sighs and I can picture her shoulders dropping.

"I'm assuming you have Mathew in your office?"

"He is up here being treated by the nurse. Unfortunately, he needs medical attention that we can't provide. We can either have him taken via ambulance or you can come get him but it appears that he needs stitches."

She's quiet for a beat.

"Stitches? For what? What happened?" she demands, the exhaustion of a few minutes ago replaced with fear.

"He got into a fight with another student who had a knife. Matt got cut on his arm."

Movement outside the door of the office pulls my attention and I watch as two police officers come in and move past the door.

Is Evan going to be arrested?

"I'm on my way, I'll be there in a few minutes," my mother says and hangs up.

Mr. Clouse looks at me with his arms clasped on his desk.

"Is he going to be suspended?" I chew on my thumbnail even though it's so short it's bleeding and sore.

"Yes," he sighs.

My head floods with schedules and how I'm going to get everywhere I need to, like practice and school, while Matt is at home. I don't trust him enough to be left unattended for that long. He'll get bored and leave the house, find trouble, and probably get arrested.

I scrub my hands over my face and wish I could disappear yet feel guilty for wanting to at the same time. Mom needs help. I get that. She didn't plan to be raising kids on her own. She didn't expect to lose the love of her life to cancer and be left with a mountain of debt.

But I also promised Dad I would look out for Char and Matt. I promised to do my best to help Mom because she was going to need me after he was gone. My entire future has been planned so that I can stay here and play hockey so I'm still around to help out after I graduate.

I want to break down. I want someone to tell me this isn't my fault or my responsibility. Matt is a dumbass and acting out for attention because he didn't process Dad's death and feels abandoned by Mom. I had hockey to focus on and use to work my grief and anger out, Charlotte did dance, Matt had nothing.

"You can go back to class," Mr. Clouse says. My stomach tightens as I force myself to stand.

"Can I check on him?" I pop my knuckles just for something to do, a nervous habit I can't seem to quit.

"Sure, if the nurse says it's okay."

I'm out the door and down the hallway in the blink of an eye. With my hand on the doorknob, I knock as I turn the handle.

"I just wanted to check and make sure he's okay," I rush the words out when the nurse, Miss Beverly, looks over her shoulder at me. "Our Mom is on her way. Can I just sit in here with him until she gets here?"

She sighs and flicks her gaze to a box of gloves on the wall. "Put those on and come here."

I drop my backpack and pull on the blue gloves.

"Hold your hand right here, keep pressure on it." She shows me how she wants me to do it, corrects my hold, then steps back. "I'm going to need a statement from both of you, the police will too after your mom gets here."

Matt's shoulders droop and he drops his chin to his chest.

"I don't want to go," he whispers.

"You need stitches, you don't have a choice. They had to call her."

With his free hand, he wipes his face then leans forward to press his head against my chest. It's the first time he's reached out for physical comfort in years. Since both of my hands are on his arm, I can't hug him back and it kills me. He may be fourteen but he's still a kid. He needs his parents.

"I'm sorry I'm not Dad," I whisper into his hair, and he lets out a little whimper like he wants to sob but won't let himself do it.

Yelling comes from outside and we both turn to watch through the door. We know that voice and that tone. Mom is here and she's pissed.

She's never been physically abusive, never laid hands on us, but words cut deeper than a knife sometimes. I was younger than Matt is now when I had to step up and help raise my siblings while also taking care of my dad who was wasting away. It took two years for him to pass. Two years for us to watch and wait and wonder if today was the day.

I grit my teeth and square my shoulders as I wait for her to come in here and tell me what a fuckup I am. Matt is desperately trying to pull back the tears but all he's doing is hyperventilating now.

Mom comes in, scared and furious with wide eyes and tension vibrating the air around her.

"What the fuck?!" she all but screams. The harsh sound bounces off the walls and makes us flinch.

"I-I-I-I'm s-s-s-sorry." Matt struggles to get the words out between the too fast breaths. My hands are still keeping pressure on his arm so I can't even comfort him. Part of me wants to punch him, though, because he's an idiot.

Mom's cold eyes flick to mine like I hold the answers. But I don't. I'm almost four years older than him.

"How could you let this happen?" she demands, shoving me out of the way and pulling the gauze back to look. "Jesus fucking Christ." She looks around the space and points to the packets of gauze for me to hand to her.

Humiliation burns the back of my throat as she gives directions and I hand her what she needs. She gets a thick patch on and tapes it down to keep pressure on it until she takes him to the hospital.

She jerks him off the table hard enough that he stumbles. Turning those cold, exhausted eyes to me, she shakes her head before she says, "All I've ever asked of you is to keep him out of trouble."

CHAPTER 1

nick

The music in the club is deafening and the writhing bodies on the dance floor means it's hot, but there's a heaviness in the air that feels like sex and pleasure. Gay clubs are a gift from the gods, and you can't convince me otherwise. It's a safe place in a world that isn't.

The bass vibrates my bones, possibility hums along my skin, and arousal hits my veins like adrenaline. It's been a long season with not much time for sexy fun times, so tonight, I'm on the hunt. I need to come, and at this point, I don't care if it's down a throat or in an ass.

Since it's December in Denver, it's cold as fuck, but as I strip off my jacket and check it at the door, I get some interested looks. A twink at the bar damn near has his chin on the floor. I send him a wink and scan the room. I'm not really in the mood for a twink tonight. No, tonight, I want a guy like me. A jock who will put up a little fight before dropping to his knees for me. I want a bit of a challenge.

My gaze lands on a few guys but none that really pull at me, so I head to the bar to order a beer. I've got time to wait for the right one.

The twink with long dark hair draping over one shoulder comes over and sits on the stool next to me. His ripped jeans look like they were painted on, and the fishnet shirt shows off his lean, pale chest. He's sexy, and he knows it.

"Well, hello there." He leans into my space, placing a hand on my knee as he speaks to me.

"Hello," I flirt a little, running my fingers along the sensitive flesh on the inside of his arm as I lift my beer to my lips.

"What are you in the mood for tonight, sugar?" He drags his lip between his teeth, looking me over again and pausing at my groin. "I promise I'm a good *fucking* time."

I cup his jaw and run my thumb across his lower lip. "I'm sure you are, sweet boy, but I'm on the hunt for a different kind of prey tonight."

He sticks his tongue out and huffs, but he wishes me a good hunt and stalks off. I'm enjoying the sway of his ass in those jeans when movement at the door catches my attention.

Who do we have here?

Looks to be about six-foot-two, solid as a brick wall, with an angular jaw and hair that brushes the collar of his hoodie which has the Darby U logo on it. That could work in my favor. His body language and the way he holds himself definitely says athlete, and I'm already dying for a taste of him.

The guy looks around, a little nervous if I had to guess. He's standing on the balls of his feet, rubbing his hands together, and his eyes are a bit wide.

I'm not trying to hide that I'm staring, so when his eyes meet mine, he smirks and heads toward the bar. He gives me some distance but watches me with interest. Okay, I can work with that.

My time on a football field, reading players, gives me an advantage. I can read people, anticipate their next moves, especially athletes. If he's at Darby, he's not a football player or I would know him. No, I'm betting hockey with that build. I desperately want to lift that hoodie and see what's under it. Taste his skin. Watch him squirm.

The man gets a beer and turns his back to the bar, looking out at the dance floor before his eyes flit back to mine. With a little head tilt and a lifted eyebrow, he asks if I want to join him among the throng of people.

I lift my chin and stand from my stool. He falls into step next to me and we move into the group of mostly dancing men.

We're forced closer together by the crowd, and at his hesitation, I reach for his arm to hook around my neck, then grip his hips, entangling our legs so our pelvises are flush. He gasps at the contact and squeezes the back of my neck.

His reaction catches me off guard. It's so *innocent*.

Leaning in so I can speak into his ear over the music, I ask, "First time?"

"No," he says quickly, but it's obvious to me he doesn't have much experience here. It wasn't what I was looking for, but I find myself wanting this anyway.

Our bodies sway, grinding, chasing pleasure to the beat of the music. In the semi-darkness of the room, where we can get lost in the crowd, I let him get used to me. He has another beer and a shot of something. The alcohol is loosening him up, but he's still in his right mind.

I'm hard in my jeans, my hands under his shirt when he kisses me. Hard, demanding lips crash into mine, and I instantly open for him. I want his taste on my tongue, his moans in my lungs.

This stranger controls my mouth while I control his body. It's a heady combination of control and submission that I've never experienced before. I didn't expect this from him, but I like it.

He cups my face in both hands, groaning into my mouth when I grab his ass and thrust against him. I need to come. Holy fuck, do I need to come. If he doesn't stop fucking my mouth with his tongue, I'm going to embarrass myself right here on the damn dance floor.

"Fuck, wait," I manage to get out, and he leans his forehead against mine.

"Don't stop," he pants. His eyes are squeezed tightly shut like he's in the sweetest kind of pain.

"I'll take care of you, come on." I kiss him quickly and grab his hand, pulling him from the dance floor and into one of the semi-private booths in the back. There's no light back here so you can't get a clear image of what's happening, but you can tell there are people back here.

I shove him in the booth and pull the little curtain closed. It's only half of a curtain so the waitstaff can see if there are people in here, but it's better than nothing. He's sitting sideways on the booth seat with his back against the wall and one foot on the floor, his legs spread for me. Luckily there's no table to get in the way of what I want to do.

"Open those pants, pretty boy," I demand, breathing hard as I tamp down my need to bend him over and fuck him senseless. No, I want his dick in my mouth. He pops the button and groans as his zipper comes down, giving his impressive cock room. Kneeling on the floor, I settle between his thighs and grip him tight as I look up at his hooded gaze.

"I'm on PrEP, you?" I ask.

"Yeah, I'm good." He nods, and I swallow his uncut cock. In one go, he's in the back of my throat, and he shouts. His hips buck off the plastic of the bench. "Holy fuck."

His cheeks are red, and he grips my hair but doesn't pull as I bob on him a few times. Saliva is already dripping down his shaft, and I want more. I let him go with a pop and pull on his pants so I can get to his hole. He adjusts to give me better access, and I suck him back into my mouth as my fingers find what I'm looking for.

My fingers freeze and my eyes snap to his when I find it wet and sloppy.

The knowing grin this guy sends me damn near has my balls seizing. He's a surprise at every turn.

"I was already fucked once tonight but couldn't come. Wanna help me out?" His breathing is ragged as I press two fingers in. He's slick with cum and I groan around his dick. How did I misread him so badly? Was he uncertain because of his need to get off? Does he have some kind of performance anxiety or was he afraid of being slut-shamed?

"If I make you come, I'm fucking you afterward," I tell him in no uncertain terms.

He smirks at me and bites his lip. "Fair is fair. Earn it and you can use me."

Jesus. Fucking. Christ.

It takes me a minute to find it, but when I drag my fingers over his prostate, he whimpers and arches into me. I smile around his dick and keep a steady rhythm on that magic spot until he can't keep still. His hips roll and his fists clench as he rides the power of pleasure. He's almost past the point of no return, and for a split second, I contemplate pulling away and letting him suffer for a minute longer. But my own need to be buried deep inside of him is too fucking strong.

"Oh fuck," he whimpers before the salty tang of his cum hits the back of my tongue, and I swallow around him. My throat milks every drop out of his balls while he buries his face in his arms and moans like the little whore he is tonight. Used and abused and sexy as fuck.

He's limp and his breathing is ragged as I let him fall from between my lips and slip my fingers from him.

He groans as I stand and open my pants. My own dick is angry and red and ready for some goddamn relief. I push his hip until he's half on his side, his shoulders still elevated in the corner, so he's looking at me as I spread his cheeks and find his hole. I waste no time working him open, just slide all the way to the hilt in a solid thrust of my hips.

"Such a good little slutty boy," I moan with one hand gripping his thigh and the other gripping his hair. I pull out slowly, and he whimpers before I snap my hips sharply, taking him deep and hard, enjoying the way his body sucks me in and holds me tight.

"Come for me," he whispers in an innocent tone that belies what we're doing. "Fill me up."

Holy fucking cum gods, nothing in my life has ever been as hot as this exact moment. I have no control over my orgasm as it bursts from my body. My knees buckle, and I have to lean on the back of the bench and his thigh or I'll fall. I've never experienced an orgasm like this, have it last this long, or have it ride me like it was going for gold at the Olympics.

I can't breathe or think. I'm barely able to hold on as my eyes roll back in my head. Someone is moaning and I think it's me, but I honestly have no fucking idea anymore. My hips buck of their own accord for long minutes until they finally stop, and I sag over his body. I don't even know his name, but I really fucking want to. I have to see him again. Just to see if it's this good a second time. This man will be my undoing if we can repeat this. And I definitely want a repeat.

CHAPTER 2

joey

As soon as he's able to stand, I pull up my pants and bolt. What the fuck was I thinking? What an idiot.

Anxiety licks at my insides as I rush from the club and call an Uber once I'm on the next block. Jesus, fuck. *Why?*

I run a hand through my hair, that my mom bitches is too long, and pull my hood up to help block the biting wind. It's winter in downtown Denver, and I'm in jeans and a sweatshirt. *Great plan, genius.* My phone beeps, telling me my driver is pulling up, and I turn around to find a silver SUV pulling to a stop next to the sidewalk. The window rolls down about an inch, and I hear a female voice ask, "Are you Joey?"

I hold up my phone next to the window so she can see I'm the one she's supposed to be picking up, and she unlocks the doors for me to climb in. She doesn't try to chat with me on the drive, which I'm grateful for. My knee bounces, and I chew on my thumbnail as I stare out the window at the city passing by me.

What if someone recognized me? I'm the captain of the hockey team at one of the biggest universities in town. It's entirely possible someone in there knew who I was. I don't want the drama of coming out my senior year. All I want is to finish the season and graduate.

My stomach clenches, and I rub a hand over it. The feel of the logo on the fabric has me looking down at it. We pass under a streetlamp, and the Darby U logo glows up at me. Holy fuck. Seriously? *Way to be inconspicuous, dumbass.*

I groan and cover my eyes with my hand.

"Hey, if you need to puke, let me know so I can pull over," the driver says, and I give her a thumbs-up instead of speaking.

Images from the club flash in my head. The flashing colored lights made it harder to see, but from what I could tell, he was beautiful. Muscular enough to push me around and do what he wanted with me, not that I fought him. I've never hooked up with a stranger in a bar before. Meeting up with some hookup I've been chatting with and letting him fuck me, sure.

But it wasn't great, and I was still horny, so I let my dick lead me to a club. A place I knew I could find someone to fuck me.

I groan again as the car pulls to a stop. I peek out from my fingers and see my dorm, so I get out and wave at the driver. All I can think about right now are my bad decisions and how much I need a shower.

Since it's almost Christmas, no one has games right now, so the jock building is only about half full. Looks like tonight is a typical clusterfuck of drinking and being dumbasses. I just don't care. Get alcohol poisoning and enjoy explaining that to Coach at practice tomorrow.

Guilt eats at me as I bypass the screaming freshmen and sophomores and hit the button for the elevator while cum drips from my ass. The doors slide open, and I step inside, grateful it's empty, and lean against the handrail on the back wall. I'm exhausted.

The ride up is quick, and my roommate is out, so I don't need to pretend everything is fine. I just strip my clothes off and get in the shower. The hot water pounding on my muscles relaxes my body. I'm almost boneless as the steam fills the room and I scrub the night from my skin. Maybe I can forget how amazing that guy felt against me, inside me. I don't have time for a relationship or even a fuck buddy, really. I'm busy until the season is over, and unless the person I'm trying to talk to is an athlete, they don't get that. Hockey comes first. It has to.

I'm pretty sure I hear my door open and close while I'm shutting off the water, but my roommate, Bryce, doesn't knock or talk to me through the door. Hopefully, he's passed out before I get out there.

I dry off and wrap the blue towel around my hips before digging in my dresser for clothes. Since Bryce is also a hockey player, we've changed in the locker rooms a bunch so none of us have much modesty anymore. Bodies are bodies, get over it.

I pull on underwear and a T-shirt and toss my towel into the bathroom. Bryce is face down in his pillow, cuddling it, and I'm pretty sure drooling, so I flick the lights off and lie down. Once I crawl into bed, my body is tired from the long season and tonight's activities, and I'm frustrated when I don't fall asleep easily.

Instead, I stare at the ceiling and replay my night. Finally, **Wants_2_Bone** and I were able to meet up. I should have known he wouldn't know what he was doing, he was too cocky, but desperate times and all that. When I was left wanting, I allowed my dick to tell me where to go. It's not often I have a free night, and damn it, I wanted to get off. When my eyes met that guy at the bar, electricity lit me up, and even though I didn't know what I was doing, I tried to play it cool. Since he asked if I was experienced, I'm guessing I failed there, but it didn't matter. His lips on mine were pure magic. The way he controlled my body while I explored his mouth was perfection. I was able to give up control to him and sink into that feeling. It was a freedom I've never experienced before.

A lot of the time, I struggle to be comfortable with someone controlling my movements. Hell, I've never been able to come so easily, especially with a partner. Was I able to for him because I was already on edge?

That has to be it. Nothing else makes sense.

Right?

I don't know him so there's no way it could have been him, and there's no way I can test the theory since I don't even know his name. Not that I would be able to ask him for a repeat. I also have responsibilities and I can't let sex distract me from them.

With a huff, I roll over and face the wall, punching my pillow into a better shape and forcing my eyes closed.

Eventually, I'm able to fall asleep but it's restless. I toss and turn all night, despite being exhausted. My alarm goes off at five thirty, and I get up. Technically, I don't have to go to the gym right now since we're on a two-week break for Christmas and New Year's, but I'm not sleeping so I might as well get my workout in. Even though we don't have practice or games, we still have to stay in shape or Coach will kick our asses. Our first practice after the break will be brutal so that he can see who stuck with it.

Bryce is still passed out, and I slap his ass hard on my way past him. He jerks awake with a yell and rubs at the spot while I change into workout clothes.

"What the fuck, man?" he yells at me through his pillow.

"Time for the gym, let's go."

He rolls over and looks at me like I've grown a second head.

"You're fucking with me, right?"

I pull a hoodie on over my T-shirt and look at him. "Do I look like I'm fucking with you?" I grab some socks and my gym shoes, then sit on my bed to pull them on. "Just because we don't have practice doesn't mean you can skip the gym. It's better to keep the routine up."

I finish tying my shoes and stand up, looking expectantly at my roommate. He grumbles but gets up and gets changed.

I pat him on the shoulder as I go to fill my water bottle. "Good man."

"Fuck off, Carp."

I stop in the doorway and point at him, "That's fuck off, *Captain*."

He throws a half-full water bottle at me, but I duck with a chuckle, so it slams into the door.

Once we find our earbuds and phones, we head to the elevator, then down to the gym. When we get inside, I'm surprised Preston Carmichael isn't on a treadmill already. He's normally finishing up as I get in, the crazy bastard. Dude is intense. There's something going on with him, Brendon Oiler, and Jeremy Albrooke, but I can't figure out what. Oiler and Albrooke were hooking up for a while, but I think that's ended. They were not at all subtle about it, though I think they thought they were. Everyone knew.

I don't know, maybe Carmichael threw a wrench in the hookups? I can't see him being a homophobe, but I've been wrong before. It's weird. Carmichael is a dick to everyone, no one is given a pass, but most of the team ignores him. Albrooke fights back, and every once in a while, Oiler and Carmichael come to blows too.

I shake off the thought as I pull my hoodie off and stretch. The pull of my muscles forces a groan from me. My ass is a bit tender this morning, which makes my face flush. I'm hoping the workout will quiet my head enough that I can take a decent nap. I'm tired.

Starting slow on the treadmill to warm up with music blasting in my ears, I'm about a mile into my run when the gym door opens again, letting a blast of cold air sweep through the space. Bryce is on the treadmill next to me, going slower than a fucking snail this morning. In the mirror that the treadmills face, my gaze is pulled to one of the guys that's just come in. The way he moves pulls at my memory, and an icy fear trickles down my back.

It can't be.

There's no way the universe is so fucked up that my random hookup is a jock on this campus.

As he gets closer, going to the locker room to get changed out of his gray sweats, our eyes lock for a second in the mirror, and I stumble. I lose my footing, hitting the belt and shooting off the end onto the floor in the blink of an eye. My forehead hits the floor with a thud, my knees sting, and my face burns with embarrassment. What. The. Fuck? I lie face down on the floor, trying to figure out what the actual fuck just happened and hoping the guys who just came in will just keep walking.

Bryce jumps down next to me, concern on his face as he asks me if I'm all right. I'm breathing too hard, wishing the earth would open up and swallow me whole, adrenaline coursing through my body like I'm fighting for my life. Fucking hell.

"Carp, you all right, man?" Bryce drops down to kneel next to me and puts a hand on my back.

"Kill me now," I groan as I force my body to move and roll over, then hiss when my knees smart from the burn the belt gave me.

"Carp?" the voice from last night questions. "Like the fish?"

No no no no no.

Why?

What did I do to deserve this?

"It's short for Carpenter," Bryce says, offering me a hand so I can sit up, which I take.

A hand comes down on my shoulder on the opposite side of Bryce, and I don't have to look to know it's *him*.

"Carpenter . . ." There's a smile in his voice, and I really wish I could disappear right now. "I'm Nick." He puts his hand out for me to shake. "It's nice to meet you."

I glance up at him, so fucking close I could lean in and kiss him.

And I want to.

This pull in my chest to be closer to him, the need to be pressed against him, is so fucking strong it steals my breath. I've never experienced it before. That romance-movie attraction to another human.

His eyes sparkle as he watches me, and his lips twitch into a small smile.

I shake his hand back, not wanting to let go of the connection.

"Joey." I swallow, my gaze still locked on his. "My name is Joey."

Nick nods, his eyes dropping to my mouth for a second, and I run my tongue over my bottom lip.

"You okay?" he asks again, meeting my eyes.

"Uh, yeah. I'm fine." I look at my knees and huff. It's not too bad, but they'll probably scab up a bit, making running and squats difficult.

"Do you guys know each other or something?" Bryce's voice cuts through the silence, reminding me we aren't alone, and I jolt.

He says yes at the same time I say no, making my face heat once again. What the fuck is wrong with me? I'm a fucking hockey captain, for Christ's sake. I am not a timid person.

Wrapping my hockey persona around me, I straighten my shoulders and look at Bryce. "We've run into each other before but never introduced ourselves."

Bryce nods his understanding and offers me a hand up. With my hands in Bryce's and Nick's, I'm lifted off the gym mats. My muscles protest and my head swims a bit at the quick change of position.

"I'm good, thanks," I tell both of them and reluctantly pull my hand from Nick's. Losing that connection is a physical pain I feel in my chest.

Bryce offers his hand to Nick to shake and introduce himself. "Hey, I'm Colin Bryce. We play hockey, you?"

"Nick Wyhe, football."

Fuuuuuuuuuck. He lives in the jock dorms. He has to. We're a Division 1 school, so all the contracted athletes live in the jock dorms.

Bryce and I shake hands with the other guys Nick came in with, making quick introductions before they head to change.

"Yeah, I'm done for the day," I tell Bryce, grabbing my shit.

"Thank fuck," he huffs and follows me to the dining hall. I'm hungry and need to get away from the gym.

We get in line and serve ourselves breakfast, mostly sticking to our diets, and find a table to sit at. The thing I like about Bryce is he doesn't feel the need to fill the silence with bullshit, so we can just eat.

I'm almost done when Brendon Oiler and Paul Johnson—two guys on the hockey team—come in and sit down with us. Oiler is talking constantly, but I have no idea what he's talking about.

"Have you gone to the gym already?" I interrupt Oiler since there's no other way to get a word in sometimes.

He stops with a mouthful of what appears to be donut and looks at me like I've grown a second head.

"It's Sunday," he says like I should understand the significance of that.

"And?"

He looks at Johnson, then back at me with a raised eyebrow. "Sunday is rest day." He shoves another piece of fried bread into his mouth. "Plus, Jer Bear is leaving today so we're keeping Preston busy so he doesn't kill himself in the gym."

Okay, now he has my attention.

"You're hanging out with Carmichael *without* Albrooke?" I clarify.

"Yup," Oiler says with a shit-eating grin on his face. "I'm going to try to get him drunk."

That's a terrible idea.

"Well, good luck with that," I tell him and grab my plate. "I'm off to shower and get changed. Make sure you hit the gym the rest of the week."

"We will," Johnson says around a mouthful of eggs.

Bryce stays to hang out with them for a bit longer, and I head back to the dorm. I don't know how long it's been since I left the gym, but I'm hoping Nick is still busy. I can't run into him again. It'll kill me.

I'll probably try to kiss him or something. Ugh.

Waiting for the elevator, I'm scrolling through my phone when I feel a presence next to me. My skin itches like someone is watching me. Looking up, I see Nick, red-faced and sweaty from his workout. Fuck, he looks good like that.

He smiles, his mouth open slightly as he pants to catch his breath, and stands next to me to wait. The elevator doors open, and we step aside to let some people off, then we climb on. He hits the third floor and I hit the fifth. The doors close and he turns to stare at me.

"I wondered when I would run into you again."

"What made you so sure you would?" I swallow nervously. No one here knows I'm into men, my sexuality shouldn't have to be a damn announcement, and I don't have time for a relationship anyway so it doesn't matter. I've always been careful to vet any hookups before meeting.

Nick smirks, obviously holding back a laugh. "You were wearing a Darby U hoodie."

I close my eyes and run my hand through my hair. Fuck.

"Listen, I get it," Nick continues. "I'm not really out to the team either, but if you ever find yourself in need of having an itch scratched, I'm in room 312."

My dick perks up at the very idea.

"Uh, 528 is my room number." My face is on fire, and I can't look at him. I can't believe I told him my room number. Shit. This is not going to end well. I can't let him distract me from the team.

"My roommate is gone for the holiday, and I'm free for the rest of the afternoon." His voice is calm like he's talking about the weather or his classes. "Do with that information what you will."

The elevator dings and the doors open onto the third floor. Nick strolls out like he has no cares in the world while I try to remove the band wrapped around my rib cage. Okay. I can do this. Having a semi-regular, casual hookup situation would be beneficial for both of us. We both know how demanding being an athlete is, so there won't be hurt feelings when one of us can't meet up.

I step off the elevator and get to my room to shower and change. The longer I think about it, the more I want to take Nick up on his offer. I have no idea when Bryce will be back, and if I text him and tell him to fuck off, he'll probably just stand outside the door and wait like a fucking creeper.

I let out a heavy sigh as I pull on jeans and a T-shirt.

Fuck it. It's break, we can just mess around while there's no practice or games then stop when it's over.

I slip on some shoes and jog down the stairs to the third floor and knock on 312.

"It's open!"

When I enter, Nick is shirtless, lying on his bed in sweats that sit low on his hips with one arm stretched behind his head, showing off the long lines of his body. His hair is still wet from his shower and combed back away from his face. I want to mess it up.

It's so distracting and unexpected that I stand there like a fucking idiot with the door open and stare at him. He lifts an eyebrow, drags his teeth over his lower lip, and slowly gives me a once-over. My cock thickens under his scrutiny, and my stomach clenches in anticipation.

"You gonna close that or are we giving the whole floor a show?"

I slam it harder than I meant to and flick the lock. "Your roommate is gone, right?"

My eyes are glued to his chest, to the way his muscles move under his skin. He slides his free hand down his torso and pushes his sweats lower, giving me a hint of the dark hair at the base of his dick.

I swallow thickly and stalk over to the bed, climbing on top of him to straddle his hips. One of my hands slides behind his head to lift his lips to mine while the other shoves inside his pants to grip his cock.

He groans into my mouth, opening up for me to explore him, and rocks against me. Nick's fingers open my jeans, and he grabs handfuls of my ass.

"You gonna give me this hole again?" He bites at my lip and pulls. I shudder at the contact, both wanting him to dominate me and wanting to do it myself.

"Fuck," I whimper, already so close to the fucking edge that it's stealing my breath. What is it about this guy that does it for me? Why does the stress and anxiety disappear with him? It's going to be my downfall.

Can you be addicted to a person after fucking them one time?

Nick pulls on my pants. "Get these off."

Grateful for the moment to gain control of myself, I climb off him and strip. Nick pushes his pants off, eyeing my dick and licking his lip.

"Do you prefer to bottom or are you verse?" Our eyes meet at his question, and I have to think about it for a second.

"Uh, bottom usually. It's not very often that I want to top."

A dangerous smile covers Nick's face before he says, "Good. Come here."

My stomach flutters with nervous excitement, and I climb back on the twin bed, this time lying next to him, face to face.

"I love the way you kiss," Nick says with his lips against my throat. He licks my Adam's apple and sucks on the skin. Who the hell knew that was erotic and didn't tell me?

My dick aches between us, my balls heavy, and I'm damn near desperate for release. I'm panting, my eyes closed as goosebumps break out along my skin, and I shudder.

"Nick," I whimper, my voice sounding to sweet even to me, and I don't understand it.

"Yeah, baby?"

"I wanna come. Please."

I feel his lips lift in a smile against me. Reaching for his head, I pull his mouth back to mine, needing the connection it gives me. I love the way he lets me control his lips while wreaking havoc on my other senses and overloading my body.

"How do you feel about edging?" He chuckles darkly against my lips, and it makes me want to sob.

"Please. It's hard enough to get off as it is." The fear of it being taken from me is so fucking real my dick actually deflates some. I hate trying to hide the fact that I didn't come or making an excuse for it. It's fucking embarrassing.

Nick draws back and looks at me with his eyebrows pulled together.

No! I don't want to have this conversation right now! I want to get off and pretend that I'm a normal twenty-five-year-old dude.

"It's hard to finish sometimes?"

Embarrassment clogs my throat.

"Sometimes. It's not a big deal." I shrug but the longer he stares at me, the more uncomfortable I get. Being naked while having this conversation also isn't helping. It makes me feel so much more vulnerable. "Can we not right now?"

My words are harsher than I mean, but I don't know how to do this. This is supposed to be an easy, quick hookup, and it's already taking longer than it should.

"Sure," Nick drags the word a little and leans in to kiss me, but that heat we had a minute ago isn't there. I'm too in my head, my dick won't cooperate, and I know I'm not going to get there now.

Fuck! I'm useless. A fuckup. Goddamn stupid dick. Why can't it just cooperate?

I try to shut my brain off and give in to the feel of his warm skin against mine, his fingers dancing along my back and over my ass, but it doesn't work. My dick doesn't even twitch.

Needing to distract him, I trail my lips down his jaw, bite at his ear, and suck on the skin of his neck. His morning stubble is rough against my tongue, but I love it.

I push him onto his back and move across his body, licking a nipple, nibbling the ticklish flesh on his ribs, making him squirm until I'm between his powerful thighs. His cock is lying against his stomach, nestled in that dark thatch of hair that's trimmed short, and demanding attention. It's thick and hard when I lick a line up the underside.

"Look at me," Nick growls, and our eyes lock as I flick my tongue over his tip. "Such a good little cocksucker."

My body flushes but my dick is finally perking up. Interesting.

With my hand around his base, I lift his veiny, uncut cock so I can suck on it and groan at the taste of him. Clean skin and man.

Nick slides his hand in my hair, then down to cup my cheek, and his hips flex. I love this part of sex, when the other person is enjoying themselves because of me. Something about using my body to create pleasure just does it for me. It gives me a sense of satisfaction I don't get from anything else.

With my hand moving in tandem with my mouth, I work all of him. Twisting and sucking, saliva dripping down his shaft until it's sloppy and my lips go numb. My free hand cups and rolls his balls, presses against his taint, and rubs circles around his rim. Nick is rocking into me, moaning and cursing.

"I'm gonna come," he warns me, and I hum. The vibration must set him off because a split second later, salty fluid fills my mouth and I have to work not to choke on it and keep my pace up. He growls, and his fingers dig into my face while his body tightens under me.

Only a few thrusts later, he relaxes and his hand falls to the bed.

"Fuck, that was good." He gives me a lopsided grin, and I metaphorically pat myself on the back for a job well done.

I climb off the bed and quickly pull on my pants.

"You're leaving?" Nick sits up, not ashamed or embarrassed by his nakedness. Not that I blame him, he's fucking gorgeous.

"Isn't that what you do after a hookup?" I chuckle, trying to not sound as awkward as I feel.

"You didn't get what you came here for." Nick stands but doesn't move to touch me or get dressed. It's a bit distracting.

I force a smile to my face that I'm sure he can see right through. "I'm fine."

With my pants and hoodie on, I grab the rest of my stuff and run. I'm a coward, but I can't face him. It's not his fault I struggle sometimes.

"Joey!" Nick's voice carries down the hallway, and I stop but don't turn around.

What the hell am I doing?

He appears in front of me a minute later with his sweats pulled back on and determination written on his face.

"I wanna talk to you about something, come on." His hand lands on my arm, turning me around, and I let him with a sigh. I can't make a scene in the damn hallway. Since most of the hockey players live on the third floor this year, I'm sure it would get around that I got into a fight with a football player real damn fast.

When the door closes behind me, Nick leans against it.

"You don't know me, and you don't want to spill all your deep, dark secrets, I get it." He crosses his arms. "But we can benefit from this arrangement, if you want."

I shove my hands in my pockets but don't say anything, just wait to see what he has to say.

"I'm sure it's just as difficult to keep a relationship for you as it is for me during the season."

I nod and let him continue.

"But I'm also happy to *explore* . . . to find what you like." He lifts an eyebrow and drags his eyes over me. "There's not much I'm against, and if it gets you orgasms, I'll call that a win."

"Why?" I stand a little straighter. "What do you get out of it?"

"Orgasms." He shrugs. "And not having to have the 'I can't, I have to go to practice' argument every day."

I snort and can't hide my smile.

"Plus, maybe we can be friends who cuddle sometimes and also fuck when the time allows." He walks up and stops when my hoodie brushes his stomach. We're eye to eye and the challenge he's wearing is almost daring me to say no so he can convince me to change my mind, but fuck, I really miss human contact.

"Cuddle, you say?" I question, and he grins.

Nick slides a hand under my hoodie and scratches lightly over my abs. I suck in my stomach on instinct and close the distance between us.

"I'm not sure how I'll keep my hands to myself, but I'm willing to give it a shot if it helps."

I smile and grip his hips. "So generous of you."

"I'm a generous guy." His other hand palms my ass and kneads the muscle. "But if you baby talk me, we're fucking."

"Baby talk?" Confusion contorts my face. What the hell is he talking about?

"Yeah. That baby talk thing you do." Nick looks at me like I'm the crazy one, but I have no idea what's happening right now. "At the club when you were about to come and earlier today before we got naked."

Oh shit.

I did do that.

"And you're into that?" I'm not sure what I want his answer to be. It's kind of weird, right? I'm a twenty-five-year-old man.

Nick grinds his dick into my hip. He's fucking hard again already.

"Oh yeah."

CHAPTER 3

nick

I like sex. I like to touch. I'm not ashamed of that, and I don't understand when others are. Humans are designed to need each other. We aren't meant to live in solitude.

I settle back on my bed, sitting against my headboard with pillows behind me, and Joey leaning against my chest. *The Amazing Spider-Man* is playing on my TV at the foot of my bed while my hand is inside the neck of his hoodie, stroking his skin.

Joey scoots up, laying his head on my shoulder, and my free hand moves to his waist to play with the exposed skin. I run my fingers through the brown hair of his happy trail and caress the skin between his hip bones.

I'm zoned out, watching the movie, the movements of my hands a comforting repetitive motion I lose track of, so it takes me a while to realize Joey keeps shifting and isn't relaxed.

Leaning my cheek against his hair, I speak quietly in his ear. "What's wrong?"

"You're driving me nuts," he grits out and grabs my wrist.

I finally tear my eyes away from the movie and glance down at him. There's a hard ridge in his jeans that makes my mouth water. I want another taste of him.

"I'm gonna make you feel good," I groan into his ear and reach for the button on his jeans. It gives easily, and I reach inside, grazing over his straining cock to cup his balls and roll them around with my fingers.

Joey moans and turns his face into my neck while his hips rock against my hand. His instinctual movements are sexy as hell. The way he moves because he just can't keep still, the way his breathing hitches, and the sounds . . . holy fuck, the sounds. I've never been with a guy who makes so much noise. I didn't know I liked it so much.

He bites my neck and moans with my skin between his teeth, sending a vibration through me.

"Fuck," I groan, wrapping my hand around his cock and pulling it from his jeans. I widen my legs to give him more room to spread his, but he doesn't take my hint. "Open up."

Joey bends his knees and lets them fall open. I love the way he listens, just submits to what I want without question. He's perfect for me.

"Such a good boy." His dick throbs at my words, and I smile. Finding out what makes him tick is fun. I tighten my grip on him, stroking him slow but hard to drive him a little crazy.

"Please," he whines, that baby talk coming out that gets me hard as fuck.

"Hang on, baby." I release him to grab the lube and chuckle when he protests. He's so needy for me. What the hell kind of partners has he been with that couldn't figure him out? Did they not care, or did he just not tell them what he needed?

I dribble some lube down his shaft and get him slicked up. He thrusts into my hand, his body moving in a rolling wave. His dick pulses as that sweet voice comes out again, desperate to come.

"Don't stop," he begs into my neck. His fingers dig into my arms as he holds on. "Please."

"Come for me, baby," I demand and pull his sweatshirt up to expose his clenched abs. "Give it to me. I want to see how much you want it."

Joey's back arches, and cum shoots out onto his stomach as he shudders and pulses against my palm. It only takes a few strokes for him to go limp in my lap, panting and sweaty. I can't help but play with his cum on his skin, dragging my fingers through it and spreading it around like I'm fingerpainting.

"I don't understand it." Joey's voice is almost a whisper.

"Understand what?" I lift my fingers to my mouth and lick him off my skin.

Joey looks at me, his head turning so he can watch. "Why it's different with you."

I release my fingers with a pop and lean down to kiss him. I want him to taste himself on my tongue. When he moans, I ache. I hold on to his jaw to keep him still and kiss him deeply, exploring his mouth and taking my time. It's not frenzied like our others have been. It's hot, sure, but it's more than that. I've never kissed a guy like this.

The last time someone meant something to me, it didn't end well. This guy is either going to be the best or worst thing to ever happen to me. I'm equally afraid of both.

We explore all the dark corners of each other's mouths, slow and deep, sharing air and learning who we are through our senses. He's a little shy when it comes to it, but I think that's because of his experiences. He smells like the ice rink and man and body wash. I don't know him in any sense other than the physical, but I already need him.

I don't know how long we kiss, but my lips are sore and chafed when we break apart.

His lips are swollen when he looks up at me, a sheepish expression on his face.

"I should clean up," he says and starts to sit up, but I tell him to wait and climb out from underneath him. "I'll do it." I grab two washrags, get one wet, and come back to him. He looks good in my bed.

Joey reaches for the rag, but I push his hand out of the way and clean his skin for him, then dry him off. He gets himself tucked away and fixes his clothes while I drop the dirty towels in the laundry.

He's sitting up, feet on the floor, looking uncomfortable as he pulls on his shoes so I pull on my sweats too.

"You don't have to leave." I shove my hands in the pockets and lean against the foot of the bed. A blush creeps up his neck, and it's fucking adorable. I know it's a stereotype to assume all jocks are dominant, bold, aggressive, dumbasses, but I've never met an athlete as soft as Joey.

Not soft like wimpy or weak, but he's not in your face. He tends to be submissive, at least with me, and it's caught me off guard. I definitely want to watch him on the ice, see what he's like. He's the captain of the team so he has to have a dominant streak in there somewhere.

"I should go." Joey doesn't meet my eyes when he stands. "I'll see you around." He does some kind of weird half-shrug thing and walks past me.

"Hey, this doesn't have to be awkward," I turn and say to his back. "I would like to be your friend."

He stops with his hand on the doorknob and sighs so heavily his shoulders drop.

"You're not like anyone else," he says to the door. "And that scares the shit out of me."

Then he's gone.

I don't know what to do with that, and it bugs me. He's not like anyone else either, but he didn't even give me a chance to tell him that. He ran. Is that what he does instead of communicating? Or is this too new, and he's not comfortable yet?

I pace my room for over an hour, going over it in my head. I'm not one to wait when a conversation needs to happen. Rip the Band-Aid off and get it over with. Deal with the problem head-on.

I hate this waiting shit.

Frustrated with myself, I grab my phone and call my best friend and former foster brother, Brent.

It rings a few times before his face appears on the screen.

"Hey, man, what's up? Must be getting laid since I don't have twelve new memes or TikToks on my phone." He shoves a bite of pizza in his mouth and talks around it. "Bad lay? It's still early."

"Would you shut the fuck up?" I scrub a hand down my face, and he snorts. He knows I'm not mad at him. "I'm in a *situation*."

Brent stops shoving food into his face to look at me. I have his attention now. "What kind of *situation*?" He eyes me with suspicion.

"Would you believe—"

"No."

"You didn't even let me finish!" I bark back at him.

"You know exactly what you did, out with it." He takes a drink of what looks like red Gatorade and gives me the hand motion to continue.

I sigh and pinch the bridge of my nose. "Okay, here it goes. I hooked up with a guy at a bar last night. This morning, I ran into him at the on-campus gym, and he's a hockey player for Darby U. I told him to stop by if he felt the need. He did. We fucked around a bit, but it got weird and not the sexy kind of kinky weird."

I really have Brent's attention now. I don't think he's even blinking.

"He was obviously into it. I asked him about edging—"

"Probably don't need to know the specifics, dude."

"—and he goes limp. Like he's done." I get up to pace my room again. "He says something about it being hard to get off, then he starts sucking my dick and runs."

"To clarify, he did not get off?" Brent asks.

"Nope." I run my hand through my hair. "I tell him to come back, let's just hang out or whatever, watch a movie. Well, halfway through *The Amazing Spider-Man,* he's hard. I get him off, it's hot as fuck, we make out for, I don't know, an hour or more? Then he leaves. On his way out, he says I'm different and that scares him."

I hate this uncertainty. It makes me fucking edgy.

"What the hell does that mean? I should go make him talk to me, right?"

"Uh, no." Brent scoffs like I'm a dumbass. "Sounds like he needs some space. You know, that thing you aren't good at? Let the guy breathe."

"Fuck you!" I snap. I'm so keyed up I can't sit still. I need to do something.

Brent laughs. "Seriously. Sounds like the guy has some baggage, and you need to tread carefully, or you'll scare him off. You aren't exactly baggage-free yourself."

"Fuck you, I let my baggage go."

He nods but it's sarcastic. "Yeah? You've dated a lot since Emma?"

The darkness that name brings is heavy but I've become a master at burying her memory in a box.

"I could convince him his baggage doesn't matter," I throw back.

"Yeah? Had a lot of deep convos in between the fucking and blowjobs? He trusts you enough to be vulnerable?"

"What the hell do you know about dating guys? You've never done it."

He rolls his eyes. "People are people. Treat them with respect, you asshole."

I drop my head back on my shoulders and groan. "I hate you."

"Yeah, sure you do. When you're getting laid by this guy you're already obsessing over in less than a week, you can thank me." The fucker hangs up on me, and I chuck my phone on the bed. What a little fuckhead.

CHAPTER 4

nick

Later that night, with a red plastic cup full of beer in my hand, I watch as the freshmen and sophomores who are still here for the winter interim run up and down the hallway of the jock building, screaming like banshees. Most students went home for the holidays already, but since not everyone can afford to fly home, there are always a few stragglers. I'm one of them. Plus, my parents' house is full of kids. They don't need another body in there or another mouth to feed.

I love my parents, they're good people. They take in older foster kids that are hard to find placements for. They're good kids usually, just misunderstood and abused. It's hard to connect with them sometimes since they have walls up to protect themselves, but it's always been worth the effort. Brent was once a foster kid in our house. He was with us for all our high school years, and since we got along so well, I shared a room with him. Mom and Dad never forced me to share my room since having the foster kids was their choice, but Brent and I were thick as thieves. He stayed in Washington for school while I got a full ride to Colorado, but I talk to him daily.

There's music playing from a speaker someone has set in a doorway, there are people everywhere, rolls of toilet paper being thrown around, and someone is puking, but I can't see them. My room isn't on this floor, so I don't care. Puke is not my problem tonight.

Unless it's one of my freshmen. Fuck.

Straightening up off the wall, I follow the sound of vomiting down the hallway, avoiding the couples hooking up and the dude passed out on the floor. He's not a football player, so he's not my problem.

I pull a condom out of my pocket and slap it against the chest of one of my freshman teammates.

"Don't be an idiot," I tell him and watch the girl for a second to make sure she's sober enough for consent.

She lifts an eyebrow at me. "What?"

"How many drinks have you had?" I ask her, but she doesn't look intoxicated at all.

"One."

"Cool." I nod and pat Chad's shoulder. He reaches for the girl's hand, and they disappear into a room. I make it a few more doors down the hallway before I find the puking kid and the one man I want to see, Joey Carpenter. I can picture how his shaggy brown hair hangs down around his collar, sharp green eyes taking in everything around him, and his cheekbones that were chiseled from granite. He's standing with his back to me, arms crossed over his chest, and he lets out a deep sigh.

This is the side of him I haven't gotten to witness yet, and I'm hungry for it.

"I swear to fuck, Riggs." Joey shakes his head. Riggs is not one of mine, but he is an idiot, and finding some of my dumbasses with him is not uncommon. Normally, the guys stick with teammates since that's who we all know the best, but a lot of freshmen have to take the same classes, so some of the guys on the team have started hanging around the hockey players.

I slap Joey's back in solidarity, and he glances back at me. His eyes go wide in alarm for a split second before he covers it with the captain mask he wears so well. I can see on his face that he feels the weight of responsibility. He's one of those that wants to save these guys from making bad decisions, but he can't.

"Fucking freshman." I shake my head, leaning my forearm on Joey's shoulder when I find the kid with his head in a trash can. "What did he drink?"

"From what I can tell, everything," Joey bites out and pinches the bridge of his nose.

The kid groans and finally stops throwing up, dropping down to his side on the carpet.

"Nope, get up." Joey grabs him under his arm and hauls him to his feet. "You're done. Go to bed."

I step aside but glance around the room to find two of my assholes half turned away from me.

"Who dared him?" I fold my arms and set my jaw, staring the guys down.

"Allen," one of the guys says, throwing his teammate under the bus.

"What the fuck, dude!?" Allen yells at the snitch.

"Allen, room." I point over my shoulder for the door. "You make bad decisions."

He stomps off, muttering something about backstabbing roommates.

"You're his roommate?" I ask Robbie, the snitch. When his eyes widen and his face pales, I know the answer. I shake my head and tsk him. "You done fucked up, A-A-Ron."

"Fuck!" Robbie takes off past me for his room, and I sigh. Bunch of idiots, the lot of them. No loyalty.

I wander down the rest of the hallway and look for more of my guys. As a senior and the special team's captain for the football team, I have to watch out for my guys too. There are six team captains this year, and it's my second year being one, so I'm used to looking out for the team, but I swear, freshmen get dumber every year.

When I don't find any more fuckery, I check the second floor, which is the female floor, and then head back up to the third. When I don't find Robbie outside the room on his ass, I assume he's okay and decide to use the stairs to get to the fifth floor instead of the elevator. I'm around the fourth floor when I run into Joey, sitting on the landing.

"Hey, you okay?" I lean against the railing, taking in the defeated droop of his shoulders and his head in his hands.

"I don't know what I'm doing," he says to the floor.

"Well, you're currently sitting in a stairwell. Does that help?" I offer, trying to lighten the mood.

He lifts his head and glares at me, completely unamused. I chuckle softly and drop down next to him, our arms brushing in the tight space.

"What's going on? You wanna talk about it?"

It's quiet for a minute before he sighs and lies back on the landing to stare at the bottom of the stairs above us.

"I'm the team captain this year. There are twenty-five guys on the team, and I'm responsible for all of them. If they fuck off and get in trouble, end up with alcohol poisoning, or drunk driving, it's on me."

"Uh, no the fuck it's not," I say matter-of-factly. "They are grown-ass adults. This is my second year as a captain, I understand the pressure you're under to make sure the team works on the field or ice, whatever you call it." He chuckles when I correct myself. "And yeah, infighting outside of the game affects performance, but if they go off and get drunk or decide to get high, that's not on you. Not once have I seen anyone turn around in a locker room and ask where the captain was when some asshole ends up in the ER for alcohol poisoning. And trust me, that situation has happened more than once."

I lie back on the floor and turn my head to look at him. We barely fit in the space, my body against both the wall and him. For just a second, I let my eyes flick to his mouth when he licks his bottom lip. My dick thickens in my jeans at the mental image of grinding against him, moans and panting breaths, deep kisses and goosebumps.

Fuck.

I turn my face away from him and force myself to breathe. Since anyone could walk in here at any time, I can't be springing a woody in here. Especially if Joey isn't out.

"What was that?" Joey sits up and leans on one elbow so he's looking down at me, and it is not helping my current situation. At. All. The urge to reach for him and lower his lips to mine is so damn strong. I ball my fists, then shove them under my ass to keep them to myself.

"Nothing." I shake my head and sit up, forcing him to move.

"Right," he says knowingly.

"Look, I'm pretty sure freshmen were created to drive the upper-classmen nuts. I know we did too. At this point, a lot of them are on their own for the first time in their lives. Much like toddlers, they're testing limits and finding what their boundaries are. We just need to make sure we set a good example, be available if they want to talk, and try to keep them from killing each other." I pat his knee, and it takes a lot of self-control to remove my hand afterward.

"How old are you?" Joey asks. Surprised, I turn to look at him.

"Twenty-two. Why?"

"I have freshmen who are twenty-one. That kid tonight, is one of two of the eighteen-year-olds I have. In hockey, it's pretty common to start college late. I'm twenty-five." He takes a deep breath. "I feel like I have nothing in common with a teenager anymore. How am I supposed to lead them when I can't connect with them?"

It's admirable that he takes this so seriously. Maybe I've taken advantage of the fact that there are five other captains to help carry the weight, but there are also a hundred and seventeen guys on the team.

"A lot of times, these guys need to learn lessons the hard way. They're going to fuck up, and they have to deal with the consequences. That's life. You can't protect them from that." Getting an idea, I slap his chest and stand. "Come on."

He sighs but stands, following along behind me to the third floor and into my dorm. My roommate is one of the lucky ones that get to leave during winter interim, so I'm alone until New Year's.

Joey drops down onto my bed, and I pull out a bottle of vodka from the mini fridge Neal, my roommate, has.

"Didn't we just tell the freshmen not to make dumb choices?" He smirks at me but takes the cup I offer him with orange juice and vodka in it.

"We know our limits," I scoff and clink our plastic cups together. I sit next to him, and we both take a drink.

Joey stares into his like it has the answer to life's questions.

"Can I ask you something?" he finally says, squeezing the cup until it makes a sound, then releasing it.

"Of course." I shrug and look at his profile. The man is gorgeous, with high cheekbones and a strong jaw. His lips look soft and a little puffy. Is that still from the kissing earlier?

His eyebrows pull together, and he lifts one hand to his mouth to chew on the cuticle that's already red and ragged.

"How. Like. When." He takes a deep breath, closes his eyes, then blurts the words out. "How did you know you liked guys?"

I wasn't sure where this was going, but that wasn't it.

He turns to look at me, and I carefully wipe the surprise off my face.

"In junior high, I was curious what it was like to kiss a boy. I liked girls, but I thought I might like boys too, but since I felt like I wasn't allowed to watch them the same way, I wasn't sure." I clasp my hands together between my knees. "In high school, a bunch of the football team was having a party, and someone dared another teammate to kiss me. We were drunk and fifteen. So he did, and that was the confirmation I needed." I shrug like it wasn't the most stressful time of my life at school. Like I wasn't terrified that it was written all over my face that I didn't hate it.

Joey's eyes drop to my lips for a second before he turns away. Fuck, I wish he would just kiss me already.

"Have you been questioning what you like? Is sex with men new for you?" I ask carefully. I don't want to spook him if he's not ready to talk about it, but knowing that much would help. "It's okay if you are or if you're solid in what you already know. Sexuality is a spect—"

Joey's lips meet mine, cutting off my rambling. The man kisses like it's his profession. It's intoxicating and all-consuming.

I reach for him, sliding my hand along the side of his neck, and dip my head to the side to change the angle and hope like hell that he doesn't run again.

CHAPTER 5

joey

Nick's warm, calloused hand holds the side of my neck, and he deepens the kiss, encouraging me to kiss him back.

Without looking, I set my cup on the floor and reach for his arm, holding on to his wrist. I need the anchor. I don't want to fuck up whatever this is because nothing has ever felt as right as Nick. No other man, no woman, just Nick.

Some piece inside my chest that I didn't even know was misaligned, clicks together. It steals my breath.

Putting my hand on the bed, I lean into him, wanting him to lie back. I want to feel him against me. I need it. This is as intoxicating as the vodka humming along my skin.

"Hey, wait." Nick pulls his mouth from mine, and I whimper. Fucking whimper. What the actual fuck was that? My face heats with embarrassment at the pathetic sound and for mauling him after leaving the way I did earlier. What the hell is wrong with me?

"Fuck. I'm sorry." I jerk out of his hold and try to flee to my own room, but Nick is just as fucking fast as I am, and he tackles me into the door. I lean my forehead against the wood with my eyes squeezed shut while trying to hold back the panic.

"I'm sorry." Heat burns my face. "I know I'm giving really mixed signals, but I can't stay away from you."

The heat of his body warms my back, and I'm not sure if I should like it or not. I do like it, more than I should since I barely know him.

"You have nothing to be sorry about." Nick's voice is soft next to my ear. We're pretty matched for height, though I'm bulkier than he is. "Trying to figure yourself out is hard. It's awkward, and sometimes you have to fight the roles society has ingrained in us with what we want or need. It's okay."

I lift my head and drop it back onto the door with a loud thud. I don't know what I'm doing or what I should be doing. I don't know anything anymore.

"Turn around," Nick demands, and my body is turning before I've had a chance to think about it. Yeah, I'm a team captain. I play an aggressive, full-contact sport, but I like when he makes decisions for me. I don't want to think anymore. It's dangerous in my head. My body reacts to him like it never has before, and I'm already desperate to see what else he can do to me.

He's smirking at me, crowding my space, and almost leaning over me. Why do I like him in my space?

"Good boy." His voice is husky, and it sends tingles deep into my gut. I swear the color drains from my cheeks. He turns serious but doesn't put any distance between us. "Listen, I know the pressure you're under. If you want to *experiment,* I would not be opposed to it. I'm not really out, but I'm comfortable with who I am, and if you need to explore this part of yourself, then we can do that. No one has to know if you aren't comfortable talking about it. We're both busy, so we can meet up when we can, and you can call the shots."

"I don't want to call the shots." The words are out of my mouth with zero direction from my brain. Come on, brain. What the hell was that? I flick my gaze to anywhere else as I die of embarrassment.

The smirk returns to Nick's face as he chuckles. "I can do that too."

"I don't want to take advantage of you." Guilt eats at me. "If I decide in a month or a week or tomorrow that this isn't it for me, I don't want to hurt you."

"I'm a big boy, I'll be okay."

My face floods again, and Nick wraps his arms around me for a hug I didn't know I needed. I bury my face in his shoulder and let him hold me, let him comfort me when my insides are a chaotic mess of what-ifs. For the first time since my dad died, someone is letting me be weak, and to take comfort. He's not demanding that I be strong and hold in my emotions. It's freeing and terrifying.

My "Thank you" is muffled by his shirt and the muscles that hide underneath.

"Your sexuality doesn't define you. You're still you, no matter what gets your dick hard."

Some of the tension in my body releases. I didn't know I needed to hear that. Nick is safe. I don't know how I know that since I met him twenty-four hours ago, but I just know. On a cellular level, I know.

We stand there for a few long minutes, just existing in the space where teammates and roommates aren't a part of the world.

"You should stay here tonight."

"I should check on Riggs," I grumble, not really wanting to, but if he's got alcohol poisoning, I need to make sure he gets to the ER.

"That doesn't answer my question." He chuckles, and it rumbles against my face.

"Was it a question?" My voice is quiet, unsure. I hate it. I'm confident in my abilities usually, but tonight, I feel so out of my depth.

"You can always say no." Nick cups the back of my head and lifts my head so I'm looking at him. "First and foremost, I know you are giving up control to me, but you hold all the power. You say no or stop, and it stops. No hesitation."

At the word power, my eyes drop back to his lips, and my tongue drags across my bottom lip. Fuck, I want to kiss him again.

"Keep looking at me like that, and I'll make sure you leave this room with a hard-on." There's an edge in his voice I've not heard before. I pull my gaze to his and see the lust burning in the dark depths of warm brown eyes. Unease and excitement war within me. A part of me likes it.

Likes that I'm turning him on, but that preteen kid that still lives in my head fears being found out.

I've seen too much shit in the last ten years of playing hockey. I've seen my teammates be attacked, and my classmates be bullied. Not that I really had time to figure out what I liked while I was still at home. Instead of risking distraction and Mom's wrath, I didn't date. At all. More than anything, I'm not sure where I fit and I hate how awkward everything feels.

Heat warms my neck and my ears the longer he looks at me. Being the sole focus of his attention is uncomfortable, but I don't want him to look away either.

Nick puts a hand on the door next to my head and leans in like he's going to kiss me, but stops just a breath away, letting me close the distance. Our breathing mixes in the frozen moment as he waits for me to decide. I search his eyes for just a second before I press my lips to his.

He groans and leans his body against mine, pinning me to the door. I love feeling his weight on me, taking what he needs from me. I want him to use me.

Reaching for my pants, I quickly unbuckle them and then reach for his. He grunts into the kiss when I wrap my hand around him and pull his thick cock out, along with my own.

I break the kiss and look down to line us up, tip to tip, and use our foreskins to create a sheath.

"Oh fuck," Nick groans. "I've never done docking before."

I wrap my hand around us and jerk us off together. A breath catches in Nick's throat, and I lean my head forward to suck on his neck. I want to leave marks, but I don't know if anyone saw us come in here, and I don't want him to have to lie if someone asks about them. So I'm careful not to suck too hard. I nip at his skin but don't sink my teeth into him.

Nick grabs my hair in a tight fist and brings my lips back to his. He pants into my mouth as I pick up speed, our hips working in tandem to get to the precipice of ultimate, mind-numbing pleasure. I want it. I need it.

"You gonna fill us up with cum?" he growls against my skin, setting off shivers.

"Yes," I whine in that little voice he seems to bring out in me.

"Good boy, do it. I want your cum all over my dick so I can use it as lube."

Tingles break out over my skin, deep in my pelvis and in my spine.

"Oh fuck, please," I whimper, needing something but not sure what. I'm so fucking close that I'm afraid it's going to be stolen from me if I don't figure it out quickly.

"Give it to me," Nick demands through gritted teeth, and that's it. I fill our foreskins with cum, my knees buckling and my mouth ravished by the only man to get this response from me.

He chuckles and catches some of the drips leaking from us in his hand.

"You look so sexy when you come, baby." Nick nips my jaw, and my hand falls from us, limp and weak from the orgasm strong enough to short-circuit my brain. He gets a good amount of cum in his palm and turns me to face the door.

"Feet apart, ass out, come on."

I bend at the hip and stick my ass out, but Nick taps the inside of my ankle with his foot to get me to open wider.

Warm, slick fluid is spread around my hole, and a finger is inserted. I bite my lip to hold in my moan. God, I love the feeling of having someone inside me. To be used for someone else's pleasure is everything. The few times I got close to coming with a hookup was when I was bottoming and being used as a cum dumpster. Last night was not the first time I had sex with more than one man on the same night. When I got to college, I went a little crazy on the hookup scene. I'm definitely not a virgin but I also didn't make a habit of hooking up with the same guy more than once.

Hockey keeps me busy half the year, not leaving much time for hookups. In the off-season, though...

Nick works me open with ease since it hasn't been very long, and he knows what he's doing. Soon, the slick head of his dick is pressing against my hole, and he slaps my ass hard enough for it to sting and burn.

"You like being used, Joey? Filled with cum and sloppy?"

"Yes," I hiss as he thrusts in.

"Good." He leans over me to brush his lips against my ear while he speaks. "I'm going to fuck you like I hate you. Make this hole gape for me."

My spent dick twitches and goosebumps break out along my skin. Nick chuckles at the shudder.

"Such a dirty boy, getting turned on by being used." He bites my shoulder and starts moving. Every thrust is harder, faster, deeper than the last until he's pounding into me like his life depends on it. I love it. I don't ever want him to stop.

"Use me," I whimper in that innocent tone that belies what I'm doing.

"I get so hard when you talk like that," Nick growls. "Do sweet boys like being used as a fuck toy?"

My cheeks heat at what he's insinuating, it's embarrassing but my cock thickens. Oh God. I reach for my dick and stroke myself, not sure I'll be able to come again but willing to try.

"Answer me," Nick demands, wrapping a hand around my throat and pulling me until my back is arched and I'm almost leaning against him.

"Yes, use me," I sob, overwhelmed but knowing I need this release, I need him to force me.

"Your hole is sloppy with your own cum, Joey."

His dirty talk goes straight to my balls. I'm achingly hard again and ready to burst. My brain can't process his words and the sensations and how much I like all of it.

"Show me how much you like being a fuck toy. Squeeze your used ass around my cock and make me come." The palm of his hand presses against my throat while his fingers dig into my jaw and cheeks. Nick bites my earlobe and pulls, forcing more sensation on my body until I can't tell which way is up and my balls empty, shooting cum onto the floor and the door. My body tightens and Nick grunts, his last few thrusts harder than just a minute ago as he fills my ass.

My knees buckle, and I fall forward against the door to stay standing. Nick leans against me too, both of us panting and sweaty.

Holy fuck, that was the best sex of my life.

CHAPTER 6

nick

After the mind-blowing sex, Joey crashed in my room. Wrapped around each other, I slept better than I ever have. I'm a little nervous at how dependent I'm becoming. How am I going to explain how attached to him I am already? The last person I got attached to was ripped away from me in the dead of night and I never knew what happened to her.

Joey quickly became insatiable. Not just wanting to fuck, but to touch, stroke, cuddle, explore. I guess we better get it out of our systems now before Neal returns and Joey has to get back to hockey. I can't wait to go to a game, though. Watching him handle his teammate on Sunday night was sexy as fuck.

It's Wednesday morning, his fucking alarm is screaming, and he's still snoring against my chest.

"Joey," I grumble, pushing him.

"Huh?" He's not awake yet.

"Alarm." My eyes are still closed, and I want nothing more than to fall back asleep, but I know it's not going to happen.

Joey reachs up and shuts off the screaming alarm. It's actually a scream. Not a normal alarm sound, but like that screaming goat sound that was all over social media a few years ago. He's a psycho. It's jarring every time.

He shoves his arms above his head and stretches. The muscles in his back bunch and flex in the light peeking through the blinds. Sliding a hand around his torso, I kiss his shoulder and pinch his nipple just to make him hiss. He slaps at my hand, and I chuckle as he rolls away, rubbing at his now sore nipple.

"You're a dick." He sits up and we both swing our feet over the edge to the floor.

I smile at him, all sleep-rumpled and sexy. "Yeah, I am, but you're still here so you don't hate it."

"It's because you dick me down." Joey stands and moves between my knees, lifting my chin so he can kiss me. It's a quick press of lips since we just woke up, but it's enough to heat my blood. "Get dressed."

He steps back and uses the bathroom as I dig out some workout clothes. I'm pulling on a shirt when he stops in the doorway and leans against the frame with his arms crossed.

"What's on the schedule today? Cardio? I have a much more fun way to get that in." I waggle my eyebrows, and he shakes his head, but he's smiling.

"It's leg day."

I pull on my shoes, grab my crap, and we head upstairs to wake up Bryce. Joey swears the guy can't make it to the gym unless he drags him, so the last few days we've been waking him up. Bryce hasn't asked why Joey isn't sleeping in their room yet, but I'm waiting for it. Maybe he texted the question?

We get off the elevator on the fifth floor and when Joey opens the door, I rush past him and jump onto Bryce's bed. Standing on his bed, I jump on the mattress and shake the fuck out of him.

"Hey, man!"

Bryce startles, yelling and covering his head so I stop bouncing.

"Time to get up." I've got a shit-eating grin on my face when I pat his shoulder.

He looks up at me, glaring. "You're an asshole."

Joey barks out a laugh as he changes into workout clothes, and I jump down.

"Yeah, I really am."

Bryce grumbles something about dickhead seniors, but he gets up to go take a piss. Joey lifts an eyebrow at me, smirking as he finishes getting dressed, and I shoot him a wink.

The bathroom door opens, and Bryce quickly gets changed, then we head down to the gym.

We get warmed up and move to the leg machines as the door opens and two guys come in, a redhead with longer hair and one with brown hair and a backward ball cap. Is it a hockey thing to have longer hair?

They come to stand in front of Joey, and I take my earbud out so I can listen to what's going on. I'm a nosey bastard.

The one with the hat on crosses his arms, and a muscle in his jaw jumps.

"Have you seen Carmichael?" Oh, he's pissed.

Joey looks between them, then stops his workout.

"No, why?"

"We can't find the dumbass and he's—" Hat Guy looks at Redhead, and he shrugs a little. "He's not doing well."

"We need to find P Dawg," Redhead says, and I try to hide my snort, but since Joey glances at me, I know I failed. "But we don't know Denver well enough to drive around and look for him."

I stand from the machine I'm using. "I can help."

Everyone turns to look at me. "I've lived here for a few years. I know how to get around the city. Any idea about what type of thing this guy would be doing?"

"Self-destruction," Hat Guy says and Redhead nods.

"Since when is Carmichael self-destructive? Dude is crazy about working out, his diet, and sleep. He won't even eat pizza." Joey stands up, looking at his teammates. The two share another look, and I'm starting to put some pieces together.

"Bad breakup or something?" I offer, watching them closely. Redhead pales a bit and bounces on his toes.

Hat Guy straightens his shoulders but shakes his head. "It's... complicated."

"You don't mind?" Joey asks me. This is Captain Carpenter, not my Joey, making sure everyone is okay.

"Yeah, I don't mind. If your guy is in trouble, I'm happy to help if I can." I shrug and look back at the duo. "Let me get changed, give me, like, ten minutes."

Hat Guy holds his hand out for me to shake. "I'm Paul," he says before pointing at his buddy. "That's Brendon."

"Nick." I shake his hand and duck out of the gym.

Once I'm changed, Paul and Brendon meet me at the curb in front of the dorms already in a blue Corolla. Now I see why Joey didn't volunteer to come with us, there's no way 5 of us are fitting in this car if we find their guy.

I climb in the back, and Paul heads to the exit.

"Okay, tell me about your guy. What kind of shit is he likely to get into? Bars? Strippers? Drugs?"

"My best guess is he literally ran somewhere, but he's been gone for hours, so the likelihood of him being injured is pretty high," Paul says and leaves the university campus to head toward downtown. "If he's high or drunk, I'm going to beat his ass."

"What's the deal? Why are you babysitting him?"

Brendon looks at Paul for a minute before turning to search out the window.

"Look, I get that you don't want to spill secrets that aren't yours, but if I have at least a vague idea of what's going on, it'll help me figure out where he would have gone." I look out my side of the car and watch for joggers. "Is he from here? Family around or local hangouts he would know that you don't?"

Paul sighs before he starts talking. "He's not from here, though his dad lives here now too. It's not a good situation, if you know what I mean." His eyes meet mine in the mirror, and I give him a nod. "He's dating our friend, Jay. Jay went back home for Christmas, and Carmichael is not handling it well."

Interesting.

The wheels start turning, and I'm thinking about the paths out of the school and where he might head. He's new to the area, probably wants to be alone and clear his head...

"Does he like getting lost in the crowd or prefer solitude?"

"Solitude," they say together.

"We're going the wrong way then." I give Paul directions to get us going the right way, and we drive around the industrial area for a while but don't see anything.

"Hey, since we're here, can we stop at that bakery? Debbi has the best cinnamon rolls." *And I want to eat one off your captain's dick.*

Brendon pops up. "Cinnamon rolls?"

Paul sighs but agrees. We get parked and head inside, the bell on the door alerting the amazing woman inside that customers have entered.

She's not out in the front, but I can hear her down the hall. Paul and Brendon look around and wait patiently.

"Nicky!" The middle-aged woman smiles wide and opens her arms for a hug which I don't hesitate to give her. "It's been a while, how have you been?"

"Good, busy." I step back when she lets me go. "You know how it is."

"Of course." She pats my cheek, and I introduce Paul and Brendon. It's not until this moment that I notice we're all wearing the same thing. Jeans and Darby U hoodies. Wow. What a bunch of dorks.

A guy in black workout gear comes from the back of the shop, dripping sweat, beet red, and obviously exhausted. Paul looks over and freezes, his jaw tightening as he turns to face the newcomer.

"What's going on, Carmichael?" Paul crosses his arms. Brendon and I turn to face him too.

Preston Carmichael is a beast of a man. He's taller than me by a few inches, wider than me, and looks like there's not any fat on his body.

"We've been looking for you," Brendon says sternly, and there's something about the way he says it that makes me feel like he doesn't speak that way very often.

Preston's jaw hardens and his fists clench. He looks like he's trying to get some control over himself before he speaks.

Paul looks between Preston and Debbi before he asks, "Do you know her or something?"

"No, she's just a woman who was nice to me. Are you heading back to campus?"

"Yeah, just grabbing some cinnamon rolls. Debbi's are the best," I pipe up, and the big man looks at me for the first time.

Debbi rings us up, and we head out of the small shop to the car. Paul and Brendon take the front seats again, and I climb into the back with Carmichael.

"I'm Nick." I offer my hand and he shakes it with a very forced smile.

"Preston."

I chuckle, "Oh, I know who you are."

Paul and Brendon are having some kind of conversation in the front with just looks, so I start rambling while Carmichael looks out the window. No one is paying me any attention and that amuses me. I could be talking about starfish orgasms, and no one would know.

Paul pulls up in front of the dorms, and I climb out with a quick "Bye" and head inside. I have a very important thing to do with Joey's dick and this amazing cinnamon roll that's still warm.

CHAPTER 7

joey

Nick comes into his room where I've been hiding out for the last few days with a devious smile on his face. Pausing *Thor* on the TV, I watch him stalk toward me with purpose, holding a paper bag.

"Whatcha got there?"

The smile on his face becomes dangerous and seductive.

"How do you feel about food as masturbatory aids?" Nick asks with a lift of his eyebrow.

Now I'm confused.

"What?"

Nick opens the bag and lifts out a big cinnamon roll. "You see, I am falling hard for your dick, and I also love cinnamon rolls. So, putting them together should be next world."

I flick my gaze between the pastry and his face.

"I'm definitely curious to see what you're going to do with that." I swallow thickly, a little nervous and a little turned on.

"Take your pants off," he demands, and I quickly shove the sweats and underwear down my legs and drop them on the floor. His eyes zero in on my half-hard dick lying against my stomach. "Get it hard."

Just giving me the command makes my dick twitch. I love when he takes charge. I don't have to think, just feel.

Reaching for my cock, I stroke myself a few times until I'm hard, and he climbs onto the bed and kneels between my legs.

"You're about to be a very messy boy," he teases, shoving two fingers into the cinnamon roll and scooping out the center piece. It's vulgar and indecent. His fingers are covered in frosting and the cinnamon-sugar mixture.

Lifting the soft, gooey bread to his mouth, he takes a bite and moans before leaning over me enough to offer me the rest of the piece.

I use my tongue to take it, chewing and swallowing quickly. When my mouth is empty, he shoves his fingers into my mouth.

"Suck them clean."

A shiver shudders through me as I hold on to his wrist and clean his fingers with my tongue.

He growls as my eyes meet his with his fingers deep in my throat.

"Such a sweet mouth," he murmurs. Removing his fingers, he leans on the bed and takes my mouth. Cinnamon and frosting dance on our tongues as we explore each other.

Pulling back, he sits up again and takes my dick in his hand, sliding the now centerless cinnamon roll onto my dick. It's still warm and sticky as it slides down my shaft.

Nick leans forward and sucks on my tip, groaning deep in his chest so it rumbles around me.

"Fuck." The word is breathy and quiet, but he hears it and looks up at me.

He moves around to get settled and bobs on my head while moving the pastry up and down my dick at the same time. It's not a tight pressure, but the strangeness of it is hot. I never would have thought to try this, but he's obviously into it, and that turns me on. The sweet mixture in the cinnamon roll makes my skin sticky, but Nick licks it off like he's catching melting ice cream on a cone.

I'll never be able to look at a pastry or ice cream again without blushing.

Nick unrolls part of the treat and wraps it around my balls, then sucks on them between nibbling the sweet bread.

Holy fuck.

My cock throbs at the gentle brush of lips and the light graze of teeth.

"You taste so fucking good, baby," Nick pants against my balls. He reaches for the lube we have stashed between the bed and the wall and pops the cap. Once his fingers are slicked up, he presses them against my hole and goes back to nibbling the dessert around my base.

My body tightens, and he smirks that knowing fucking smile that tells me he knows exactly how good it feels.

"Think you can come from just my fingers in your ass?"

I have no fucking idea, but I'm willing to let him do anything he fucking wants to me right now.

"Or should you fuck this pastry while I fuck you?" Nick curls his fingers, searching for my prostate, and I brace for it. It's such an intense pleasure. It's almost too much, but if I relax into it, it's so fucking good. "I do love when the devil comes disguised as sweets."

My back arches, and I let out a pathetic whimper when he finds it.

"There it is," he says, and I don't have to look at his face to know he's grinning. The fucker loves watching my face when he's toying with me.

"What do you want, dirty boy? Do you want me to fuck you? To fill you up? Or should I drag it out until you're desperate?"

"Uh. Hng. Hu." I can't form words. I can barely make sounds, and he wants to have a fucking chat?

"Drag it out, it is."

With his fingers slowly dragging over my prostate, his hand stroking my sticky dick, and his mouth on my balls, I'm not going to last long. I'm overstimulated and drowning in sensations.

I slam my eyes shut to focus on my breathing, but it's useless. All it does is let the thoughts in. Is he going to let me come if I get there, or will he back off at the last second?

The what-ifs start circling my brain, and I can't stop them. Fuck. The anxiety starts swirling, and I can feel my hard-on deflating. Clenching my fists, I try to only think about the sensations, but I can't block out the nagging voice telling me I'm going to disappoint him.

"Joey," my name is a command, and my eyes pop open, meeting Nick's hard gaze. "Eyes on me."

My breathing slows a little, and the noise in my head quiets as I watch him touch me. His mouth wraps around my dick, sucking and bobbing until I'm hard again, and my hips jerk off the bed.

"Come in my mouth, give it to me." His fingers stroke me inside while his mouth and other hand work together to fuck me—and I'm done. The hot, wet suction of his mouth while he plays with my hole is too much. I fill his mouth only a few pumps later, my hips thrusting my dick deep into his throat, but he takes it and keeps going. He sucks my soul from my cock, leaving me panting and weak.

"Holy fuck," I groan, dropping my arm over my eyes.

Nick chuckles and slides up my body. "I'm going to fuck you, Joey, while you're weak and your cum is on my tongue."

He kisses me hard for a minute, and the click of the lube bottle sounds just before his slick tip presses against me.

"Yes," I moan against his lips. "Use me."

Nick shudders as he sinks all the way in, then grinds against me for a minute.

"You like being used, don't you? My little gutter slut," he growls, and goosebumps break out across my skin.

"Yes," I hiss. My dick twitches like it's going to try to rally, but it doesn't matter if I come again, it feels so fucking good to be used without having to worry about it. The pressure is off, and I can just enjoy the way he feels. The grip of his fingers on my flesh, the slap of his pelvis against my ass, and how full I feel with him buried deep.

Nick pulls the cinnamon roll off my dick and drops it onto the bag, then leans over me, pinning my wrists to the bed and teasing my mouth while he brutalizes my ass.

"Come for me, use me. Please," I whisper against his lips, and he shudders. "Make me your cumwhore. I want it."

He trembles and grinds against me, then fucks me harder as he comes. Heat blooms inside of me, and he moans the sexiest sound before dropping down onto my chest, panting. His grip on my wrists lessens, and I pull them away to wrap my arms around him and run one hand through his hair slowly.

"Fuck, that feels good," he mumbles into my neck, and I smile as I close my eyes. I could fall asleep like this. Warm, sated, relaxed. His weight is comforting, and I find myself starting to drift off, but when he sits up, my eyes open.

"We should clean up, and we can't let the cinnamon roll go to waste." Nick climbs off the bed, and I look at the poor dessert that we violated. It's falling apart and messy but will probably still taste good. Is it weird to eat food that was on my dick? I'm not going to think too hard about it.

Nick goes into the bathroom and comes back with a wet rag and cleans me up. I like that he takes care of me afterward. I've never let anyone else do it before, but he insisted, and after just a few days, I've started to look forward to it. Why is it so easy to let him take care of me? To give up that control? How does he know I need it?

He kisses me soft but deep while he drags the warm cloth over my skin. He lingers, enjoying my body in the relaxed state he leaves me in.

While he puts the rag in the laundry, I grab my clothes and get dressed.

We sit on the bed and eat the pastry without talking much, just sharing knowing looks and quick smiles. My cheeks are a little red, but I'm surprised at how not embarrassed I am by this.

"You know I'll never be able to look at one of these again, right?"

Nick laughs, his shoulders shaking as he shoves another bite into his mouth and licks his fingers. "Yeah, that's the point." He looks at me. "You can't ever forget me now."

"I don't think that would be possible, even before this." I nod at the food in his hand.

"Why's that?"

I take a minute to answer him, not sure what to say or how to say it, I guess. I'm afraid it'll sound weird or clingy.

"I—" I cut myself off and take a deep breath. "You make me feel worthy? Important?"

His eyes meet mine, questions and determination swimming in the depths. "What do you mean?"

"I obviously had sex before we met." I shrug and try to hold his gaze but end up looking down at my lap. "No one cared enough to make sure I got mine or noticed when I didn't, but even before we got to know each other, you cared. You made sure I was good."

"Sex is only good if both partners are satisfied." He lifts my face to see him. "Otherwise, why would you go back for more? I knew after that first time that I needed more, so I made sure I gave you a reason to come back."

I smile at him and give him a quick kiss, just a brush of lips.

"I appreciate you."

Nick winks at me and offers me the last piece of the cinnamon roll, but I shake my head, and he eats it.

"I should take you to meet Debbi, she will like you." Nick lies down on the bed on his side and pats the mattress in front of him.

"Who is Debbi?" I lie in front of him, and he pulls me flush against his chest. Nick settles his face against my neck and kisses my skin.

"She makes the cinnamon rolls," he says around a yawn.

"I can never meet her!" I turn my head to try to look at him, but he holds me tightly so I can't roll over. "I violated her masterpiece!"

Nick chuckles and throws his leg over my hip. "It'll be fine. She's supersweet, you'll like her."

He quickly falls asleep, wrapped around me like a damn octopus, and I can't stop myself from following him.

The next day, we head down to the dining hall after our workout. The moment I step inside, I smell it and my face heats. Cinnamon.

I stop dead in my tracks and look at Nick with what I'm sure is a horrified expression. We can't eat in here. My dick is already thickening just from the memory the smell brings flashing into my head.

"Let's find a diner or something." I grab his hoodie sleeve and pull, but he doesn't budge.

"Cinnamon roll day is my favorite." Nick is smiling so big it reminds me of kids on Christmas. I'm going to kill him.

"Nick!" I whisper-yell as he pulls out of my grip and hustles toward the line. Oh, fuck my life.

I get in line behind him, cursing him under my breath and thinking about hockey stats to stop my head from going to sex, but I can still feel how hot my damn cheeks are.

Nick loads up on food, and of course takes a damn cinnamon roll and throws me a wink, the bastard.

Once I've gotten food, we find a table and sit down. I glare at Nick while he smiles like the Cheshire cat as I shove eggs into my mouth.

Since I'm staring at Nick, I don't notice anyone approaching, so I jump when trays hit the table. Oiler and Johnson drop down next to us, obviously in the middle of a conversation.

"Movie marathon today," Oiler mentions and shoves food into his mouth as Johnson nods.

"What are you guys going to watch?" I ask.

"*Star Wars*," they say together.

A woman walks past us with what looks like the center of a cinnamon roll on her plate, she dumps it in the trash and puts her plate into the dirty dish bin. The memory of eating that same part from Nick's hand, then sucking his fingers clean hits me like a freight train. It's immediate and overwhelming. My face flushes and my breathing shallows as I relive it.

Nick makes a sound of disbelief, and it pulls me from the memory playing like a movie in my head.

"Why the fuck would anyone throw away the *best* part? Is she broken? What kind of trauma does that to a person?" Nick is so shocked by this that I laugh. He turns on me with wide eyes and indignation flaming his words. "That is a crime against humanity!"

"Dude, chill." Johnson is looking at Nick like he's crazy, which isn't wrong.

Nick looks at me half crazed and shoves two fingers into his cinnamon roll like he did yesterday and scoops out the center. Our eyes lock as he shoves his fingers into his mouth and sucks the sweetness from his skin. A groan gets stuck in my throat, making a weird squeak sound instead.

"Uh, are you having a moment with your breakfast?" Oiler's voice pulls my gaze from Nick. "Did you ask if it consented to public violation?"

I. Am. Horrified.

My eyes are wide and the blood drains from my face. I grab my tray and start to stand, but Nick puts his feet in my lap. The bastard is smiling like this is the funniest thing he's ever seen while I'm trying to forget that I have a hard-on in the dining hall in front of my teammates. My knee starts bouncing, and the pressure around my ribs increases. I'm not ready for the team to know about this. While I don't think they'll care much, you never really know how someone is going to react.

"I *really* like cinnamon rolls." Nick winks at Oiler, and Johnson snorts. "All warm and gooey and sweet." Nick hums, and I have never wanted to punch him, but I do right now. He's about to learn how violent hockey gets.

Oiler looks skeptical, but he's eyeing the pastry like he's considering it.

I can't sit here anymore. Standing, I grab my tray, and Nick's feet fall to the floor. He watches me with a lifted eyebrow and a smirk on his face. He thinks this is hilarious while I'm trying not to panic. Great.

I deal with my tray and leave the hall toward the dorms. It's probably time for me to sleep in my own room. Why does that thought make my chest ache?

There's a dull pain in my breastbone that I rub the heel of my hand against as I open the dorm building door.

"Hey!" With the door handle in my hand, I turn to see Nick jogging to catch up. Why does my heart hurt? That was a close call. I'm not ready for anyone to know yet. Fuck, I don't even know if this is anything more than just sex while we're here on break with nothing else to do.

We walk inside and wait for the elevator in silence, but it's not comfortable, at least not for me. He's watching me from the corner of his eye, so maybe he's as uneasy as I am. The doors open and we step on, then I reach for the five button, but he grabs my wrist.

"We should talk," he says, not giving anything away in those three words. Is that a *we're done* talk or a *let's label this* talk?

I nod and he pushes the three. When the doors close, he threads our fingers together and holds my hand. Slowly, I drag in a deep breath and let it out. Why does his touch soothe me like this? This can't be bad, right? He wouldn't be trying to comfort me if he wanted to end it, right?

When the doors open a minute later, he gives me the chance to pull away, but I don't want to. Am I ready to tell everyone I'm sleeping with him? No, but right now, I need his comfort more than I need the secret.

He gives me a small smile and leads us to his room.

Once we're safely inside alone, he turns to face me and wraps me in a tight hug. I breathe him in and relax in his hold. How did he know I needed this when I didn't? Can he read me that well already?

"No one on the team knows you like men, right?" he says while keeping me tightly against him.

"No."

"I'm sorry I pushed it." Nick cups the back of my head and leans his forehead against mine. "That was a dick move, I'm sorry."

I nod and press a light kiss to his lips.

"I don't want this to stop," he says against my lips. "It feels too important to let go."

"I don't either."

Our breaths mix between us, and the warmth of our bodies surrounds us.

"I can wait until you're ready." Nick holds my gaze. "I'm not exactly out either, but I just don't care. I'm not going to make an announcement to the team, but if someone sees me with a boyfriend, I'm not going to lie either. You know?"

"Yeah, I get that." Some of the tension drains away. "I kind of like that. My sexuality isn't an announcement, but I don't think I want to hide who I'm with either. That's shitty. But I don't want the questions."

"If you need to wait, it's okay. I understand. You get to decide who knows and when." Nick kisses me again. "But I don't share."

I smile. "I don't share *you*."

"Good." Nick slides his hands down my back and cups my ass, rubbing our hips together. "I need you."

I chuckle and bite his lower lip. "Again? You got off two hours ago."

"Cinnamon rolls now give me a hard-on."

I drop my head back and laugh at the most ridiculous sentence I've ever heard but let him push me back onto the bed and welcome his weight on me.

We don't have to have all the answers right now, we have time to figure it out, and together, we'll do just that. We are worthy of love and happiness.

CHAPTER 8

joey

Classes start again in a few days which means Nick and I won't have a room to ourselves at all hours for long. No more sleep-overs in our boxers like our current situation.

Nick's warm, sleep-loosened body is pressed against my back, his arm under my neck, and his knee between mine. I thread my fingers through his, a slow smile lifting my lips when he stirs a little. Nick pushes his face into my neck and grumbles something about morning people.

His other hand slides down my stomach to run along the waistband of my underwear.

"I thought you hated morning people?" I close my eyes and lean into him.

"If I have to be awake, I might as well get an orgasm out of it." Nick bites my ear and scrapes my neck with his prickly face. He slides his hand inside and pumps me slowly. A shudder has goosebumps breaking out on my skin and I can feel Nick smiling against my skin. "I love the way you react to me."

"I love the way you touch me," I groan.

I roll my hips and close my eyes, letting myself get lost in him. We both know this can't last, we have to get back to school and I still have hockey for another two or three months, and his roommate is going to be back in a few days. But right now, today, in this moment, I can just enjoy him.

It's still early enough that I don't need to worry too much about being quiet so I don't hold back my moans or the hitches in my breathing that sound like whimpers.

"Hmm such a needy boy," Nick says against my neck and squeezes the base of my dick. In the blink of an eye, his hand is gone and he's settling between my thighs. I reach for him, wanting to feel his weight against me, but he doesn't seem to want to give me what I want.

"Nick," I whine while wrapping my legs around his hips and grinding up against him.

"Pull your dick out, stroke it for me." The demand in his voice has my hand doing exactly that with no hesitation. My brain doesn't even try to process it, just reacts.

For once in my fucking life, I don't have to think about the consequences, implications, what is expected of me. All I have to do is feel and let him take care of me. It's a completely foreign concept. No one takes care of me.

"Look at me," Nick growls and I focus on him. I didn't realize I had zoned out and got lost in my head. He's released his own cock and wraps his hand around both of us to show me what he wants. "Jack us off, make us come."

Using both of my hands, I grip us tightly as he lets go and thrusts against my hands.

With his eyes locked on mine, he forces pleasure onto both of us. His pupils are blown with arousal and a light sheen of sweat covers his skin. This guy is gorgeous and for whatever reason, he wants to be with me. He puts up with my baggage.

I can feel my dick softening in my grip and embarrassment heats my cheeks. Fuck! Why? This is not how I wanted to start today!

Nick leans over me, his lips a whisper above mine. "Do you need to be filled, stretched, and taken?"

I bite my bottom lip and whimper in that pathetic little voice he says he loves.

He smirks, it's a promising lift of his lips, and he licks my throat.

"It's fine." I grip him hard in my hand, working his dick quickly so he'll come.

"Joey," he lifts my chin and waits until I meet his gaze before continuing. "If you want to slow down and work yourself back up, it's okay. Trust me. It's no hardship to have my hands on you."

This can't last, can it? My chest tightens with fear and embarrassment and feelings I don't have any right to have. Lifting my arm, I drop it over my face to cover my eyes before I start crying like a big baby.

Why do I have to be like this? What twenty-five-year-old has problems keeping their dick hard? Why do I have to be broken?

A soft mouth brushes mine below my arm, then the tip of a tongue runs along the ridge of my bottom lip. I let him distract me, use him to get out of my head. Sliding my arm off my face, I run my fingers through his hair and cup the back of his head.

Nick puts more of his weight on me and fucks into my mouth with his tongue.

His hips slide against mine in a slow roll until I'm panting.

"I have an idea." Nick wags his eyebrows and hops off the bed to dig through a box under his bed. He's back in a flash with a silicone-covered bullet vibrator and a couple clothespins.

I look at him skeptically. "You do know that I'm no stranger to sex toys, right?"

He scoffs and settles between my thighs. "When was the last time a partner used them on you?"

Okay, he may have a point there.

Nick leans over me to suck on my nipples. He doesn't touch anything else, only his mouth on the sensitive skin.

I know the bite of the clothespin is coming and anticipating that pain is doing weird things to me. I want it but I'm almost afraid of it at the same time, which is confusing my dick.

I hiss at the pinch when he clamps the pin on my skin. He gives the other nipple the same treatment and my dick twitches. With a devilish smile, he kisses me and flicks the pins, making my back arch off the mattress.

I'm panting and half hard when Nick sits up and reaches for the lube.

"I'm still good from last night, I don't need prep."

Nick lifts an eyebrow and meets my gaze. "You sure?"

"Just fuck me, Wyhe."

With a smile, he coats his thick cock and pushes against my hole.

I groan at the slight stretch as he thrusts in and grinds against my ass.

"Please," I beg in that little voice. I don't know why it comes out with him but I love that he likes it.

His nostrils flare and he sets a quick, hard pace. This isn't soft, slow morning sex, this is the kind of fucking that proves a point.

I grip my dick, stroking fast until I'm finally hard again.

Nick grips my hips, changing the angle just a little to get deeper, and I arch off the bed. My orgasm is building, my muscles tightening, and tingles spreading. He rips off the clothespins and the new sensation shoves me over the edge.

"Fuck." That sweet voice only he can pull from me comes loose as my body tightens with my orgasm. "Daddy!" The word flies from my mouth as warm cum lands on my stomach and my fingers tighten in the sheets until my knuckles are white. There's nothing past Nick fucking me, the endorphins flooding my brain, and my harsh breathing.

"Oh, duuuude." A voice I've never heard before comes from behind Nick and we both freeze. I can feel my eyes getting wide as I stare at him in horror. Nick's entire body is tight with tension as he quickly looks over his shoulder.

"Shit," he snaps and pulls out of me. "Dude! Get the fuck out!" Nick yells at whoever that is and pulls up his boxers. "Joey, you're okay."

I barely hear the words as I scramble for clothes and shove past Nick's roommate, running from the room. There's nothing in my head except the need to get away. My brain is telling me I'm in danger and need to run, need to get away. I make a break for the stairwell and run as fast as I can down them, then push my way outside into the cold air. The icy concrete seeps into my feet and helps calm me. The swift change in my environment pulls me out of my fight-or-flight response and lets me breathe.

My breath is a cloud in front of me and my bare arms prickle as I cover my face with my hands.

Fuck. What the hell am I going to do? Did Nick's roommate recognize me? Would he if he saw me again? I can't risk it and go back to Nick's room. I guess what we were doing is done now.

It was never supposed to be anything major. I don't have time or energy for a relationship. I have to focus on finishing up my hockey season and graduating. Helping Mom and Charlotte with Matt. Coming out and having a boyfriend is drama I don't want to deal with. I haven't heard many homophobic slurs in the locker room this year but that doesn't mean a closet homophobe isn't lurking. Sports are notorious for toxic masculinity and homophobia.

Then why does the idea of not seeing him again hurt so much?

I rub at the ache in my chest and force back the tears that threaten to fall.

"Yo! Carp!" A voice behind me makes me jump, my heart pounding as my body prepares for an attack. "What are you doing out here with no jacket, man?"

Bryce cocks his head with a confused expression on his face.

"And where are your shoes?"

"Oh, uh." I look down at my feet, at my toes that are an angry shade of red that's starting to turn purple. Oops. "I needed to cool down for a minute."

He shrugs and holds the door open as I hobble toward him. The small pebbles on the concrete are like knives on the bottoms of my feet. I guess they aren't quiet numb yet.

"Joey." Nick bursts through the door of the stairs and makes a beeline for me. I quickly put my captain mask on. We both knew what this was when it started. We were just fooling around during the break and maybe a random hookup or two during the season when both of us had time and an itch to scratch.

"Hey, what's up?" I shove my frozen fingers into my pockets and cringe as the rough fabric scratches my sensitive skin.

Bryce is standing by the elevator pretending like he isn't listening, but he clearly is.

Nick grabs my arm and pulls me into the stairwell.

"Are you okay? My roommate is cool, he won't say anything."

"How do you know that?" I cross my arms over my chest like it'll help protect me from my feelings. It's laughable, really. I'm an adult, yet here I am, wishing things could be different. Life isn't easy for me, it never has been, so why did I think this would be any different?

"Because he's on the football team and is an underclassman trying to get to first string. If he causes problems, he won't make it."

I can't meet Nick's eyes despite how desperately I want him to hold me right now. But I can't give in.

"Well, we knew this was a limited time thing anyway, so it's fine." I shrug and force myself to straighten my shoulders. I'm twenty-five, the captain of the Darby U hockey team, and a senior. I will deal with this head-on and stop running. "I'll see you around, I guess."

I push past him and hate myself for the hurt I see in his dark eyes and the droop of his shoulders. I can't have the distraction of a relationship. There's too many things at play here, and I need to focus on my responsibilities. Once I graduate, I have to make sure my siblings are taken care of, make sure Mom can retire eventually. I don't have time for a boyfriend.

Doesn't matter how safe he makes me feel. Or how seen. Doesn't matter that he's the first guy to give a shit about what I need and not make me seem like a freak.

My gut clenches as I hold back the emotions.

This is why I do meaningless hookups when the need gets to be too much. There's nothing but lust and hopefully an orgasm or two before we part ways.

"Everything good?" Bryce gives me a chin lift and I nod.

"Yeah, no big deal." I sigh and push the button for the fifth floor. "He wanted to check in on our dumbass freshman that got drunk a few nights ago."

I catch Nick's gaze through the glass in the stairwell door as the elevator closes and I hate how much I want to reach for him.

CHAPTER 9

nick

I'm numb as Joey walks away from me. What the fuck just happened?

He steps into the elevator and hits a button but as the doors close, his eyes find mine. My soft boy that just wants cuddles and attention is hidden behind the hockey player mask. That side of him isn't mine. It never was.

The only part of him I got was the one he keeps locked in the dark. I guess even that is gone now.

Somehow, in two weeks, my feelings got involved, and he became more than a fuck. I told him we could be friends, but now I'm not so sure of that. If I see him with someone else, it might break me.

With a sigh, I run my hands through my hair and head back to my dorm, taking the stairs. The fear on Joey's face when Neal caught us will forever be etched in my memory. I never want to see that look on my lover's face. Ever. But especially while we're in bed.

I find my way back to my room in a daze. If anyone spoke to me, I didn't hear it or acknowledge it. Was there even anyone in the hallway?

Neal flicks his gaze to me for a second before looking back at his phone. "I see your winter break was more fun than mine." He does something on the screen then huffs and puts the device down. "I *got* to see my sister have a baby then spent every day with her, the crying lump of flesh, and her obnoxious husband."

I don't know what to say but his sarcasm isn't lost on me. *Don't tell anyone* seems obvious, but he's also not freaking out, so I kind of want to thank him for that...

"You don't like babies?" *Really, brain? That's all you got?*

"No, kids are gross, messy, usually sticky or smelly, and loud." The big man ticks things off on his fingers. Being a defenseman means he's got weight to throw around and he's a hairy bastard on top of it. He's solid as a boulder and probably twice as thick as I am.

I laugh in my head at the unintentional dick joke.

"So are ninety percent of the guys on our team." I scoff and run my hand over my hair. I want to find Joey and demand that he listen to me, but I doubt he will. I don't know enough about his history to be able to figure out what's going on in his head right now.

I need out of here. The longer I stay in here, the worse I'll spiral. "I gotta go," I mumble before I grab my shoes, a hoodie, and my phone, then leave. I can't be in here where I can still smell Joey on my pillow. Where I can picture him lying in my bed, hear his sweet voice in my head.

It's cold outside since the temperature has dropped below freezing, but I don't care. I just start walking. The wind bites at my cheeks and nose, my breath a cloud in front of my face, but I keep going with nowhere in mind.

The streets are busy, people are in a hurry like always. It's easy to get lost in the crowd and let my mind wander.

I'm not typically a relationship guy because football takes up so much of my time. Spring training, summer training, the season, practice, traveling, and gym time all take up a lot of my energy. Add classes on top of it and I'm not left with much else. Most people want to spend time with their boyfriend. Most athletes' significant others don't last long. Once the season starts, they bounce.

Pulling my phone from my pocket, I text Joey.

NICK:

This doesn't have to change anything. We can still just mess around when you get that itch.

I wait for him to see it but either he didn't hear the notification or he's ignoring me.

NICK:

We can be friends, like we agreed on.

Fuck, I sound desperate. Clingy.

I scrub a hand over my face and call Brent. He won't bullshit me.

It rings a few times before his face comes up on the screen.

"What's up, numbnuts?" He smirks at me and my bright red cheeks.

"Neal caught me having sex." I sigh.

The smile on my best friend's face falls and his eyes widen.

"Oh shit, with that hockey player?"

I pinch the bridge of my nose. "Yeah. He panicked, ran, and said we're done."

"Sounds like you were more than hooking up, man." He pauses for a second, then the light behind him changes as he moves. "You catch feelings or did you just not want to tell me the whole truth?"

As I walk along, I find a bench and sit down. The cold seeps through my jeans so fast I'm afraid my ass is going to get stuck to the metal.

"I offered to let him explore some shit with me, told him I wanted to be friends." I look up at the gray clouds that are just as stormy as my head. "He's an athlete. He knows how hard it is to keep relationships up, so it was a good deal."

"Right..."

"Shut up. It was a good plan!"

"Yet here you are looking like a kicked puppy. Something isn't adding up, dude."

I huff out a breath in agitation. "All right. Fine. I caught fucking feelings, you jackass. Happy now?"

"Uh, yeah, actually, I am. 'Cause I'm right." Brent reaches across himself to pat his own shoulder.

"Yeah, great, yay for you. How do I fix this?"

"Fix it so you can have an actual relationship or so you can fuck him again?"

"I really fucking hate you." I switch hands holding the phone and shove my now red fingers into my armpit to warm up. "I want an actual relationship but if all he's willing to give is sex, then I'll take that."

"Does he want a relationship? Isn't hockey still going?"

"Dude. I'm real tired of your logic right now." I take a deep breath and think about his question for a minute. "I don't know if he's against a relationship or not, and yes, hockey is still going, but I understand the lifestyle he has to live right now. I'm not going to be whining at him because he doesn't give me enough attention."

"You're *literally* doing that right now."

"Why do I talk to you again?" I stand and head back toward the school. It's too damn cold for this.

School doesn't start for another few days, which means Neal will be in our room constantly. Looks like I'm about to get a new hobby.

CHAPTER 10

joey

Waking up without Nick sucks.

Not cuddling with Nick sucks.

Not getting off multiple times a day sucks.

It's truly amazing how quickly you get used to something. It's been barely past two weeks since Nick and I started messing around and already I miss not having him around. It's been a few days since I ran from his dorm room like my ass was on fire, and it feels like there's a weight on my shoulders. Well, more weight.

Char texted to tell me that Matt was arrested and thrown into the drunk tank. Again. Mom keeps letting him back in the house even though he doesn't help out in the slightest and makes a huge mess.

I've been told that she blames his lack of work ethic on me.

Somehow, I'm supposed to fix my brother's issues while playing hockey and going to school, from four hours away. Great.

Nothing new there.

With a sigh, I drop onto my bed and hold my head in my hands. I should be packing for our away game tomorrow, but I just don't care.

Albrooke and Carmichael are a thing now, I guess, Oiler and Johnson are being weirder than normal, and I don't have the energy to care about either situation. Carmichael is still a raging asshole and I'm tired of hearing it.

Bryce comes in and sits on his bed across from me.

"You okay?"

I sigh and sit up, faking a smile. "Yeah, today's workout was just a rough one. I'm fine."

He gives me a sad kind of smile. "You can just tell me you don't want to talk about it."

Damn it. My shoulders droop as the energy leaves me.

"That's fair. Thanks for asking, but I'm not ready to talk about it."

He nods and pats my shoulder. "I'm gonna grab lunch. You wanna join or are you gonna continue to sit here and sulk?"

I chuckle. "Lunch sounds good."

Though I would rather sit here and sulk in my loneliness, I don't really get that option. I have guys to look after.

In the dining room, Oiler and Albrooke are having some kind of heated discussion about bread while Carmichael looks bored and Johnson laughs.

Bryce and I sit and watch as we eat.

"Texas Roadhouse rolls are far superior to Olive Garden breadsticks!" Oiler says with a mouthful of...something.

"Nothing beats Red Lobster's Cheddar Bay Biscuits, is all I'm saying!" Albrooke yells.

"Neither of you should be eating this much bread," Carmichael says, but everyone ignores him.

"Adding cheese to anything makes it better!" Oiler scoffs.

"Not pie," Johnson retorts.

"Cheddar cheese on apple pie is pretty good, actually," Oiler says.

"I don't think I would like cheese on cake or ice cream," I offer.

Oiler groans and tosses his head back. "You guys are missing the entire point. We're talking about bread, not desserts!"

"How about you shove more food in your mouth and shut up," Carmichael says.

"Why don't you make me?" Albrooke turns to Carmichael and the look they share is terrifyingly sexy.

"Make sure you guys are packed for tomorrow." I take a bite out of my apple and Carmichael turns back to the table, but Albrooke has a flush on his cheeks that I don't want to think too much about.

Bryce chuckles but doesn't chime in to the chat, just eats and watches the chaos. The team really is a bunch of good guys this year. The young ones are *very* young but they aren't troublemakers. Carmichael is the biggest asshole I've ever met, but I'm starting to think he means well.

All in all, I'm proud to say I'm on the team with these guys and I'll miss them next year when I'm forced into the working world.

My phone starts ringing and I hold my breath as I pull it from my pocket. Charlotte. Shit.

"I gotta take this," I say, not waiting for a response, and leave the loud dining hall as I accept the call. "Hey, Char, what's up?"

"I swear to God!" she yells in my ear. "I don't know how you did this for so damn long but I'm going to kill Matt, maybe Mom too!"

I close my eyes and lean back against the rough stone wall. I hate that the pressure of taking care of Matt has fallen on her shoulders since I left. Guilt eats at me for leaving her. She doesn't deserve to be responsible for him. She's twenty-four and should be living it up with her friends, establishing a career, and getting married. Instead she's pulled back into cleaning up our brother's mess, all while Mom does nothing to help and even accuses her of not doing enough.

"What happened this time?"

"He was court ordered to go to AA, right? Well, he showed up drunk and pissed in a plastic plant in the meeting hall. Piss everywhere!" She's so angry I can picture steam coming out her ears. He's a fucking mess and guilt weighs heavy on me for that too. "Guess who they called to come clean it up? Me! And I had to take him home. They told me I was *lucky* they didn't call the police and have him arrested for public indecency and public intoxication. Lucky! Do you believe that shit?!"

"I'm sorry, Char, I would have taken care of it if I were there." My shoulders fall and I want to slide down the wall to sit on the ground, but

I don't. "Just a few more months and I can move back home and try to find a job. Then it won't be on you to deal with all this."

"That's not the point! Neither of us should be dealing with Matt's bullshit. If Mom doesn't want him falling on his ass, then she needs to be the one to deal with him."

I nod, though I know she can't see me. She's right. Mom should have always been stepping up and taking care of her kids, but instead she buried herself in work. I don't really blame her. The medical bills from Dad's treatment and the funeral costs were insane, but she checked out on us. Somewhere along the way, she blamed us for not being perfect, for having trauma and scars. I waited as long as I could to go to college. I found a team I could play on close to home that wouldn't ruin my chances of getting into a good school. While I was there, I honed my skills, and made sure my brother graduated high school before I left. Fuck, I even got him a job, but it all fell apart when I moved out.

Now he's found himself at the bottom of a fucking bottle and he's only twenty-two.

"I don't know what to do anymore." Her voice is quiet now. Tired. Sad. "I don't want to bury him, Joey."

Sadness clogs my throat at her words. She's only a year younger than me, but she had to grow up too fast. In times like these, she's a little girl again. Lost and in need of someone to give her a hug, tell her it's going to be okay, that we'll figure it out together, but I'm not there to do it.

"I don't either."

"He's wasting away in front of me. He's so much worse than the last time you were home." She sniffles and it breaks my heart. "We're going to lose him."

"Just a few more months. I graduate in June and I'll come home for spring interterm to help out."

This right here is why I can't date. I don't have the time or the energy to give more of myself to someone. There's nothing left. I'm being crushed under the weight of everyone else's expectations. I don't know who I am or who I'm supposed to be anymore.

CHAPTER 11

nick

I'm watching the hockey game on the TV at the foot of my bed. The last few days I've been *researching* Joey's games on YouTube and shit. Getting a good feel for how he plays, the way he thinks out there, and learning some of the game rules. Sort of. They're weird.

I've watched so many clips of his games that as I'm watching this one, I can tell he's having a shit night. He's frustrated and maybe distracted. The team as a whole looks great, though. They've gotten a few goals and not too many fights have broken out.

They do that thing where the guys switch out in the middle of whatever is happening on the ice and Number Twenty-Two, a big fucker, is hit hard by someone on the other team. He falls awkwardly onto someone behind him and doesn't get up. Another Darby U player skates over and offers him a hand up.

The announcers say something about a possible injury, the whistles blow on the ice, and what looks like medics and the coach hurry out.

We get a commercial break and I'm bouncing my knee as I check the roster on the team's website. Preston Carmichael. That's the guy I found at Debbi's with the redhead and hat guy. What the hell were their names? Peter and Brian?

I chuckle when *Family Guy* pops into my head. Definitely not Peter and Brian. Patrick? Parker? Phillip? I think the P name was hat guy. Redhead started with a B. Brant? Blake? Braxton?

It doesn't matter.

The announcers tell us that Carmichael was taken for a shoulder injury and the game continues. Shit. That's going to stress out Joey.

I open up my texts and send a message, even though he hasn't looked at the previous ones.

NICK:

Hey, I'm watching the game. I know you're stressed. Take a deep breath. Call me if you want to talk about it.

I hit send without thinking about it too hard. I want him to call so fucking badly it aches. I can't even get updates about him via social media because he doesn't post anything. Literally nothing. His last IG picture was from eight months ago. Eight.

I toss my phone on the bed and scrub my hands over my face. I have to go out and do something tonight or I'll sit here and obsess over my damn phone.

Changing into jeans and pulling on shoes, I give myself a stern talk. *I will watch the rest of the game, then go out and find something to do. Play pool or darts or something. It doesn't matter.*

My phone rings as I'm pulling my last shoe on and I scramble for it, answering it before I look to see who it is.

"Hello? Joey?"

"Who's Joey?" My mom's voice filters through the speaker and I wince. Shit.

"Hey, Mom. What's going on? Did you get a new kid? How's Alice, she still having trouble in school?" *Please let her get distracted and move on...*

"Nice try, Nicholas."

I sigh heavily and close my eyes. "It's just...some guy I'm trying to be friends with." I shrug even though I know she can't see it.

"Friends or *friends*?"

"Nope. I'm not talking to you about this." I shudder at the very idea of telling her I want to hook up with Joey. I love my mom and I know I can talk to her about anything, but no thanks.

She laughs and it comforts my heart. I miss her warm hugs and gingerbread cookies. It's not Christmas until she makes saffron bread for Saint Lucia's Day on the thirteenth. It doesn't matter that we aren't religious. She started baking it because of a second-grade school project I had and just never stopped. I've missed it every year since I went away to school.

"We haven't talked in a while so I'm just calling to check in on my kid now that football isn't keeping you busy."

I flop back on my bed with a sigh. "I'm okay. I'm going out tonight and hanging out with some people."

"That sounds legitimate and not at all made up," she scoffs and I laugh.

"No, really, I'm going out tonight. I just don't know where or who with. I made the decision about two minutes ago."

The conversation drops off into silence as I get wrapped up in my thoughts of Joey again. How much I miss being around him, his smile, the smell of his skin when he's fallen asleep against me...

"Nicky?" Mom says my nickname that I haven't heard in too long.

"Yeah?"

"I think you should come home on your next break. Something is going on with you and I think you need to ground yourself."

I know she means well and she's probably right, but my gut says no. I don't want to be that far from Joey. What if he needs me and I'm not there?

How did I let him get so far under my skin? Why am I so obsessed with him?

"I'll see if I can. I can't promise anything."

"Okay, baby, let me know, okay? I'm worried about you."

I smile a sad, one-sided smile. "I know, Momma. I love you."

My parents are amazing. I know I'm lucky to have them. I've seen firsthand what happens to the kids whose parents weren't around or abused them. How the system designed to help them has actually forgotten them or doesn't care. My parents cared and did everything they could for the kids' lives they touched. A lot of them keep in touch after leaving, whether they went back home, got moved to another house, or aged out.

But maybe they meant more because they were broken and I wasn't.

"I love you too."

I end the call and open my message thread with Joey but he hasn't opened it. Not surprising. I think the game is still going on. With nothing in mind, I slip down the stairs, shove my hands in my pockets, and wander around. I'm not hungry so I don't go to the pizza place. Not feeling social, I skip past Rocky's. It's cold, though, and I want to go inside, so I end up in a coffee shop on campus.

It smells like coffee beans and something sweet, maybe cookies? It's hard to tell over the overwhelming coffee scent. A girl in a black apron and a high ponytail smiles at me as I walk toward the counter.

"Hi, welcome to Roasted Mountains. What can I get started for you?"

Her apron has Carly stitched onto it.

"Roasted Mountains is a horrible dad joke." I smile at her, knowing she probably hears it multiple times a day.

She chuckles and nods. "You aren't wrong."

"I don't really drink coffee...I'm more of an energy drink kind of person." I look up at the chalkboard menu and none of this shit makes sense. Americano, flat white, latte, cappuccino? What's the difference?

"So you came to a coffee shop, why?" The smile on her lips is flirty and while a part of me wants to flirt back because flirting is fun, I don't have the energy for it.

I shrug and lean against the counter. "Just needed somewhere to go."

Her smile falls to contemplative and she cocks her head while she studies me. "I have an idea. Any food limitations?"

I shake my head.

"Have a seat, I'll bring it over in a minute."

There's a few people taking up the booths and bartop stools, so I head to a corner where there's a couch and some armchairs. One is facing the big floor-to-ceiling windows, so I take that one and scooch down until the back of my head is against the cushion. I don't want to stare at my phone, obsessing over Joey not looking at the messages, or watch the game.

There's a light dusting of snow outside and now that everyone has taken down the Christmas decorations, it's just depressing. Something about the twinkling lights brings a sense of magic. I guess it's one more tally against me today.

Carly pops up next to me with a tray. "Spiced hot chocolate with one shot of espresso and a warm chocolate chip cookie." I take the short wide mug from her and the matching white plate.

"Thank you."

"You're welcome." She smiles and goes back behind the counter. I have to admit it smells amazing, sweet, and comforting. The whipped cream is melting into the hot drink and when I take a sip, the cinnamon and cloves make me groan. There's more in it that I can't pick out but it's perfect. The espresso cutting the sweet just enough that it isn't overpowering and is rounding out the flavors.

I turn in my seat to see Carly watching me.

"You're a coffee witch!" I raise my mug at her and she laughs. "This is amazing."

She exaggerates a bow. "Thank you, kind sir."

Sitting up in the seat, I look around and find a small table to put my drink on while I eat my cookie, but of course my damn phone rings.

With a huff, I pull it from my pocket and groan at Brent's stupid face.

"What?"

"Nice to talk to you too, ass."

I sigh and wait. I know Mom called him. He's the only one who could talk me down when the urge to fight kicked in. It didn't always work, but he had a better chance than anyone else, especially since he knew the root cause of my issues.

I was in love with a girl I couldn't save.

"Mom called," he says, not beating around the bush. I appreciate that about him.

"Figured as much." I shove a piece of my warm cookie into my mouth. "I'm fine."

"I doubt that," he scoffs but doesn't push. Not yet.

I sigh and pinch the bridge of my nose. "I'm just in a bad mood. I'm allowed to be."

"So you aren't treading water in the deep end of the feelings pool over this hockey player walking away?"

I grit my teeth. "Fuck off."

"Good. Just so we're clear, you caught feelings like it was mono at an eighth-grade sleepover playing spin the bottle, and now that you can't play with your favorite toy, you're sulking."

"For fuck's sake, Brent. Stop." I really don't want to picture thirteen-year-olds making out.

He sighs and his tone is softer when he talks again. "It's okay to have feelings for this guy."

"You're really stuck on the feelings, aren't you?" My gut tightens and tears knot in my throat. "He's not interested."

The line goes silent for so long I pull it from my ear to check and see if the call dropped.

"Can you hear me?" I ask.

"Uh, yeah. That's not the impression I got from him basically living in your room over break." I can picture the confused expression on his face. While I'm my parents' only biological child, this guy is my brother through and through. He knows everything about me, my ride or die.

I look around the coffee shop and there's too many people in here for me to be comfortable having this conversation here.

"I can't talk about it right now."

"Fine, but I expect you to talk to me. Today."

I huff but agree. It'll probably be good for me to talk to someone but my instincts tell me to bury it. Feelings are dangerous.

"Look, I'm out right now. I'll talk to you later." I don't want to do this right now. Or ever. I want Joey back and for him to promise he won't ever leave me again. Right now, I feel like I'm drowning in anger. Or loneliness. Hopelessness. Feelings make you weak and I can't be weak again. Never again.

CHAPTER 12

joey

Everything is falling apart.

I was the only one at tonight's game that didn't have my shit together. Oiler, Johnson, and Albrooke were on fire. Willis and Carmichael were a force to be reckoned with. Our goalie, Chris Austin, was killing it. Then there was me. Tripping over my own fucking skates, missing passes, passing to the wrong fucking team. I'm a joke.

The bite of cold cools my heated skin as I watch my teammate get carted off the ice. Carmichael is a tough bastard, so if he needed help up, he's hurt bad. Fuck.

The crowd stands and claps in respect for Carmichael but my gaze goes to Albrooke. He looks like he's going to be sick. The two of them fight during practice like they get off on it. Oiler and Johnson surround him and get him somewhat settled, but I can tell his head isn't in the right place anymore.

I chew on my mouth guard as I wait for my turn back on the ice. The refs get the boys set and restart the game. The puck is flung to a

Providence player and the fight for the goal starts once again. It's a constant battle and we're all hungry for it.

At least, we usually are. Most of the team is, but not me. I'm hungry for something else.

For the escape only one person has ever helped me find. For the release of all my responsibilities for just a few minutes.

Normally, when my skates hit the ice, I can tune out all of life's bullshit. My brother's problems, my mom blaming everything he does on me, the weight of everyone around me to be perfect all the damn time. But I can't today. Today, all I want is for Nick to wrap his hand in my hair, make me look into his eyes, and have him tell me that I'm enough.

Why can't I ever be enough?

Coach yells for a line change and I stand to get ready to head back out on the ice. The defenders come off and my skates hit the ice. I take off toward the other side of the ice and try to focus. The puck is on our side and I hustle to block a winger trying to get to the goal. There are bodies everywhere, sticks and skates making it hard to get the puck to move. I shove the player in front of me hard enough to get him out of the way and Matthews, my other defender, flings the puck back to the other side where Louis grabs it and scrambles across the blue line with Kendall.

The first line wingers, Kendall and Louis, pass it back and forth a few times before aiming at our center, Yaw, who manages to get the biscuit in the basket and the lamp lights up!

"Fuck yeah!" Matthews hollers, his hands in the air. Relief surges through me that I didn't fuck up the play, and I head back to the bench.

"Good teamwork, boys," Coach says as we come off the ice, but he's not looking at us. He's watching our second line get set for the puck drop.

It's rough the rest of the game but we manage a win. It was hard and we're all exhausted by the time we get to the locker room. Adrenaline keeps us standing but once we hit the showers and get changed, most of us just want to eat and pass out.

I overhear Albrooke on the phone and turn to watch him grab Carmichael's stuff then take off.

Johnson and Oiler share a look that I'm sure is them deciding if they are going to go to the hospital as well. If I were close to either Albrooke or Carmichael, I would go.

"Hey, Coach," I holler when I see him enter the locker room. He turns and stops when he sees me. "Any update on Carmichael?"

"Dislocated shoulder. He'll be out probably the rest of the season."

Shit.

I nod with a boulder in my stomach. I'll have to help Coach rearrange the lines. While I don't make those decisions myself, Coach does take my opinion seriously when it comes to who works best together.

We climb on the bus and head back to our hotel for the night. We have strict rules about going out since we have another game tomorrow and I'll have to check rooms to do a head count at nine fifteen.

I head up to the room that I'm sharing with Bryce and change into flannel pajama pants and a Darby U hockey T-shirt. I'm not going out. My stomach is in knots and even though I'm tired, my body wants to move.

I end up pacing the length of our room. Bryce comes in not long after me and eyes me while he gets changed, but he's used to my pacing.

"You all right?" he asks, sitting on his bed to pull on sneakers.

"Fine," I sigh and turn to head back in the other direction.

"Because you always pace when there's nothing wrong."

Bryce comes up behind me and when I turn, he grabs my shoulders.

"Losing Carmichael sucks, but we'll be okay. Injuries happen, man." He squeezes my shoulders and I want to melt into the comfort he's offering, but I don't. I'm the captain and a senior. I have to be strong for the underclassmen.

"Of course. We'll manage." I nod and step around him. I can hear him sigh, but he leaves with a quiet snick of the door.

I want to scream, destroy the room, and let out the frustration the last week has left me with, but I can't.

My chest tightens until I feel like I can't breathe and tears threaten to fall down my cheeks. I miss Nick so much. It's physically painful, but he's too much of a distraction. Hockey and school has to come first, and after graduation I have to move back home. Char can't keep taking care of Matt. She deserves to live her own life, be happy, get married, and have babies if she wants.

That's not in the cards for me. Matt doesn't want to grow up so I'll spend the rest of my life taking care of him. Not to mention when Mom gets too old to take care of herself, I'll have to take care of her too. It's only fair, right? Since she took care of me, I should take care of her.

My phone pings and with anxiety and guilt weighing heavy on me, I pick it up. At Nick's picture, a sob escapes me. He's the only one who has seen me for who I am on the inside. He sees the mess, how overwhelmed I am, and takes the burden from me.

In a moment of desperation, I unlock my phone and call him.

"Joey." His voice shows his surprise and the background is loud.

"Help me." Tears are running down my face and I'm barely keeping myself from a full-blown meltdown. "I-I-I—" I can't fucking breathe.

"Joey." That demand in his voice cuts through some of the panic. "Where are you?"

I close my eyes and slide down the wall until I can pull my knees up to my face.

"Ho-hotel." I hate how broken my voice is. How weak.

"Are you alone?" The noise in the background is gone suddenly and I can hear his breathing.

"Yes," I whisper. So very alone. Even when I'm with my teammates, I'm alone. I don't have friends, not really, not anyone who knows me. Only Nick.

CHAPTER 13

nick

"Yes."

That trembling, whimpered word breaks my heart.

My poor boy. I don't know how to help him in the long run but I can get him out of his head for a few minutes. That he reached out to me when he needed it means he still cares about me, right? We can't be over if he still needs me, right?

"Switch to video." I'm not sure he'll agree but something in my chest loosens when I see the screen loading, only to be heartbroken when his wet face appears. He's rubbing at his eyes, making his face redder than it was. "You need a release, baby?" he nods his head. "You worked hard today, so it's time to relax."

He sniffles and clears his throat.

"Please." His voice is that small tone he uses when he's close to coming. The one that turns me into a feral beast.

My balls tingle and my dick thickens as I duck into an alley for privacy. What I wouldn't give to sink into him right now when he's needy and salty from crying.

"Do you have lube?"

His breathing shudders but he shakes his head.

"Lotion? There's usually some from the hotel." He hasn't let go enough to blindly follow directions yet. "Go find it."

He looks at me in the screen for a second then everything is blurry as he stands and walks.

"I found lotion," he mumbles and looks down at the phone.

"Good." I smile at him. "Strip and get comfortable. I'm not leaving until I see you come."

He shudders and his breath catches. It turns my smile predatory. Fuck, I wish I were there with him right now. I would use him until he's too exhausted to think and passes out against me.

Joey bites his lip and moves back to the bed. I stare at the sky while he undresses and the camera bounces a bit when he gets back on the mattress.

"Okay," Joey says, still using that little voice that makes me ache.

"Show me."

I see a little peek of a smile before the camera switches and his bared body is displayed for me. Long legs and perfect skin that I swear I can smell through the phone.

"How much time do you have before your roommate comes back?" I want to draw this out but I doubt I have that kind of time.

"I don't know."

"Are you being a dirty boy, Joey? Trying to get caught playing with yourself?" Is he into exhibitionism or is the threat of getting caught a turn-on? God, I want to explore all the facets that make him, him.

His dick twitches and I smirk. "Open your legs like you would if I were there to see your slutty hole."

Joey groans and bends his knees to open his thighs wider. My own dick hardens and I rub the heel of my hand against it through my jeans.

"So hard for me, baby boy." I can almost taste him. Like the ghost of a flavor that I'm desperate for but can't have. A tease. "Slick your hand with lotion and push your cock into it."

The phone gets put down again and while I listen to the pop of the cap, my screen is black. It doesn't take long for him to pick up the phone again and fill my screen with his dick.

"Set your phone up on the bedside table so I can see all of you."

His hand freezes at the tip of his dick and he groans as I make him wait a few more seconds, but he does what I've instructed. Joey props up the phone and adjusts the camera so I can see the length of the bed and his stretched-out body.

"It's unfair you can touch what belongs to me when I can't." I growl and he shudders.

"I want to touch myself. Please, can I?" His chest is rising and falling rapidly with his breathing.

"Thrust into your hand. Let me see you fuck your fist." My own breathing has gotten faster and I pull my dick out to jack off right along with him. I miss him. I miss his need for me. His earnest submission.

Joey whimpers and arches, watching himself appear and disappear in his own hand.

"Look at me." The demand in my voice is harsh but I want—no, *need*—his eyes on me. I need to be his entire fucking world and it hurts so goddamn bad that I'm not. So I will take every second he gives me, demand he not forget me when he's desperate and aching.

His eyes flash back to the screen and I see it, the pain, the frustration, the need to give himself to me.

"Good boy." I soften my tone and his face relaxes just a little, like he needed those words more than I needed to say them. "You're so hard for me, Joey. Are you getting close? Do you want to come and show me how much you like being at my mercy?"

"Huuung. Yes, please. I want to come for you." God, what that voice does to me. I throb in my own hand.

"Ask nicely."

He closes his eyes for a second, pulling his plump bottom lip between his teeth for a moment before his eyes pin me through the screen. "Please, Daddy?"

My balls seize and I'm hit so hard with my orgasm my knees buckle. I groan, long and loud, leaning against the wall and spilling cum onto the concrete.

"Oh fuck, baby. You're such a good boy, come for me. Show me how much you wish I was there to fuck you to sleep." My voice sounds like I've run a marathon, panting and airy, as I try to recover, but it has its desired effect and I watch as cum shoots onto Joey's stomach and chest as he cries out for me. I want to lick him clean, kiss him deep and slow with his taste still on my tongue.

When his body relaxes, he tosses an arm over his face as he pants. I love seeing him like this, wrung out and relaxed. Post-orgasm is the only time he's not *on.* My poor boy is a people pleaser and can't let a text message or a phone call wait unless I'm commanding his attention. It's the only time he lets himself go and just feels.

I unashamedly watch as he grabs his T-shirt to clean himself up some and pull on some pajama pants. In front of my eyes, I watch him sink back into himself and it makes me want to rampage. He doesn't want to look at me but knows he has to find a way to end the call without being rude. God forbid he hurts someone's feelings. It didn't take me long to figure that out about him. He doesn't know how to stand up for himself, but I desperately want to teach him.

"Joey, look at me."

He sits on the bed, shoulders rounded and head dropped toward the floor. I wait for him to get the courage. It's fascinating to see this insecure side of him when he's such a beast on the ice. Captain Joey Carpenter and my Joey are two very different sides to the same coin and I enjoy both of them.

Finally, his head lifts and he looks at me, chewing on that damn lip again.

"I'm glad you called."

"I shouldn't have. I don't want to give you mixed signals or whatever." He sounds miserable.

"Is it because my roommate knows?" I want to understand his thought process. Maybe then I'll be able to find peace.

He sighs and drops his head again. "I don't have time or energy for a relationship, even a casual one. I have to focus on my classes, hockey, and my family. There's nothing else for me."

His family?

"Your fam—"

"Listen, I'm tired and I just want to sleep. I have another game tomorrow. Thank you, for tonight, but I really need to go."

The call ends and I'm left staring at my phone in the alley behind a bar with my dick out and cum drying on the dirty concrete. What a time to get a backbone. The one time I don't want him to stand up for himself, he does.

What the fuck am I doing?

CHAPTER 14

joey

Carmichael dislocated his shoulder, a story about his father abusing him went viral, and we've been hounded by reporters for days now. Mom has texted me no less than eight times to tell me what a piece of shit Matt is and how it's my fault because I'm selfish and went away to go to college instead of working a dead-end job the rest of my life and taking care of *her* child.

Saying I'm on edge is like saying the sky is blue. Fucking duh. At twenty-five, I shouldn't be responsible for my brother who is also a legal adult. I shouldn't have to flinch every time my phone pings because I know it's someone wanting something from me. So I put it on silent and only have Coach, Char, and a few players as my emergency contacts that my phone will make noise for. I can't handle anything else. Even with only a handful of messages, I'm damn near pushed into a panic attack when it goes off.

The urge to call Nick, to have him meet me somewhere, is so strong it physically hurts not to, but I can't. I can't keep using him. It's not fair. What I said to him last time I talked to him was true, I don't have the time or mental capacity for anything else. I'm barely keeping the balls in the air that I'm already juggling, and if I add any more, I'll drop them all. Getting laid isn't worth it.

It's more than just getting laid and you know it.

The heartbroken look on Nick's face still flickers in my mind and causes my chest to ache. I wish more than anything that I could give myself to him and know I would be there for him. But I can't take on any more.

I feel like I'm in sinking sand, holding weighted plates that push me down farther. I barely have my head above the sand, one more push and I'll be lost forever. My house of cards will fall and I'll be left scrambling to collect them all before I lose them.

At our next practice, I've got my gear on and head out to the ice before everyone else. I need a few minutes to clear my head. Some guys run, some lift weights, some drink themselves stupid. I skate until I puke. The sound of my blades on the ice and the bite of the cold on my skin centers me. I skate around the rink, letting the familiarity take over and the muscle memory move me while my body warms up.

The smell of the ice centers me as I push myself to go faster, turning and twisting, and coming to a sharp stop before taking off again. I run through skating drills one after another, mindlessly, like a routine, until I'm sweaty and panting. Skating to the bench where I left my water bottle, I suck down a mouthful and wipe my mouth with the back of my hand as the team files out onto the ice.

"Warm up, let's go," I call to the boys who are just standing around on the ice, chitchatting like this is social hour. They start moving, skating along the edge of the rink in a big oval to get their muscles warmed up. Oiler rides his hockey stick and Albrooke shoves Johnson, setting off in some kind of race.

Carmichael steps into the bench box with a stern frown on his face, and I sigh. He's going to be even worse now that he can't be on the ice. No one can control him and he can't seem to keep his mouth shut, so we all have the *joy* of hearing him berate everyone.

He flicks his gaze over me, taking in the sweat on my skin, and nods subtly. "At least someone on this team puts in effort."

I turn my back to him, not wanting to get into a fight with him this early in practice. Putting my water bottle down, I join the guys on the ice. It doesn't matter that I'm already warmed up, I'm not above them. Albrooke and Oiler are fucking around, racing each other now and laughing. Usually, I find their antics amusing and can laugh along with them, but not today. Today the unread texts on my phone and the weight my mother refuses to remove from my shoulders is heavy.

There's a pain in my chest that I rub at while we line up to start suicides. With the team split in half, each of us on blue lines, Coach chirps his whistle and my line races for the center line, comes to a hard stop, and hustles back while the other line rushes for us. Over and over the whistle blows and we move. Most players hate these but there's something about them that I like.

Maybe it's because there's no time to think about anything else. My muscles scream, sweat pours from my skin, and my lungs are begging for a break, but we keep going. When Coach finally blows the whistle to stop, we all collapse on the ice, gasping for air.

"Walk it off before your muscles seize," Carmichael bites out, and I lift my hand to flip him off. A couple of the guys chuckle and I smile to myself.

But unfortunately, he's right, so I force myself up.

"Come on, guys, on your feet."

Coach blows the whistle again and they groan and grumble about having to move but they get up, grab a drink, and move on to the next thing. We're still adjusting to the change in defense lines since Carmichael is out and we've only had a few practices.

On our next water break, Bryce slaps my shoulder. "You all right, man? You seem off."

He's a perceptive little shit and since he's my roommate, he probably knows me better than anyone else.

"Yeah, just busy in my head today." That was more honest than I meant to be, but oh well. Too late to take it back now.

"You wanna talk about it, after practice?" He chugs water and I shake my head. There's nothing anyone can do and talking about it just makes me feel worse for burdening them.

"Nah, I'm all right. Thanks, though."

We get back out onto the ice and Coach breaks us into groups. One defense versus two offense. I'm up first to protect the net, and the goal is for the offense to pass then shoot.

Albrooke and Oiler are up first and I miss the puck.

Riggs and Willis are next and I miss it again.

I'm frustrated at myself and gritting my teeth. I'm not a goalie, but seriously?

Johnson and Bryce come at me and I finally stop it, but I slap at the puck and end up sending it flying into the bench box. Oops.

After practice, we get showered and changed. Some of the guys have night classes, some have plans, but I head straight back to my room.

Waiting for the elevator, I overhear a voice I recognize.

Turning far enough to see Nick's roommate laughing with a group of guys, my back stiffens. Will he recognize me? Say something?

I'm embarrassed by the possibility. I hate myself for it. For the weakness.

Heat flares up my neck and I grit my teeth. I can't afford to get in trouble for fighting if he comes for me. Not this close to graduation.

The doors to the elevator open and I step on, jamming my finger at the fifth-floor button and hoping they don't get on too.

I'm not that lucky. The group gets on and I'm forced back into the corner, listening to them discuss blowjobs and who would be better at giving, men or women. No one sounds disgusted but actually curious...

As the doors are closing, Nick slides in too. His eyes meet mine and his roommate slaps him on the back.

Nick looks around the group of guys and gets a knowing smirk on his lips.

"What are we talking about, guys? Sounded like a fun conversation." He looks from one guy to the next, but they don't say anything. Are these more football players? Are they embarrassed to ask because at least Neal knows Nick likes men?

"Who gives better BJs, men or women?" I repeat the question.

Nick's smile widens. "Oh, interesting question. It really depends on the human sucking the dick. There aren't many women who love cum and, let's be honest, enthusiasm is what can make or break a blowie. Girls who are open to all kinds of things usually give great head, but men are just that much more comfortable, typically. If you like a rougher touch, men are my vote."

The elevator is so quiet you could hear a pin drop as they stare at Nick, but it looks like Neal is trying to stifle a laugh. I can't help but snort at the self-satisfied smile he has on his face. The doors open on the third floor and the group steps off, Neal finally letting his laugh out and dropping his head back on his shoulders.

Nick catches my gaze again and my smile falls. I want to reach for him, press my forehead to his, and wrap my arms around him, but I can't be what he needs. I can barely deal with my life as it is and it's not fair to drag him into my bullshit.

He steps off the elevator and the doors close with a finality I can feel in my bones. Tears burn the backs of my eyes and when the doors open again on my floor, I beeline for my room and drop onto my bed. Shoving my head under my pillow, I let the tears fall.

The need to be held, to be weak for just a few minutes, seeps onto my sheets, but there's no one here to tell me it's okay.

CHAPTER 15

nick

I hate how this feels.

This bone-deep ache to touch, to hold, hell, even just to talk to him. I would accept a fucking text message at this point. It's been weeks of this—of nothing.

Picking up my phone, I flip it over and over in my hands, just for something to do.

My phone rings and looking at the screen, I sigh but answer the video call.

"What's up?"

"Why are you moping?" Brent asks. "Get your ass out of your room and go do something."

I glare at my best friend. "Fuck off, I'm not moping."

He scoffs. "Really? So you aren't sitting in your room, pining after a guy you can't have, and not doing anything fun?"

"Fuck off." That's exactly what I'm doing and it fucking sucks. Seeing Joey in the elevator, seeing him smile, made the ache in my chest worse. Why can't we just be friends? Would it hurt to see him with someone else? Definitely, but at least I would get something, right?

"Earth to dumbass," Brent says, snapping his fingers in front of the camera.

"Jesus, dude, what?" I look back at the phone and the teasing look on Brent's face falls.

"Seriously, are you all right? You aren't acting like yourself."

I sigh and drop my head back on my shoulders. "I don't know. Something about this guy has me fucked up." I let my shoulders sag and the sadness I've been carrying around show. "But he walked away, told me he doesn't have time or whatever, so there's nothing I can do about it."

My chest aches and I rub at it even though I know it won't help. Part of me wants to know that Joey is mine. I want to claim him, tell everyone to keep their damn hands off, but the other part of me wants to be his comfort. He puts so much pressure on himself that he doesn't need, taking responsibility for other people, and I want to be the one he leans on when that burden is too heavy.

I just want to hold him.

My throat tightens with the urge to cry.

Why am I so fucked up over this guy? Usually, my little obsessions burn out in a week or so and it's on to the next thing, but Joey dug his hooks into me and won't let go.

Except he did. He cut the lines holding me to him but left the hooks he implanted in my heart so I'm adrift without him.

"You're really hung up over this guy," Brent says more to himself than to me. "It's been a lon—"

"Don't." I can't hear her name whispered in my head. I can't be thrown down that memory lane because there's no one here to pull me back. I'm already spiraling, and I don't know how to stop. "I know, okay?"

It's quiet so long I finally look up to check my screen and see if the call dropped, but Brent's knowing green eyes are watching me. Is that why I'm so obsessed with Joey? Because he reminds me somehow of the girl I tried to save but was ripped away from me instead?

"I wish there was something I could do from here."

I nod and force myself to swallow past the lump in my throat. I need a fucking hug. One of the best parts of sharing a room with Brent during my teenage years was having someone there who knew me and wasn't all about toxic masculinity. Sometimes, guys need hugs too. On the bad nights, we would share a bed just so we didn't feel so fucking alone.

When the nightmares would haunt one of us or my parents would miss something important to me because a foster kid needed something, we had each other. It feels so petty, so childish, but I needed my parents too, and they weren't there. Not for me. Not when I wanted them.

"Do you have any close friends you can hang out with? Anyone who *knows* you?" I know what he's hinting at. Is there anyone here I can be weak in front of. The answer is no. Not really. If Joey won't even open a text message, I doubt he'd cuddle me.

But it's been too long since someone touched me.

Fuck it.

"I gotta go, B." I hang up and head upstairs to the fifth floor and hope he doesn't turn me away.

With a shaking hand, I knock on the door, tears threatening to fall down my cheeks, and wait.

And wait.

And wait.

Nothing.

Fuck!

He's not even here.

The urge to break down and sob is damn near overwhelming.

Losing my cool for a second, I slam my palm against the door and let out a yell until my lungs are heaving.

I swipe at my face quickly and turn to leave, to run back to the stairwell and break down, but run face first into him.

"Whoa there," he says, grabbing my shoulders. He takes one look at me and hauls me against him. Joey wraps his arms around me and I sink into him. He smells like soap and Tide and mine. I shove my face into his neck and drink him in, needing this so much more than I thought I did.

"Hey, you're okay." His arms tighten around me when I grip his shirt in my fists. "Let's go inside, come on."

Keeping one arm around me, he backs me into his room and closes the door.

"What's wrong?" This is Captain Carpenter, not my Joey, but that's okay. Right now, I need him to be strong for me.

I shake my head and let the tears fall. It's been so long since I've felt this out of control, this needy.

"I'm sorry," I cry into Joey's neck. "I just need a minute."

His arms tighten around me again, holding the broken pieces of me together while I fall apart. It's been so long since I gave myself permission and even longer since I let someone hold me while it happened. Not since I left home to come here for school.

I tremble against him, against his strength.

"It's okay, you're okay," Joey says into my hair. "Do you want to talk about it?" He cups the back of my head and kisses my temple, which only makes more tears fall. Why can't he be my person?

"I don't have the time or energy for a relationship."

Joey's words flitter through my mind and I take a deep breath. I shouldn't have come here. Shouldn't have come looking for him. But fuck, I just needed a goddamn hug.

Forcing myself to get control, I release him and step back but don't meet his eyes. "Thanks and sorry. I just needed a minute."

I turn to leave and the door opens, Bryce stops in the doorway and looks between the two of us.

"Hey, Nick, haven't seen you in a while." He closes the door and slaps me on the shoulder as he moves past me. I miss the comradery of teammates. I should text some of mine and see if anyone wants to do something. Go play pool or get a beer or go to a movie. Something to get me out of my dorm.

"Good to see you, man. Later." I give Bryce a head nod and leave, needing to get away from the room that smells like the one person I can't have.

Joey calls my name and it's a knife in my heart, but I keep walking. I shouldn't have come to him anyway. Finding comfort in him is only going to keep my obsession with him going longer. I have to find a way to get past it.

Even if it kills me.

CHAPTER 16

joey

What just happened?

Nick's tears dampen my shirt but he's walking away. What was that? Why did he come to me? I want to go after him, make sure he's okay, but does he want that?

I don't know what to do but I want him back in my arms. It felt so good to have him against me. In my space. Breathing my air. Sharing a heartbeat.

He's the only person since my dad died that has let me break, let me be weak. The only person to see that I needed it.

Instinctually, he took care of me, giving me the space, the safety, to take up room with my emotions, my needs.

But who looks after Nick?

Who does he go to when he needs to feel?

"What's up with Nick?" Bryce asks while he spreads out on his bed with homework.

"I don't know, he was here when I got back from practice." I don't want to turn away from the door, like if I move the feeling of him clinging to me will disappear too.

My heart aches for him. I want him to come back, to tell me to lie down, and wrap himself around me again. To need me.

"I haven't seen him around in a while. You guys get into a fight or something?"

I shake my head, remembering the last time he touched me. The pain in his gaze when I told him we were done.

"You know how it is during the season." I rub at my breastbone, at the pressure lingering there.

Seeing him snap like that, yelling and hitting the door, it was so out of character for him.

My phone chimes in my pocket and I sigh. Probably Char.

Turning away from the door and what I can't have, I check my phone and see a message from Mom.

MOM:

Matt is drunk at work. I have to leave work to go get him and take him home.

Guilt eats at me. Somehow, it's my fault. Matt's drinking problem is my fault. The way he can't keep a job is my fault. If only I raised him better, put more time, energy, and effort into him after Dad died, he would be better. Char is a responsible adult, so how did I fuck up with Matt?

Bryce grabs my shoulder and I jump since I didn't hear him move.

"Breathe, man, you're okay."

Looking up at my teammate—my roommate—through watery eyes, I realize maybe I do have a friend. If he wasn't my friend, he wouldn't care, right?

I nod, unable to speak around the knot blocking my throat.

"You want to talk about it?"

Sucking in a deep breath, I toss my phone on my bed and pop my knuckles.

"No. Thanks, though." I crack my neck. "Family shit will wait until after the game tomorrow."

"Do you need to work it out? Like, go for a run or go skate until you puke?"

I laugh and shake my head. "No, I have homework to do and just want to crash."

Once I'm settled on my bed with my homework spread out around me, all I want to do is go to sleep.

No, I want to go find Nick, make sure he's okay, and fall asleep with him. I haven't slept for shit since being kicked back to my own room. Since I've had to put the weight of everyone's world back on my shoulders.

The team depends on me to lead and keep my cool. I've been failing on both points lately. I don't have words of wisdom or helpful insight. The guys must have noticed since they aren't coming to me, and I'm not sure if I appreciate the break or hate that they don't feel comfortable talking to me. Matt has fallen off the wagon and is going to hurt someone. Mom is constantly telling me how I'm ruining everyone's life by trying to have one of my own.

Yet Nick came to me today because he needed a fucking hug.

I need to check on him.

Leaving all my shit on my bed, I leave the room and jog down the stairs toward the third floor. As badly as I want to just barge in, I knock. Neal is back and I don't know if Nick actually wants to see me.

"Yeah," comes from inside, and I square my shoulders before entering.

Nick isn't there.

The room smells like him but only Neal is here.

"Never mind." I step back out and close the door without another word.

Bryce lifts an eyebrow when I get back to our room, but I don't respond to it, just shove everything off my bed and climb in with my phone.

I open up the thread of messages I have from Nick that I've ignored.

Asking if I'm okay, if I want to hang out, if we can still be friends.

My heart breaks. I want him so much more than this. More than friends and text messages, but I can't bring him into my bullshit. Too many people rely on me, demand my focus, that I don't know who I am anymore. I'm a shell of a person. Aren't you supposed to find who you are and who you want to be while in college?

CHAPTER 17

nick

Joey is struggling and it hurts to watch.

I'm at every home game since the season started again because I can't stay away from him. Even not being a hockey fan, I can tell he's spiraling. Over the last few weeks, his playing has gotten worse. Little mistakes have become big mistakes that lead to penalties. As an athlete, I know that who you are on the field isn't who you are off of it. Joey has so many fascinating parts of his personality that I want to deep dive into. He's the captain and responsible for the harmony of his team, he's an aggressive but controlled player, and he's my sweet boy. I need him just as much as he needs me. It's clear as day.

I don't know what made him think that everything is his responsibility all the time—probably being the oldest sibling, if I had to guess—but with me he lets go and allows himself to be cared for. Who else does he have in his life that takes care of *him?*

I know the answer. I spent two weeks with him, every day, every night, and no one asked about him. He got text messages and phone calls from people needing him to fix things but no one asked how they could help him. He needs a break.

We're in the final period of the game against Miami and Joey has already been in the sin bin twice. The coach has yelled at him, the other players are giving him a wide berth, and he's throwing things around and jittery.

I have to stop it.

The clock counts down and when Darby gets the next goal, I can see the relief on his face. They're up by a point and have to hold it for three minutes.

It's a mad dash when the puck drops, purple jerseys versus green-and-teal jerseys scrambling for the puck. It's chaos. Skates and sticks everywhere, people getting shoulder checked in the chest. Moves that would be penalties on a field.

Even from up in the stands, I can see the strain on Joey and I just want to give him a break for a few minutes. I need him to need me. To give me a fucking purpose. I'm drowning out here alone. It's a physical weight on my chest and pain in my heart. Once again, I'm not important to the person that became everything to me. He walked away instead of being taken from me, but the pain is just as sharp.

There's only a minute left of the game and I get up to leave. Not only do I not want to deal with the crowd when the game is over, but I can't watch him anymore. Not tonight. Not when I'm almost close enough to touch him.

I end up back at Roasted Mountains and drop down into the same chair I claimed last time. My knee is bouncing as I stare at the windows. It's dark and cold. The glass is getting foggy around the edges and a part of me wants to put my fist through the panes. It won't fix anything, but for a minute I might feel something besides the rage that's bubbling under the surface.

My phone chimes and I pull it out to find a text message in a group chat of teammates. It's probably my own fault that I don't have anyone that I can call a friend here. I was one of the captains, but I spent more time dealing with freshmen than anyone else and since the season is over, my role is done. I graduate in a few months, so I won't be part of spring training.

The team doesn't need me either.

PATTERSON:

Anyone want to meet up?

He's one of the special team's guys and always up for something. The guy doesn't know how to sit still or relax.

The group goes back and forth, deciding when and where to meet up. They decide on Rocky's and I sigh. It's going to be full of the hockey team and puck bunnies.

I drop my head back onto the chair and close my eyes.

Just go and talk to him. See for yourself that he's okay.

WYHE:

I'm coming.

By the time I get to the bar, the hockey team has ascended and it's chaos. There are girls everywhere, hanging on to every big guy they can get close enough to, beer and shots everywhere.

The big guy that doesn't know how to smile is trying not to stare at someone, but I can't tell who it is. The redhead and baseball hat guy are at the bar with a girl hanging on the redhead. What were their names? Paul and.... Brandon?

"Wyhe!"

I turn and see my teammates—well, former teammates, I guess—and head that way. There's a group of them taking over a few tables, most have drinks already, so I order myself a beer.

For a few hours, I manage to fake a smile and a good time. Some of the guys take pictures or videos and post them on social media. My phone keeps pinging with notifications of the tags and probably Brent asking me what the hell I'm doing. I can't lie to him tonight, though.

My bladder is demanding attention, so I head to the bathroom to take a piss. It's surprisingly empty, only two guys at the urinals.

I take the one on the end and handle my business while I let the mask fall for a minute. I'm exhausted from the energy it takes to be here.

As I'm washing my hands, the door opens and my eyes clash with Joey's. His cheeks are pink from the alcohol and he drags his gaze over me.

"Hmm..." He steps closer, the rich scent of his cologne tickling the edge of my senses. I want to bathe in it, roll around and cover my skin in it.

"Joey." I clear my throat and dry my hands. "Congrats on the win."

I shove my hands in my pockets to keep from reaching for him. He looks around the bathroom and reaches to the door, turning the lock. With his lip caught in his teeth, he comes for me. He grips my head and crashes his lips to mine.

My heart pounds as I inhale him. His chest is pressed against mine and he backs me up to the wall, leaning hard into me. It's intoxicating. It's everything I've wanted for weeks.

Wrapping my arms around him, I hold him just as tightly, needing him for just a minute. I know this can't last, we're in a fucking bathroom, but he's my damn weakness.

"Touch me." Joey rests his forehead against mine. "Please."

I can't resist him when he talks to me like that.

"Not in here, baby," I say and press a kiss to his lips. "Meet me in the back alley in, like, five minutes, okay?"

He chews on his lip again and nods. My poor boy.

He slides his hand down my neck, my chest, and around my hip to my ass to pull me closer.

"I need you, please?" That little voice comes out and warmth blooms in my chest.

"What do you need from me, sweet boy?" I drag my thumb along his mouth.

Joey's face turns a darker pink, almost red.

"Escape. Release. To not be in control."

My lips quirk up in a small smirk. "I can do that."

I kiss him deep but quick and unlock the door. Bryce is standing there with an eyebrow raised but doesn't say anything. I push past him and head toward the back where the alley exit is. Anything Bryce thinks he heard or knows is not my problem, it's Joey's.

It's cold, my breath fogging in front of me while I wait, and wait. He needs me. He said it himself. Does that mean he'll stop ignoring me? That he'll find time to let me in?

I'm afraid to get my hopes up but at this point, I'm fucking desperate. The heavy door squeaks open and Joey steps out in his hoodie and jeans. He looks so fucking good.

I reach for him, jerking him toward me, and spinning us to put him against the wall.

Joey shoves his hands under my shirt, raking his fingers down my ribs then back up to hold on to my shoulders. He's not releasing control, but making demands. Is that really what he wants tonight? If he needs it, I'll let him take the lead, but that's not normally how we operate.

He whimpers, grinding his hard-on against my hip. His panting breath fans over my lips and I suck it deep into my lungs. I want him to consume me in every way. This moment with him is the most alive I've felt in weeks. It's fresh air and sun on my skin. A healing balm where I've been cracked and bleeding.

I don't want to think too hard about how quickly he was able to hook himself into the walls of my heart, my soul.

"Please, Da—" Joey cuts himself off abruptly but my eyes snap to his at what I think he was going to say.

"Say it," I demand, though my voice is quiet. I need him to say it. The memory of him saying it the last time we fucked slams into me. In the fear of being caught and the pain of losing him, I had forgotten about it. But now, I need to hear it. I need him to acknowledge who I am to him.

He clenches his jaw and closes his eyes, dropping his head back against the brick wall. Joey's cheeks are already pink with arousal but the color deepens now.

"Are you embarrassed?" I open his jeans and slide my hand inside, gripping him firmly. He throbs in my palm. If he's embarrassed, his dick isn't. "Say it, baby."

His cock pulses again when he whispers the word, "Daddy."

I groan into his mouth, ravaging his lips and stroking him. "That's right, Daddy's going to take care you."

"I-I-I—fuck." He's trembling against me and it's everything I need. *I need him to need me.*

"Are you gonna come, dirty boy? Are you that close already?"

"Yes." Joey's hips roll and thrust against me. The arousal coursing through him and stealing the ability to keep still. I drop to my knees and pull down his pants and underwear to get better access to him.

"Tell me." I tighten my grip on him and say my next words against his hip. "Tell Daddy how badly you want him to make you come."

A strangled sound leaves his lips as my mouth envelops him. Salty cum fills my mouth so fast I almost choke on it. I watch him ride the pleasure, the tense set of his shoulders, and the lines around his eyes loosen as he sags against the wall. So fucking pretty. *Mine.*

CHAPTER 18

joey

I shouldn't be here with him.

He feels too good. Like that first gasp of oxygen when you've held your breath too long and your lungs are screaming for air. He's a drug I've become addicted to and I can't afford the distraction.

Nick stands with a confident smirk on his angular face. I'm weak right now, mentally, and he knows it, but I know he won't take advantage. I can trust him.

I do trust him.

He covers my body with his, grasping my hand and intertwining our fingers together above my head as he kisses me. It's slow and deep and everything I need right now. The salty flavor of myself on his tongue is sexy as fuck. How does he always know what I need? I can't even anticipate my siblings' needs and I grew up with them.

"Joey." My name is a whisper on his breath, and I snap back to the present. Our foreheads are pressed together like he can create a world that's just us. How true I wish that was. I would give my left nut to not be responsible for anyone but me. No siblings, no team. I love them, but the weight of them is so fucking heavy sometimes.

"Baby, are you with me?" His lips are a ghost on mine. "Nothing matters but me."

He has no idea how true that statement is. It's so hard to fight it. Even when he's not around.

"Yes," I mumble across his jaw.

"Good boy."

The simple praise brings warmth to the frigid chunks of my heart that I shut the door on a long time ago. I don't have time to want praise. I don't have time for my own needs, only everyone else's.

I can't need him.

It hurts.

My chest constricts, not letting my lungs get enough air. I can't do this. Not again. It's been weeks of trying to get him out of my head and I've failed in every way.

"Nick. Wait. Stop." There's a panicked edge in my voice, a weakness that I despise, but he immediately freezes.

"What? What's wrong?" He takes a step back and cups my cheek, searching my face for some clue as to what changed.

"I can't do this, I'm sorry." It hurts to talk around the knot in my throat and the tears pricking the backs of my eyes, but it has to be done.

It takes a few seconds but he steps back, wrapping a mask around himself as he gets his clothes situated again and shoves his hands into his pockets.

"Okay." He looks at my shoes and nods. "I don't know how to prove to you that I can handle your life, to prove that I understand your responsibilities, but when you're ready to let me try, you know where to find me."

Nick walks away, leaving me in the dingy alley with my dick out.

I DON'T GO BACK into the bar, but back to my room. I can't fake it anymore and my buzz is fucked. I don't say goodbye to anyone or let them know I'm leaving, I just bounce. It's fucked up but I don't have the mental energy for it.

With the door closed and the lights off, I strip down to my T-shirt and underwear and lay on my bed. But I don't sleep. All I can do is stare at the ceiling and wish life was different. Wish my brother wasn't an addict. Wish my mother would take responsibility for her own kids. Wish my sister could get away from it all too.

My phone buzzes and I sigh. This late, it can only mean one thing. Matt is in some kind of trouble. Why am I the one who's called? There's nothing I can do about it. I'm at school. Since I'm not sleeping, I pick up the stupid phone and check it. Char sent me a voice message which means one of two things: either she's driving or emotional. Or both.

Hitting play, I hear my sister's voice thick with tears and the rumble of road noise.

"Well, Matty is fucking drunk at work. Again. Why he hasn't been fired is beyond me. And is it my fault? I brought his stumbling ass home and Mom starts in on me. Why aren't I a better sister? How could I let him turn out like this? Why aren't I helping him? It's bullshit. He's a grown-ass adult! I have my own fucking life!" She sucks in a shuttering breath. "I swear to God, I'm going to stop answering the phone. You should too. He needs to fall on his ass. He'll never get better if we keep bailing him out."

The weight on my shoulders pulls harder on me. Char doesn't deserve to deal with all this shit. I'm failing everyone and I don't know how to fix it. I'm hours away from home with no car but I have to find a way to get some of the pressure off her. She has a fiancé and a full-time job and is trying to live her life.

Instead of sending a message, I call her. She needs the connection.

"Yeah?" Her tear-laden voice cracks when she answers.

"Hey, I'm sorry you had to deal with Mom and Matt today." I pinch the bridge of my nose and close my eyes. "Only a few more months and I'll be back so they won't call you all the time."

She sniffles and I can picture her wiping her eyes. "You shouldn't have to deal with it either. Don't come back here."

"I can't abandon you like that. I'm coming back and you need to leave. Leave town, the state, whatever it takes. Go live your life."

"What about you? Being back here will suck the life out of you. You barely escaped to go to college. Seriously, Joey, don't come back."

She doesn't understand. I made a promise to Dad that I would take care of the family. I promised to be the man of the house.

"Don't answer the phone when they call anymore. Ignore texts and voicemails. You should cut ties with them, for your own well-being." It hurts my soul to say it, but I know it's for the best. If Mom wants to baby Matt, she can do it herself.

"I can't." The choked words gut me. I hate that I can't give her a hug right now.

"Are you back home?" I realize I don't hear the road noise.

"Yeah, I just pulled into the driveway when you called."

"Good. Go inside and hug Jack, then go to bed." I sit up when I hear noise in the hallway outside my room. "Mom is wrong. You did nothing wrong and Matt's choices have nothing to do with you."

The door opens and Bryce comes in, looking at me with a lifted eyebrow.

"Love you, Joey."

"I love you too."

I end the call and wait. I know Bryce will have something to say. He always does.

"Why did you bounce?" he asks over his shoulder as he starts getting changed.

I shrug, knowing he can't see it. "I just wanted the quiet."

He turns and pins me with a look. "Riiiight."

I put my phone back on the bedside table and rollover. I don't have the energy for this.

Bryce doesn't say anything else, just climbs into bed and is snoring in a frustratingly short amount of time. Yet here I am, staring at the stupid wall, wishing Nick was wrapped around me. It felt so good having him touch me. I miss him. Miss the peace he brings. Miss the way he takes care of me for a change.

A tear falls across my nose and down my opposite cheek onto the pillow.

Cutting him off completely isn't working. Would I be able to handle being his friend? Who maybe gets cuddles . . . I miss hugs. And kisses.

And orgasms.

I haven't been able to get myself off without thinking of him, and even then it's maybe a fifty percent success rate.

Rolling back over, I reach for my phone.

"I thought I saw Nick tonight." Bryce's statement makes me freeze. When did he wake up?

"Okay?"

"Just thought it was interesting, is all."

Interesting, my ass.

Pulling up my message thread with Nick, I finally open it. There's several messages I haven't read and I hate myself for it. Nick deserves better than to be ghosted.

NICK:

Are you okay?

We can still be friends without sex.

I miss you.

Seriously, please let me know that you're okay.

Can we meet up for drinks or food or something?

My hands tremble as I type out my first message to him in weeks.

JOEY:

I'm sorry.

Immediately the dots pop up and I hold my breath.

NICK:

For what?

JOEY:

For being an asshole? For ghosting you when all you wanted was to make sure I was okay.

NICK:

Are you?

Okay I mean.

That damn knot is back in my throat again, making it ache. How does he still care? I don't think I would.

JOEY

Total honesty? No.

The message goes through, Nick sees it, and the bubbles pop up then disappear. That's not the response I expected. A boulder drops into my stomach and I force back the disappointment. I don't know what I expected, but nothing was not it.

I turn off my screen and turn to put my phone back when there's a sharp knock on the door. My head pops off the pillow to stare at it, excitement and hope trying to bloom in my chest.

"You expecting someone?" Bryce's voice comes from his side of the room and I toss off the blanket, hustling for the door.

When I rip it open, Nick's hand is raised to knock again. Our gazes lock for a long second before he's pulling me against him in a tight hug. Fuck, I missed his hugs. I burrow my face into his neck and inhale the spicy, warm scent of vanilla, nutmeg, and amber that is Nick. The ache in my chest loosens and I sag into him, but he holds me up. I'm exhausted and just want to sleep next to him, but I can't. There's nowhere for us to do that and not have awkward questions. I don't think Bryce would really care, but it's not a conversation I want to have right now.

"You're okay, sweet boy, I've got you." The urge to sob into his warmth is almost more than I can take. All I've wanted since I was a child was for someone to see me, to want to take care of me. Does that make me weak?

Nick kisses my temple and I smile into his skin.

"Thank you," I mumble against his throat.

"Can we talk for a bit?"

I nod and straighten up. Nick's eyes travel down my body and he smirks when he gets to my legs. When I look down and realize I'm standing here in my underwear, my face heats. Shit.

"Hang on." I hurry and grab some pants and a hoodie. "Do I need shoes?"

"Nah, we'll stay in the building."

"Jesus fucking Christ!" Bryce snaps. "Would you shut the fucking door? I'm trying to sleep!"

Oops.

"I'm going, calm your tits."

Nick chuckles and moves to let me into the hallway. We take the stairs because that seems to be our thing, and stop partway down to sit.

My heart is fluttering in my rib cage.

"Listen," I start once we're sitting down next to each other on a step. "I can't afford the distraction of a relationship." I lean my elbows onto my knees and try to find the right words.

"Joey, look at me." Nick waits until I turn to him. "I know. Your family asks a lot of you and your season isn't over. I get it. I understand."

Ever so slowly, Nick moves his hand toward mine, the back of his toward the back of mine, slowly dragging his finger between the veins of mine until he can hook one of my fingers with his. It's cute as fuck and sweet. Makes me think of first loves and first kisses.

"I don't know why or how you got under my skin as fast as you did, but I hate not talking to you," I admit, wrapping my finger around his.

"Good."

I laugh at his response, the weight on my shoulders a little lighter than it was an hour ago.

"If you don't want a relationship, that's fine. But when you need a hug, someone to vent to, or you need to fuck, call me."

A blush heats my face again, both embarrassed and turned on. I got off earlier but he didn't. It bothers me that he didn't, and I want to fix it.

Releasing his finger, I place my hand on his knee and his eyes darken. His breathing deepens.

"Did you jack off after the bar?" I lean into him until our breaths become one.

Nick leans back on his elbows against the stairs behind him. "No."

"Hmmm..." I want to touch him, to get lost in him again just for a few minutes. I move to kneel between his spread thighs with only my hands on his knees. "Can I?"

"Can you...what?" The lift of that one eyebrow tells me exactly what kind of mood he's in and fuck if I don't want it too.

I invade his space but don't touch him anywhere else but his knees. It's close though, so fucking close.

Dropping my chin, I look up at him and drag my lip, between my teeth. "Can I suck your cock, Daddy?"

His pupils blow wide and his next inhale is sharp, moving his entire body with the force of it.

"Fuck, you have the dirtiest, sweet mouth." Nick's thumb brushes along my lip then slides it inside. I suck on the rough digit, swirling my tongue around it and scraping my teeth over it while pulling on his pants. He lifts his hips and I get everything pushed down past his knees.

His cock pulses where it rests on his lower belly. The short dark hair at the base of his dick calls to me. I want to nuzzle it, bury my face in it, and breathe him in.

"Go ahead, pretty boy." Nick pulls his finger from my mouth and I lean forward to inhale him. The smell of skin is so strong here, I want to roll around in it so he's everywhere.

He cups the back of my head tenderly and when I look up at him, his expression has morphed into something soft. Nick watches me watch him for a minute before pulling on me. "Come 'ere."

Crawling up his body until I'm straddling his lap, I expect him to kiss me, grind against me, but he doesn't. Nick wraps his arms around me in a tight hug and just holds me. Chest to chest. I slide my arms under him, taking advantage of the space left by the steps, and hold him just as tightly.

"Are you okay?" I mumble against his neck after we've been sitting like this for a while. The metal edge of the stair must be digging into his back but he doesn't complain or move.

"I am now," he sighs, and the tension in his body melts away. I sink into his hold, his comfort, and just let him be in this moment. It's hard to sit in this space and just be, knowing I can't be what he clearly needs, but I can give him this. He gives me so much, cares too deeply, and giving him a hug is the least I can do.

I wish I could be what you need.

CHAPTER 19

joey

When my alarm goes off the next morning, I'm somewhere between content and hung over. My stomach isn't happy with me and I've got a headache looming, but my heart is calm. I can't let myself get wrapped up in Nick. Doesn't matter how badly I want to. How desperately a part of who I am calls to him.

My soul is tired.

I sit up and shut off the second alarm. Another day, another workout. Time stops for no one. That's a lesson I learned early in life. The world keeps turning, even when you're mourning, even when your mom is burying herself in work because she can't deal with life, even when you're left to raise your siblings because there's no one else to do it. Life keeps going.

Somewhere along the way, I stopped living and just started surviving. I don't know what living feels like anymore.

"Bryce, time for the gym." I pull the blanket off my sleeping roommate and change into workout gear. Bryce is still snoring and I'm tired of having to do this every single fucking day, so I leave him. He can get in trouble with Coach today. I shouldn't have to baby him.

I grab a protein bar and my water bottle before opening the door and sighing. If Bryce doesn't show up on time, everyone will look at me like I'm the dick for not helping a teammate out.

Growling to myself, I turn and throw a water bottle from Bryce's desk at him.

He jolts and covers his head. "What the fuck, man?"

"Get up." With that, I leave the room and head down the hall. I'm apparently not hiding my frustration if the side-eyed looks from my teammates are anything to go by. But I don't pay them any attention. With music blasting in my ears and agitation burning in my blood, I push myself harder than normal. Since we're done with last night's game, we're working toward the ones next weekend, and I know I shouldn't push it right now but I need to burn off the frustration before I do something stupid, like find Nick.

Sundays are supposed to be rest days but I typically do something light, not today, apparently.

I'm pouring sweat down my face, soaking my shirt, on the treadmill when Bryce steps in front of it and folds his arms on the rail.

I glance at him for a second and see the raised eyebrow and set jaw. He wants something or is expecting me to do something. Great. What am I missing? I slow my pace so I can stop panting enough to talk to him.

"What?"

"You what?" he barks back. Bryce is not typically a hothead, so him being upset is…concerning.

"What the hell does that mean?" I slow the treadmill even more until I'm walking comfortably.

"What's the deal with Nick?"

I look around the gym, but it's empty except for us. "What are you talking about? There's no deal."

He looks at me like I'm an idiot and I grit my teeth. This right here is why I don't want people to know. I don't want to deal with the intrusive questions and snide remarks. It's only a few more months until I graduate and I don't have to deal with this.

"You really expect me to believe there isn't something going on? Really? Do I look like a dumbass to you?" I open my mouth to respond but he holds up his hand. "Don't answer that."

I snort and a smile starts to turn up one side of my mouth. "Nick and I are friends, kind of. You know how it is during the season, shit is busy and we really don't have much time for anything besides school and hockey." I shrug, trying to play it off like it's not a big deal, but the ache in my stomach is a weight trying to pull me into the core of the earth.

"Bullshit."

I stop the treadmill and stare at him. "Excuse me?"

"Bull. Shit," he enunciates. "You mope around the room when you aren't in here or in class. Everyone else has a social life. Every. One. Else." He takes a deep breath and watches me for a minute. "So, go shower, get changed, then go away. I'm kicking you out of the room for the day."

"You can't kick me out of my own room." I step down and wipe my face on my T-shirt.

"Watch me. I'll get the guys to help me carry your ass out if I have to."

"What the hell am I supposed to do all day?"

"I don't care."

He turns and leaves me in the middle of the gym contemplating my reality. Would he really call the guys on the team to physically remove me from the room? Yeah, he probably would.

With a sigh, I head to the showers to get cleaned up and changed.

When I step out of the gym, clean and free of my shit since Bryce took my gym bag, I look around and just start walking.

When was the last time I just existed? Where I did what I wanted and didn't worry about my siblings or teammates? I've been so wrapped up in taking care of everyone else that I don't know what to do or who to do it with.

Okay, I want to call Nick.

Maybe today I should test if we can really be friends...

JOEY:

Hey, what are you doing today?

NICK:

Checking myself into a mental hospital because I think I'm hallucinating?

I chuckle and start to form a plan.

CARPENTER:

Hey, can I borrow your car for a while today?

JOHNSON:

Why? You okay? Do you need a ride?

CARPENTER:

I'm good, just want to get off campus for a while.

"Carpy Carp!" Oiler's singsong voice has me turning to see him and Johnson coming from the dining hall.

Johnson reaches into his pocket and hands me his keys with a hockey puck key chain on it.

"You sure you're okay?" He eyes me skeptically.

"Yeah, I'm good. Thanks."

My phone pings with a new message.

NICK:

Uh hello? Was that a figment of my imagination?

JOEY:

Get dressed and meet me by the dorm parking.

NICK:

You're not luring me to murder me, are you?

JOEY:

You're a heavy bastard, I would need help carrying the body.

I head toward the dorms with Johnson and Oiler, but I'm not really paying attention to what they're talking about. Oiler seems to be in a chatty mood today, so he's probably changed topics five times since he saw me.

But I have a smile on my face that doesn't feel forced when I get to the dorms and see Nick pushing out the door, only to stop when he sees me with my teammates.

"Nope. I'm not dying today, fish boy!" Nick yells from the door.

"Fish boy! 'Cause we call him Carp! Like the fish! Why didn't I ever think of that? That's genius!" Oiler slaps his own forehead and Johnson shakes his head.

"You better hope he forgets about that or it's going to be everywhere." Johnson pats my shoulder and follows his redheaded cohort.

They wander off and I wait for Nick. With a smile on his handsome face, he approaches but stops far enough away that I hate it. I want him to touch me.

"You look...happy." He looks me over and his shoulders drop a little like he's relaxed knowing that.

"Well, my roommate kicked me out of our room for the day and I haven't had a free day to do whatever I wanted in a long time, so I was hoping you could help me find something." I bite on the inside of my cheek before speaking again. "We can be friends, right? You said we could do that?"

"Yeah, friends is good." Nick nods as a huge grin splits his face. I haven't seen a smile like that since before classes started and as much as it hurts, it lights up a part of me I didn't realize was dark.

"Friends that sometimes cuddle, though, right?" My voice is quiet and I can feel my cheeks heat.

"I don't have friends I don't cuddle with." He steps a little closer.

I narrow my eyes and think about it for a minute. "Are you a cuddle whore? Cuddling people all willy-nilly?"

Willy-nilly? Seriously? Ugh.

"I am a cuddle whore who is lacking work."

I snort and reach for his hand, but stop myself and look around before clearing my throat and step back. I turn toward the parking lot and motion for him to follow me. He clearly saw what I was going to do if the look on his face is anything to go by.

Do I really care what people will think if they see me holding hands with him? No. Yes? I don't know. I don't want to care but there's a part of me that's scared. Which is stupid. It's not like I couldn't take on someone in a fight if they got in my face or ran their mouth. I know I can take a hit and stay standing.

But I don't want to deal with it. I have enough on my plate.

I'm tired of having to deal with everyone else's shit.

We climb in the car, and I have to adjust the seat since my legs are longer than Johnson's. Nick smirks at me as I get it adjusted and start the car. Since it's winter, it's cold as fuck and the engine doesn't want to turn over, but with some coaxing it comes to life. The heat is turned high so it feels like an industrial fan is blowing cold air at my face.

"What the fuck?" I find the knob and turn it off. Nick has his hands on the vents, closing them so they stop blowing at him as well.

"So, what's your plan?" he asks as I pull out of the parking lot to head toward downtown.

"I'm hungry, so food."

"I know of a mom-and-pop diner that makes amazing biscuits and gravy."

My stomach grumbles and I send Nick a quick smile. "Sounds good."

He gives me directions and we get lucky to find a parking spot up close. Most of them are taken, so it must be a good place if there's this many customers.

"Nick!" a happy male voice booms as soon as we enter, and I turn to see a man through the kitchen window with a big smile on his face looking at us. He's an older man, probably in his sixties with smile lines by his mouth and at the corners of his eyes. From what I can see, this is a happy man. I like him already.

"Jim! How's it going?" Nick waves to him.

"It's been a while. You good, kid?" He looks genuinely concerned about Nick and a pang hits my chest. How does Nick know this man? Why has it been a while since they saw each other?

"I'm good."

"Seat for two?" I turn to find a young woman with a nice smile but a no-nonsense energy and blue hair pulled back in a French braid. I nod and she leads us to a booth in the back, drops our menus on the table, and tells us our server will be with us shortly.

"You come here often?" I ask as I hide behind my menu. I know I have to keep my distance from him, emotionally, but there's so much I don't know about his life.

"I used to work here during the off-season."

I look over the top of the laminated paper to find him leaning on the table, watching me.

"I guess that means you know what you're going to order?"

His smile is wide when he answers. "Biscuits and gravy."

Oh yeah. Duh.

"Me too." I put aside the menu and feel awkwardness crawling up my spine. Why is this so weird? I hate this.

Nick opens his mouth as his phone buzzes loudly on the seat next to him.

He lifts it and denies the call.

"Relax," he says as he slides his foot against mine under the table. My neck and face heat at the simple touch. "It's okay."

His phone vibrates again, and he huffs, his eyebrows pulling together. "Sorry, it's my brother, just a sec."

I nod and watch him, even though it's rude, but I don't think he's ever mentioned a brother.

"Hey, nut sack," coming from the phone makes me jump at the volume.

"Fuck," Nick mutters and turns it down. "I'm at breakfast, what do you want?" It's quiet for a minute before he lifts an eyebrow at the screen. "What?"

"That's not on campus. Are you at Jim's?"

"Yes, I am. What do you want, Brent?"

"Brent? Did you just government name me? What the fuck, dude? Am I interrupting something? Trying to get laid?"

I snort, trying to keep my laugh in, and cover my mouth with my hands. Of course now is when the server comes up to us.

"Good morning, what can I get you to drink? Are you ready to order?" The young man looks uncomfortable, like he's new and not used to randomly talking to strangers.

"I'll have a coffee," I tell him. "And biscuits and gravy."

"Who is that?" comes from the phone again. "Did you find a friend? I'm so proud of you, lil Nicky." Condescension in those words makes me laugh again.

"I'll have the same," Nick says to the server with a tight-lipped smile and turns back to his phone. "I'm hanging up now. I hope your asshole itches all day."

He puts his phone back on the seat and sighs. "Sorry about that."

"It's okay, I'm kind of surprised my sister hasn't texted me yet." I check my phone just in case and breathe out a sigh of relief when there's no messages.

"Brent is my best friend and while he's an ass, he means well. Usually." He shrugs but it's obvious that he cares deeply for him. I wish I had that kind of relationship with my brother. I can't remember the last time I talked to him on the phone since it got shut off a few months ago.

I also don't have a best friend. Not anymore. Not since I moved away for hockey and college. I have my teammates that I know I can talk to, but no one I'm particularly close to.

Nick's foot rubs against the inside of my ankle and I lift my eyes to meet his.

"I'm glad you have him," I say quietly.

"Who do you have?"

I don't want to say the words out loud and find that I can't when I try, so I just shake my head and shrug. Pathetic. Who doesn't have a friend? Just one friend they can talk to? This loser.

CHAPTER 20

nick

Breakfast with Joey is...different. I can't stop myself from touching him under the table. A simple touch, just my ankle against his, but it's the connection I've been craving. What is it about him that makes my fingers reach for his? That makes my heart ache for him to be close?

We talk about his family and mine. The way we had to grow up too fast and take care of others, put our needs on hold or pretend we didn't have any.

When we're done eating, I clear our table and dump our dishes in the dishpan, then head back to the kitchen with Joey on my heels. He seems interested to learn about me, so I want to keep showing him.

"Hey, Jim," I call over the noise of the kitchen when I push through the door. There are two cooks in here, busy with prepping orders. One I recognize as his son but I can't remember his name at the moment.

"Nicky!" The big man turns and gives me a quick hug before turning back to the hot grill he's cooking up a couple of burgers and toasting some buns on. "How've you been?"

"I've been okay, trying to keep my head in the books so I can graduate on time."

"Good, good." He pats my shoulder and gives it a squeeze. This man was the father figure I didn't know I needed. "Who you got with you?"

With a half-smile, I look behind me at the man who means too much to me. "This is Joey."

He steps forward and offers his hand, but Jim pulls him into a quick hug too, patting Joey's back with his big mitts. I chuckle quietly and lean my arm on his shoulder when Jim lets go of him.

"Nice to meet you," Joey says with a smile.

"You see," I pat his chest, "Jim is Debbi's brother."

At Debbi's name, Joey's eyes widen and his cheeks pinken.

"You don't happen to have any of her pastries left, do you?" I ask Jim but he shakes his head.

"No, we ran out early today."

Damn.

"All right, I won't take any more of your time." I step in for a hug and he holds me tight for a second longer than I expected, but damn do I need it.

"Come in any time, you hear me?" He pats my back and squeezes me one more time.

"I hear you."

Joey lifts his hand in a wave and we leave the kitchen, heading out to the parking lot after paying for our food.

"What's next?" I ask when we get into the car but he doesn't start it.

With his hands in his lap, he stares out the windshield, and sighs. "I don't know."

It's quiet for a while before I reach for his hand and thread our fingers together. A shy smile lifts one side of his mouth and I want to kiss it so bad it hurts. He's so damn cute.

"In a perfect world, where you could do anything, what would you do right now?"

Joey looks at our hands before he answers. "Cuddle."

Hmmm...maybe...

Sliding my hand into my pocket, I pull out my phone and text Neal.

NICK:

What are you doing?

NEAL:

Jacking off, what's it to you?

NICK:

Awfully quick response time for a jerk session.

NEAL:

What do you want?

I glance at Joey who's watching me before telling my roommate to get lost.

"Back to the dorm, driver." I buckle my seat belt, which sucks one-handed, but get it done while Joey watches me uneasily.

"What about your roommate?"

"I told him to fuck off for a few hours, so he left." My phone pings and I glance quickly at it. "And he even sent me a picture to prove he left." I chuckle and show Joey the image of Neal in the elevator.

The tension in Joey's shoulders lessens for a split second before guilt mars his face.

"I'm sorry." He shakes his head. "You deserve better than to be a dirty secret."

I squeeze his hand and lift it so I can kiss the back of it. "You have a lot going on and coming out can be...a lot."

"Why are you so...accommodating?" Joey demands, clearly irritated. Isn't accommodating a good thing?

I turn in my seat as far as the seat belt will allow me to and look him in the eye. But he's turned his head away from me and is chewing on his lip. Reaching for him, I turn his chin toward me and brush the pad of my thumb over his lip. There's a glassy sheen of held-back tears over his eyes and it breaks my heart.

"I don't know why you are so determined to keep me at arm's length, but I respect your decision." Dropping his hand, I cup his face with both of my hands. "You deserve good things, Joey."

A tear slips slowly down his face, and I bring his forehead to mine.

"Letting yourself be cared for doesn't make you selfish. Wanting your own dreams doesn't make you selfish. Wanting your family to figure their own shit out doesn't make you selfish."

He closes his eyes and sags into me, crying quietly on my shoulder while I hold him.

"Why am I so weak around you?" The words are mumbled into my shirt, but I hear them.

"Because it's safe to. You know, somewhere in your head, that I've got you." I kiss the side of his head, the only part I can reach, and run my hand down his back. "Everyone needs a person that's safe."

He lifts his head and I know his question before he says it out loud...

"Who's your safe person?"

I wipe the moisture from his face before answering. Brent is as close as I have to a safe person, but not having him here with me makes it hard. When I don't want to be alone, who do I call? No one.

I clear my throat and try to force a smile, but it's not convincing. "My brother, Brent."

"He's in Washington, right?"

I nod, wishing I could teleport us to my dorm so I didn't have to let him go, but Joey sits up and buckles his seat belt.

"Yeah, he stayed close to home."

Is it home, though? I love my parents, they are amazing people, but...they never noticed when I needed them to.

Joey starts the car, then seems to hesitate for a minute before reaching for my hand to put on his leg. He doesn't look at me, just nods his head, and pats my hand before pulling out of the space. I give his thigh a squeeze and sit back with a sense of contentment settling in my chest.

Once we get back to the dorms, we hurry into my room before anyone can see Joey and therefore need him for something. He breathes a sigh of relief when we get there and Neal isn't around. As much as I want to lock the door, I'm pretty sure that would be more suspicious, so I don't. The urge to hide him from the world is strong, though. He needs a break.

After stripping my hoodie off and changing into sweats, I sit back on my bed and turn my TV and Xbox on. Joey stands in the middle of the room looking awkward as fuck.

I raise an eyebrow at him. "Whatcha doing?"

He rocks back and forth a few times and shoves his hands in his pockets before he finally blurts out, "I don't know how to be friends with you. I don't know where to sit or how much touching is too much or—"

"Joey." My hard tone makes him stop rambling, hopefully stops the spiraling thoughts in his head. "Come here."

As if on instinct, he walks to the bed and stops when it's touching his legs but doesn't climb on. He's breathing too hard and there's a crease between his eyebrows. My poor boy is locked in his head and fighting himself on what he wants versus what he thinks is okay.

Sitting up on my knees, I shuffle toward him and grab the front of his hoodie to jerk him into my space. "I have no limits on you touching me. I *need* touch. So sit on this fucking bed or wrap yourself around me like an octopus, I don't care. Get out of your head and do what you want to for once."

With his gaze locked on mine, he slowly lifts his hands to my cheeks, and leans down to press his lips to mine. His eyes don't close, so I force mine to stay open too. He doesn't deepen it, just a gentle press, hold, and release before he starts again. It rips my chest open to see him hesitant. Like he's afraid I'll take back what I said and push him away or demand more. There's already too many people demanding too much of him. As much as I want him to be mine, I can't have him. Not really.

Once again, someone who means the world to me doesn't need me like I need them.

The thought steals my breath, aches in my bones, and despite knowing it's going to hurt later, I reach for him. Sliding my hands under his shirt, he gasps into my mouth when my palms meet his flesh.

I need him to need me.

The contact doesn't turn frenzied, or lust-driven. He's hard and so am I, but neither of us move to take the step. I think we both just need *this* right now. The contact, the anchor into this moment where there isn't sports or family or obligations.

This...whatever it is, was supposed to be easy. No feelings, just pleasure. Why did that have to change? Why did my heart decide that we couldn't live without this man?

I slide my hands up his back and dig my fingertips into his muscles then drag them back down. He groans into the kiss and pulls back to lean his forehead against mine.

Joey's eyes are shut now and his forehead is scrunched up like he's confused or fighting something in his mind.

"What is it?" I whisper, nudging his nose with mine.

"I feel like I'm leading you on or taking advantage because I don't know what I want. Everything you've offered me seems too good to be true and I'm waiting for the other shoe to drop. I'm waiting for you to get fed up with my crap or get taken from me." He takes a deep breath and his shoulders sag in defeat. "I'm afraid of you."

He's so fucking perfect it hurts.

"Let me worry about me. I know you just need to *be* here, and that's okay." I grip his waist and bite at his chin to get a chuckle from him. I smile when it works. "You don't owe me anything, Joey. You don't have to be any certain way with me. Just be you."

He runs his fingers through my hair, then pushes me back on the bed. I settle back against the pillow I've wadded up and watch him strip off his hoodie before laying down on top of me, shoving his face in the crook of my neck and sighing. His arms slide under me and he cocks one leg between mine. It's really fucking comfortable and even though I planned to cuddle while watching a movie, a nap sounds perfect.

He settles and adjusts a little before his breathing evens out, and I find myself slipping into sleep too.

CHAPTER 21

joey

The shrill ring of an old-fashioned phone wakes me from the best sleep I've had in weeks. Nick's cologne fills my lungs and I don't want to extract myself from him. He's warm and comfortable and here.

The ringing stops but immediately starts up again. Shit. That means it's either Charlotte or Mom. I kiss Nick's chest and force myself to get up. He grumbles and tries to roll us onto our sides, but I manage to get off the bed and dig through my hoodie before it hangs up again.

"Hello?" I try to whisper, but my sleep-roughened voice cracks and I have to try again. "Hello?"

"Where the hell have you been? Mom is losing it!" Charlotte is damn near hysterical and I'm instantly awake.

"What happened?" I pace the length of the dorm room and my gut clenches. Did Matt finally hurt someone? Did he hurt himself worse than usual?

Charlotte breaks down and sobs for a second before pulling herself back together.

"He ran a fucking backhoe into a tree because he was high. This time the police were called, so he was arrested after getting treated for a concussion!" she all but screams into the phone and my stomach sinks to the floor. Motherfucker. What the hell is it going to take for that kid to get his shit together? Does he realize he could have hurt someone, not just himself?

Frustration burns through me and makes my hands shake. I want to punch something, yell, cause damage. There's nothing I can do. Literally nothing. I'm hours away with no car, no money, no means to help him.

But his face when he was fourteen and scared, waiting for Mom after getting cut at school, pops into my mind. The trembling lip, the tears on his cheeks. He's broken and hurting and somehow I didn't teach him how to deal with any of it the right way. So he turned to drugs and alcohol to feel better. I failed him.

"Charlotte," I say her name, but she's still ranting. "Charlotte!" This time I bark her name and she stops. "Go home. Matt is not your problem. I'll see what I can do to help him, but you're going to stress yourself into a literal heart attack if you don't stop."

"I can pay for his bail—"

"No." My tone says this is not a negotiation, but Charlotte was never good at following orders. "Go. Home. Take a shower, hug your fiancé, read a smut book, or watch a true crime documentary. Whatever it is girls do to relax."

"How am I supposed to relax when my little brother is in jail and my mom won't stop blowing up my phone about it?" She sounds like a little girl. Unsure and scared. Not the bold, fierce woman I know she is.

"Turn your phone off." It sounds so simple but I could never do it.

"Are you going to turn yours off?" There's the sass I expect from her.

I sigh and Nick slings an arm around my waist, forcing me to stop pacing. He brushes his lips against the back of my neck and I let myself lean on him. This man. He deserves so much more than I can give him. Nick is too good of a man to come last.

"You know I can't do that." Even I hear the resignation in my voice. I'm burned out. Ready to snap.

"It's getting turned off," Nick says loud enough for Char to hear it.

"Who's that?" I can picture her perking up to dig for information.

"It's—" just a friend. "Nick."

I can feel his smile against my skin and it makes my heart happy to know I made him smile, but it hurts too.

"And who is Nick?" Charlotte is not going to drop this and I don't know how to explain him to her.

"Good night, Char." I end the call before she can get started but before I can slide the damn phone into my pocket, there's a ping from a message. I groan and drop my head back on Nick's shoulder.

"If she's anything like my brother, that was the worst thing you could have done." Nick's hand slides under my shirt and strokes down my chest. It's not sexual, just comforting. "Turn it off."

"I can't." I turn and bury my face in his neck, breathing him in on a deep inhale. "What if someone needs me? Coach or one of the guys?"

"They can be grown-ups and deal with their own shit." His tone has just enough of a hard edge that I know he'll take the damn thing from me and turn it off himself if he has to. Grabbing it, I give it to him.

"Can you just put it on do not disturb and check it every once in a while?" I drag my nose up the column of his throat. "In case there's an emergency."

He shudders but does it and tosses the device onto his bed. With strong pressure, Nick slides his hands up my back, making me groan. Fuck, that feels good. He chuckles and does it again, pushing me into him while he digs into the muscles of my back and shoulders.

"Who knew you were so noisy?"

I grumble but keep my cheek pressed to his shoulder as I relax into his hold. It feels so good to be seen. To be taken care of.

"What do you need right now?"

My head spins with everything I don't know and lists of things I need to do, people to call—will Matt need a lawyer?

"Joey." That commanding tone shuts off the spiral and I drag in a deep breath laced with his scent. "What do you need? Food? Go back to sleep? Work out? An orgasm?"

I smirk into his skin at the last offer. An orgasm sounds fantastic, but I don't think I could keep my head quiet long enough to get there and that will just frustrate me more.

"Maybe a run."

Nick runs his hands down my body again and slaps both palms on my ass. "Okay, let's go for a run."

The tightness in my stomach relaxes when it hits me that he means for us to go together. I wrap my arms around his neck and kiss him. He's too perfect.

"You said run but I'm happy to supply orgasms." He smiles against my lips.

"Stop being perfect."

Nick bites at my lip and kisses the tip of my noise. "I'm only perfect for you."

CHAPTER 22

joey

We're on our Saturday game against Vegas and we're struggling. Something has Oiler and Johnson distracted. Albrooke is confused, which means I'm not the only one, and Carmichael is hell-bent on making sure we all know how much he hates us tonight.

During a break in the game, Willis slides up next to me sweaty and panting. "What the fuck is his problem tonight?"

"No idea. Ignore him."

The puck drops and the game takes off. Normally I love the fast pace of the game. There's no time for anything but this. Watching the puck, anticipating where it will go next, who will try to block or steal. If your head isn't in the game, it's obvious. To everyone.

At the first break, I smack Oiler and Johnson upside the helmet as we head toward the locker room.

"What was that for, Carp?" Oiler looks over his shoulder at me.

"I don't know what is going on with you two tonight but get your shit together. It's clear you aren't in this game," I snap and shoulder past them.

Shit. I'm not normally one to yell. I'm calm under pressure, keep my head in high-stress situations, but I just lost my cool.

I drop down in front of my cubby and take a long drink from my water bottle. I'm sweaty and sore from yesterday's game but I've got another fifteen minutes of game time to do tonight. Closing my eyes, I force myself to take a deep breath. And then another.

The room is loud around me, Coach is yelling while also giving a pep talk, and all I want to do is curl up in bed with Nick.

Focus on the game.

When I look around the room again, Bryce is watching me with a strange expression but doesn't say anything.

As we make our way back down the hallway, I realize that I don't find freedom in hockey like I used to. For years, I lived and breathed this game. I did everything I could to make sure I could play. I played sick, I played hurt, I played exhausted, I played while my siblings were sick in the stands. Hockey was my life.

Now as a senior in college, it's just something I do.

Something I used to love.

I love the guys on the team and I'm glad I'm able to play with them, but I'm not hungry for it like I used to be.

I'm just...tired.

Carmichael spends the next ten minutes of playtime yelling at everyone, until I snap and yell back.

"Carmichael, fuck off! You aren't helping!" He's right behind the glass in the stands and if looks could kill, I would be bleeding out right now. If he wants to be mad at me, fine, go ahead. I don't fucking care anymore. I'm over his shit.

"Poor Jer Bear is in for a long night," Oiler sighs and shakes his head.

"What?" I turn to look at him and Albrooke winces.

"Yeah, thanks, Cap." He looks behind me, probably at Carmichael, then back to the ice. "Way to rile him up before bedtime."

"You could sneak some melatonin in his food," Willis offers, and we all turn to stare at him in horror. Even I wouldn't do that. "What?"

"You really think I could get away with that?" Albrooke lifts a skeptical eyebrow at him. "If I managed to do it and he fell asleep, he would murder me in the morning. If he caught me, I would leave the hotel in a body bag."

"Also, now I feel like I need to watch my drinks around you, man." Brendon puts his hand over his water bottle and turns away from him. "Consent is sexy, dude."

Bryce hops over the wall with the other second lineman and drops down next to me while the first linemen and the second line defense go out. Willis is immediately thrown into the boards but bolts toward our goal to help Austin.

We're quiet as we watch the battle on the ice, Austin doing his damnedest to keep the puck out of the crease, but the Vegas left winger manages to get the puck on his stick and fling it into the goal. The lamp lights up and we groan.

That's that. We're down six points with two minutes remaining.

This is not how I expected my senior year of hockey to go. When the season started, I was hoping to make it to the Frozen Four again. But I doubt we'll even make it to finals.

When the final horn sounds, signaling the end of the game, everyone is depressed. It's never easy to lose. It doesn't matter how many games you play, how many times you walk away with an L, it feels personal every time.

We all skate out onto the ice to shake hands with the other team, saying shit like "Good game," but what we all really want to do is duck into the locker room and not look at them.

I get to the Vegas captain and give him a smile. "Good job out there."

He smiles back and pats my shoulder. "You too. You guys didn't make it easy for us."

I want to scoff but manage to keep it inside. I was a clown out there. A petulant child throwing a temper tantrum because things didn't go my way.

I'm an embarrassment.

Coach gives us the 'keep your chin up' speech and we all get in the showers. Most of the guys are talking about going to find a bottle to sink into, a few are talking about strip clubs and puck bunnies. Riggs is trying to hang with the big boys tonight, the twenty-one-plus group, so I snag him on his way past me at my cubby.

"No."

He opens those big puppy dog eyes at me like I just took his candy. "But, Cap..."

"If you want to drink, find a dumbass to sneak it into your hotel room like the rest of us had to do. If you get caught sneaking into a bar, Coach will have your ass." I look at the crushed dreams in his eyes and fuck, he reminds me of Matty. Just a little, when he lets the walls down. "And you don't have enough money to keep strippers interested. Find a bunny if you have to, but seriously, stay out of trouble. Vegas will eat you up and spit you out, and not in a fun way."

He snorts and nods as he walks off, no longer striding around like a dickhead. I haven't looked at my phone, but the blue light is blinking, telling me there's something there. A message or twenty. Some crisis that I'm going to be blamed for not being there to fix. I'm sure the fact that it happened is my fault too.

I get my tie done, pull my shoes on, and slide into my jacket, only to be held up from leaving by Coach.

"Listen up, boys," he growls and looks around at each and every one of us. "If you aren't on that bus at seven sharp, I'm leaving your ass behind."

The room erupts in groans of "Yes, Coach," but he's not done.

"And it better not smell like a brewery!"

There's more grumbling but everyone acknowledges him, and we head out to the bus that will take us back to the hotel.

We all sit in basically the same seats every time, so I find mine and drop into it with a sigh. The notifications on my phone are burning a hole through me. I know I have to look at them. I know I will have to deal with whatever it is, but I'm so fucking tired of being the punching bag of my family.

"Your mom is going to need you when I'm gone."

Dad's scratchy words run through my head. It's the only time I can still hear his voice. I don't remember his laugh or stern 'get your head out of your ass' tone, only this one sentence from his deathbed. He died three days later.

It's not fair. None of it.

That we lost him. That we had to watch him wither away. That I had to finish raising my siblings in his place. Everything from getting to school to heartbreaks to nightmares. I did it all. Mom kept a roof over our heads and food in the house, but she was checked out the rest of the time. I don't remember the last time she went to a game or an open house at school. I did all of it. Char was always in the stands during home games and when Matt wasn't getting into trouble, he was too.

They deserve better.

Tapping my phone screen to bring up the notifications, I sigh when I see Mom has called three times, Char has texted me five times, and Nick has texted me twice. Tears burn the back of my throat and I hate myself for wanting everyone to leave me alone.

"Yo, Cap!" Bryce calls from two rows ahead of me.

I give him a nod, telling him to continue.

"You coming out with us?" He motions to a few of the guys who are also looking back at me.

I shake my head and he sighs. I know he can tell something's up with me and is trying to help by getting me out, but I don't have the energy. All I want is to hide in my room with Nick wrapped around me. I want a hug. And cuddles.

And maybe an orgasm.

"If you change your mind, text me and I'll send you our location."

I give him a thumbs-up and lean my head back on the seat. Life has beaten me and I'm so tired of fighting.

Every part of me is exhausted. There's nothing left to give.

Everyone gets off the bus and heads into their rooms to get changed. No one wants to hang out in these damn suits.

When I get to my room, Bryce on my heels, I drop down onto the end of my bed and put my head in my hands.

Bryce sits next to me, shoulder to shoulder with his hands clasped between his legs. "You want to talk about it?"

"There's nothing to say." There's a knot in my throat and pressure on my shoulders. I want to yell, scream at the world to fuck off, but it won't do any good. Bryce also doesn't need me to unload all my bullshit on him.

"Is there anyone you talk to? Anyone you can vent to?" He leans into me a little.

Immediately, Nick pops into my head but he doesn't really know what's going on either. Not the details, anyway. It's too much to unload on another person. It'll just sound like I'm complaining anyway, like I'm a downer. No one wants to be around someone who complains all the time.

"I'm okay." I sigh and sit up. "Just an off night."

Bryce scratches his jaw and looks at me like he's about to call me out. "Been having a lot of those lately."

Yeah, thanks for that.

"You're a good captain, man, a great player, but you're in your head."

He's not wrong and that pisses me off. But it's not his fault.

"I know." I scrub my hands over my face. "I'm sorry I'm letting you guys—"

"Shut up, Jesus fucking Christ. That's not what I said." He shoves me and I almost tip over off the bed. "Everyone can see you're struggling but no one knows how to help because you won't let anyone in."

I thought I was hiding my bullshit, but I guess not. Shit.

"So, stand up and give me a hug or punch me in the face, whatever it takes to get that damn look off your face." Bryce stands and opens his arms wide, watching me unblinkingly.

"You look like an obsessed stalker right now." But I stand and without thinking about it, I hug him. He doesn't hesitate to wrap his arms around my shoulders in a tight hug and slap my back.

"I know we're supposed to be all emotionless Neanderthals, beating our chests and whatever, but it's okay to need to talk to someone." He squeezes me tighter and I take the comfort he's offering.

When I let go, he does too, and I force a little smile on my face. "Thanks. I guess I needed that."

"Well, hugs are all I got so if you need something else, find someone else." He holds his hands out, palms toward me.

I chuckle and think of Nick. There are messages on my phone from him that I'm both excited and a little scared to look at. Did he watch the game? See me fucking up?

"Hey, hey!" Bryce slaps my chest. "Stop looking like someone kicked your dog. Get changed, eat something, hydrate, jack off if you need to, and go to bed."

I lift an eyebrow at his suddenly stern tone. "And since when are you the boss of me?"

"Since you've been taking shitty care of yourself and it's starting to show."

Ouch.

Bryce steps around me and starts loosening his tie, so I do the same. In the quiet, we get changed, hang our suits up in the garment bags, and I put on pajamas while he finds jeans. All the while, I'm thinking about calling Nick. I wonder if he'll be able to talk me through an orgasm again. It's pathetic that I can't get myself off. Frustrating and sad and pathetic.

"You sure you don't want to come out?"

The question throws me off guard and I blush for a second. Come out? No, I'm not coming out. No one needs to know who I'm having sex with. Why would he ask that?

"What?" I don't turn toward him, just stay frozen facing my bag.

"Are you sure you don't want to come get food and a beer?" he says again, enunciating every word.

I want to sigh in relief but I don't.

"Uh, no, I'll order something here and crash." I sit on the bed again and grab the remote. "Don't stay out late or tomorrow will suck."

He pats me on the shoulder on his way out the door, double-checks that he has his room key, then leaves.

I flop back on the bed and stare at the ceiling.

I'm a fucking mess.

CHAPTER 23

nick

I want to call him. The game ended over an hour ago, so he should be at the hotel by now. But he hasn't opened my messages yet.

Did something happen with his family that he's trying to deal with? Did he crash as soon as he got back and is asleep? Did he finally put his phone on silent or turn it off so he can get some peace?

Do I have the right to demand he talk to me? Of course not, but I fucking want to.

I sigh and toss my phone onto my bed. This is what he was talking about when he said he didn't have time for a relationship. Does he realize that by leaning on me, making me a priority, he wouldn't be dealing with everything else alone? I can carry some of the burden so it's not so damn heavy for him. He has zero boundaries with anyone and I can help him with that too.

Fuck it.

Picking up my phone, I find his contact and push call. It rings a few times before a rough voice says, "Hello?"

"Hey, baby, you okay?"

I can hear him sniffling and what sounds like him wiping his face.

"Yeah, I'm fine. What's up?"

What's up? Is he serious?

"Are you at the hotel?" Is he around someone he can't be candid with? Maybe? Hopefully?

"Yeah." He sniffles again.

"What's wrong?" I lean against my dresser and wait. Having someone care about him is so foreign to him that he doesn't know how to handle it when it's presented to him. Fuck, I wish I were there with him right now. "You sound upset."

He clears his throat before he answers. "Nothing, just a long weekend. You know how it is after a game and the adrenaline crash."

I do, but this isn't that.

"Joey." There's no anger or frustration in my tone, even though I am frustrated.

"What do you want me to say?" I hate hearing him sound so small, so broken.

"The truth, sweet boy." I close my eyes and try to picture him alone in his hotel room, upset and needing comfort. This is all I can do for him right now and it's killing me. "Talk to me."

A little sob escapes him and it breaks my damn heart. "There's voicemails and messages on my phone from my family and I don't want to open them." His voice cracks and he lets out another sob that I feel in my chest. "But I feel like a shitty person for thinking it. They need help and I should want to help them. They're my family, my responsibility, and I'm failing them."

He's sobbing now, no longer able to speak through it. I hate that I can't help him, can't hug him in this moment. He can't see how strong he's been for so long and I don't know how to show it to him.

"Joey, listen to me." I wait until I hear him suck in a deep breath. "They are *not* your responsibility. They never should have been. I can almost guarantee that your dad did not mean for you to raise your siblings. He didn't mean for you to take the brunt force of your mom's failings. He didn't want this for you."

Joey's breath shudders and he sniffles. "I want to make him proud."

It's so clear that he had to grow up before he was ready. He has wounds from his childhood that are still open and festering. I hate it for him.

"Baby, I may have never met him, but he would be *crazy* not to be proud of you." I hate how far apart we are. "Think about all the things you've done." I start ticking them off on my fingers even though he can't see them. "You survived losing your dad, got your siblings through high school, got onto a college hockey team where you then became the captain. You're about to graduate college, while playing hockey, and dealing with your family's shit." He's a fucking rock star. "Those guys on the team with you? They're proud of you, and I bet they don't know what you're dealing with personally. I'm fucking proud of you. The fact that your mom can't see how much you've taken on, how much you've done for her, is her short coming, not yours."

The sigh he releases sounds defeated and I want to shake him.

"I wish you were here." His voice is small, like a child who's scared of being in trouble. It makes my heart sing to hear him admit it, though.

"You are not alone in that want." I smile to myself. "I would give my left nut to be there with you right now."

Joey chuckles, and I can hear the stubble on his face scrape across his hand as he wipes his face. "Why the left one?"

"So, my swimmers know how to act right, duh."

He snorts this time, laughing and finally breaking some of the tension. I love when he laughs. It doesn't happen often and I can almost picture his face in my mind. Eyes sparkling, tension lines gone, a warmth to his cheeks.

"Oh man, I needed that. Thanks," he says on a sigh.

"Anytime. It's what I'm here for." I sit back on my bed until my back is against the wall and I can relax. "I'm here for you, whatever you need. You know that, don't you?"

"Logically, I do but..."

"But what?"

"I don't know how to rely on anyone." His voice is soft, almost a whisper.

"I'll teach you."

Leaning my head against the wall, I thank whoever was responsible for sending Brent to my family. I don't know how I would have survived without him during my hardest years.

"Why?" The question comes after it's been quiet and it catches me off guard.

"Why what?"

"Why...me? I'm a mess of baggage and issues. You can find someone easier."

There it is. What's really been holding him back. He doesn't think he's worth it. "Can you switch to video?"

"Uh, I guess, hang on."

In a minute, Joey's handsome face is on my screen, full of trepidation. He's tired, the circles under his eyes are dark, and there's a raggedness to him that I want to erase.

"There you are." I smile at him, happy to see him even if the circumstances suck. "I wanted you to be able to see me when I tell you this. Are you ready?"

I wait for him to nod. "One, you aren't the only one with baggage. I've got some too. Second, having issues or baggage or whatever doesn't make you undeserving of love or affection or friendship." His eyes fill with unshed tears, and I pause to make sure I'm really about to say this. To be vulnerable. "I don't want someone easier. I want you. Just the way you are."

My heart is pounding in my ears, I can feel it pulsing in my neck as I wait for him to say something. Instead, the tears trail down his cheeks and he covers his face with his free hand.

"You're worth everything." I don't know if he'll let me show him or if he'll decide it's all too much and ghost me again. I don't have answers to what happens later, in the future, after graduation, but I want to figure it out with him. He hasn't given me a chance to love him but right now, there's no doubt in my mind that I do. If he walks away from me again, it'll crush me.

CHAPTER 24

nick

All day, I've been bugging Joey for estimated arrival times. I need to see him. Hug him. Kiss him.

I check my phone for the time for what feels like the hundredth time today and groan.

"I'm about to put you on the chain outside in the yard if you don't knock that off," Neal says from his desk without taking his eyes off the computer.

"Excuse me?"

"You're annoying as fuck today with all this moaning and groaning and pacing. Checking your damn phone every seventeen seconds isn't going to make time go faster." He turns and pins me with an exasperated glare. "Go jack off or something, that'll kill, like, two minutes."

I laugh even though I want to be offended. "First off, fuck you and your two minutes—"

"If that's what it takes to make you shut up, I'll take one for the team." He sighs and stands up, pulling on his shirt.

"If you come any closer to me, I'm pissing on your pillow."

Neal contemplates that for a second before shrugging and sitting back down. "Don't make me get the chloroform."

That makes me pause my pacing. "We don't have chloroform on campus."

"That you know of..."

Well, that's terrifying.

I look at my phone again and groan but grab my shoes and leave the room. Unfortunately, Neal is right and pacing my room doesn't make the time go by any faster. I take the stairs just to take up more time and head to Roasted Mountains for that drink thingy the coffee witch made for me. I should probably remember what that was...

When I enter, the coffee witch is behind the counter and lifts an eyebrow at me.

"Back again, I see." She smiles at me when I come to the counter.

"Yeah, I'm killing time. Hey, do you remember what concoction you brewed for me? Something with hot chocolate, I think?" I put my palms together like I'm praying and try to look desperate. I mean, I am desperate, so it shouldn't be hard.

"Yeah, I got you." She puts in the order and asks me for a name.

"You're a goddess." I bow to her and tell her my name while she shakes her head and walks away. She loves me. I can tell.

A minute later, she calls my name and gives me the to-go cup and a cookie. I love cookies. I should take Joey to meet Debbi and get more pastries to eat off his dick...

"You're the best, coffee witch!" I holler as I leave and she shakes her head but I hear someone laugh in the back.

After wandering around campus for a while, I make my way back to the rink where the buses will drop off the players and all their shit. I've finished my drink and the cookie and now my stomach hurts from all the sugar, but oh well.

The bus finally pulls into the parking lot and I swear my blood starts vibrating. What if he doesn't want me here when he gets off the bus? Is it weird that I'm just standing here waiting?

I look around and there's a few girls hanging around too, but I'm guessing those are either puck bunnies or girlfriends. Fuck. This looks weird. I should have just waited at the dorms. Too late now, I'm sure I've been spotted.

The bus stops and though I can't hear what is said, the head coach is saying something. Probably along the lines of "don't be idiots, you have practice tomorrow" since that's what we were always told.

I shove my hands into my pockets and bounce on my toes, just to have something to do. The team streams out, the storage under the bus is opened, and everything is put on the sidewalk for the guys to grab. Joey's eyes meet mine as he steps off the bus and a smile tries to lift his lips but he tamps it down. From where I'm standing, I can watch the blush pinken his cheeks and some of the nerves in my stomach settle.

It's dark and cold since the sun went down a few hours ago and it's February, but I don't let it bother me. They've been on the bus all day, they're tired, achy, and probably hungry.

With surprising efficiency, they clear out the personal bags, and the equipment manager deals with what is left.

Bryce gives me a head nod on his way past me but I can't take my eyes away from Joey. The big man with a soft heart and the need to help holds my attention like nothing else ever has. I'm obsessed.

He makes his way toward me with his head dipped a little, not looking me in the eyes, and a shy smile on his lips.

"Hi," he says, glancing up quickly before looking back at my shoulder.

"Hi." I want to reach for him, wrap him in a hug, hold his hand, but I don't know how he'll react. "Are you hungry?"

His stomach growls and I chuckle. "I guess that answers that." I tap his chest with the back of my hand and turn toward the dorms. "Let's put your bag down and feed you."

It's quiet for a minute but it's not uncomfortable. I can tell there's something rattling around in his head that he wants to say, so I just wait. When we hit a spot outside of the lamppost, he grabs my arm and pulls me off the path into the dark. My back hits the brick and his body is pressed against me, his lips claiming my own, and his hand is on the back of my neck. I swallow his groan when I kiss him back, taking control of his body while he ravages my mouth.

His skin is hot under my hands when I slide them under his shirt.

He shudders under my touch, goosebumps popping up against my fingertips as I reach for every inch of his flesh I can reach.

"Fuck," Joey pants against my swollen lips. "I needed that."

I smile and bite at his pouty lower lip. "Kiss me like that anytime."

He rocks his hips against mine, a soft moan falling from his lips when the ridge of his erection drags against my hip.

"Are you needy, baby?" My voice drops and I grip his hips, grinding myself against him.

"So fucking needy." His whimper is music to my ears and adrenaline in my veins.

"I need you to make me come."

Both of his hands cup my head and he fucks my mouth with his tongue. God damn, if he doesn't stop, I'm going to come in my pants.

I grip his throat and force him off my mouth. "I'll take care of you, horny boy. Inside."

Joey groans with his whole body, his shoulders dropping and his head falling back a little, but he grabs the bag he dropped and my hand, pulling me toward the dorms.

"Is your roommate out? I don't know what Bryce is doing."

I already have my phone in my hand, texting Neal to get lost for a while.

"Already on it." When my phone is back in my pocket, I slow down until Joey turns to look at me.

"What are you doing? Is something wrong?" He glances around before looking back at me.

"You're holding my hand. In public." I lift our hands to show him, as if he can't feel my palm against his. "Are you okay with this?" I wave our hands a little.

"I—" His eyebrows pull together as he looks at where we're touching. "I didn't think about it, I guess."

"I'm fine with it, if that's what you're worried about."

In the harsh glow of a streetlamp, I watch him shut down. He's not ready, and that's okay, but he's now feeling guilty about it; it's written so clearly on his face that it may as well be written in text.

"Hey," I release his hand when his grip loosens, "it's okay." *Yet my heart hurts anyway.* "I'm not rushing you." *Please pick me. I need someone to pick me for once.*

"It's just that we don't—we haven't—I don't—"

"Joey, take a deep breath. It's okay." His anxiety over hurting my feelings or whatever cools some of the hurt.

"Damn it. I'm sorry." He runs his hands through his hair and pulls on the strands. "I don't know what I'm doing anymore."

I look around quickly then step in closer to him, almost touching but not quite. "You don't have to have answers right now, just do what feels good." His gaze drops to my lips and he licks his own. One side of my mouth turns up in a knowing, carnal smile. "I want to make you feel good. Watch you come. Hear that sweet voice beg when you get close to the edge."

He sucks in a sharp breath and his shoulders tense. "Yes. I want it. All of it."

"Good boy." I pat his cheek and lead the way to our dorm building. He follows along like a puppy and when I glance back at him, his eyes are on my ass. Hmm, interesting. Is he feeling toppy tonight? I wouldn't be opposed to that...

My phone buzzes as we step onto the elevator and as I'm looking at the screen, Joey grabs my hips and presses himself against my back and ass. He's breathing hard against my ear and neck, making my skin pebble, and my dick ache.

"Neal left the room, it's ours," I groan when his hard cock rubs my ass cheek. "Do you want to fuck me, sweet boy? Do you need to be inside me tonight?"

He gasps as his body is rocked by a shiver and he bites my neck. "Yes, please, Daddy."

The smile on my face is feral and I don't need a mirror to know it. I need my boy and if he needs to pound me into the mattress, I'll let him.

The doors open on the third floor and we hustle to my room. For once, the hallway is empty and we aren't stopped ten times. I push open the door and when Joey steps through it, I slam it closed and lock it. In the same instant, he drops his bag and we're on each other. We're ripping at clothes and savagely kissing, groping, grinding. It's been too long since we were together, too much hurt and distance between us.

Joey palms my ass, gripping and kneading the muscles. Anticipation flutters in my stomach. Fuck, I want him.

I turn us and walk us to my bed, pushing Joey down when his knees hit the mattress. After tossing the lube on the bed, I climb onto his lap, straddling his thighs. He holds my hips and I wrap my hand around our dicks in a tight squeeze.

Joey gasps, watching my hands on us. I roll my body, thrusting into my hand and dragging my cock against his. His fingers flex into my skin, digging in and probably leaving marks.

With my free hand, I reach for his nipple and pinch it hard. He sucks in a hiss between his teeth and his body tenses, but his dick throbs and his hips jerk up.

I'm getting too worked up, too close to the edge, so I release us both and lean over his broad chest to kiss him. He works my hips, pushing up against me to get some friction on his aching cock, but I lift up so he can't get what he's searching for. I chuckle into the kiss when he groans with frustration.

"Please," he whines, desperation dripping from him. "Daddy..."

I nip at his jaw and neck, moving to his ear. "Don't worry, sweet boy, I'll take care of you." I grab the lube and slick up his cock, stroking him slowly. "You're going to stretch me open, fill me with cum." Joey whimpers and he thrusts into my grip. "I love the burn of the stretch. It hurts so *fucking* good."

His face is bright red, his neck and chest too. His fingers are digging so deep into my flesh it aches, but I welcome it. It's proof that he's here, that he wants this, wants me.

I add some lube to my hole and test myself with a finger and then two. Fuck it, I want the burn. Lifting his cock, I position myself over him, letting his head tease my hole. Pushing against it and lifting off, once, twice, before letting the head in.

The stretch stings but it doesn't dissuade me from wanting more. Wanting everything.

I can't stop the hiss when I take more.

"You don't have to." Joey's panting and starting to shine with sweat. He's wrecked and we've barely started.

"Do you want to stop?" I lean on his chest, holding myself still.

"I don't want to hurt you." The man looks so conflicted. He wants to fuck, it's clear on his face, but he wants to take care of me. I can't have that, not in this moment.

"That's not what I asked. Do you want to stop or do you want me to sink down on your cock and ride you until all that exists is pleasure?"

His hips move involuntarily. "Pl-please, ride me."

With my eyes on his, I force my body to relax and take the rest of him. It burns, stings, but watching his eyes cross and roll back is worth it.

I start easy, grinding my ass down against his hips, keeping him as deep as he can go. Joey's legs move back and forth across the mattress and his fingers flex. My boy is so turned on he can't keep still. It's my favorite part. Where arousal and desperation crash, taking away the ability to control your body.

All the nerve endings in my body are sensitive and on high alert as I build up speed and lift off him. Soon my body is slapping against his, moans and whimpers and panting breaths fill the space between us. We're riding a high, chasing the inevitable end, and hoping not to drown in the undertow.

I brace my hands on his chest and his eyes open, watching me take him. His eyebrows pull together, then he clenches his eyes shut. Something's changed and I don't know why or what caused it.

He's thinking too hard.

Joey's dick doesn't feel as full as it was a minute ago and the strain in his muscles isn't from holding himself still.

"Look at me, baby." I stop moving, sitting on his hips, and wait. "Joey." This time I put some command in my tone, he's too far down the rabbit hole already.

His chin lifts and his warm eyes meet mine, making my heart ache. Without a word, he's begging me for help, for guidance, for reassurance. This time, I don't know how to fix it. Does he need praise? Does he need degradation? Does he need comfort?

"You feel so fucking good, baby." I circle my hips and his breathing hitches, but it's not what he needs. "Such a dirty little fuck toy—" His dick twitches. "—letting me use your body any way I want to get off." I wrap my hand around my cock, jacking myself as I grind on his dick, and our gazes locked. "Just lying there and taking what I give you. My jizz trap, hungry for me to mark you with cum."

Joey reaches for me, pulling my mouth to his in a punishing kiss as he thrusts up to meet me. He's hard now and breathing too fast. Part of me is relieved I didn't make it worse, part of me is proud I figured out what he needed, part of me wants to come.

"Daddy." That innocent voice is spoken against my lips and my heart sings. "I need to come."

"Fill me up, baby." I stroke myself quickly, twisting my hand around the head. Joey tenses, back arching, pounding into me for a few thrusts before he grunts into my mouth and finally relaxes. He goes limp, breathing hard and cum-drunk. His blissed-out expression and sleepy smile push me over and I come on his stomach and chest.

CHAPTER 25

joey

I'm on the verge of sleep where I feel like I'm floating but heavy. Time doesn't exist and I'm so warm and comfortable and relaxed. Have I ever been this relaxed before?

Soft lips press against mine and I hum at the contact.

"Sleepy boy," Nick singsongs. "Neal is going to be back here soon so unless you're okay with him seeing *everything,* you gotta get up."

"Noooo," I whine and reach for him. "Come back to bed, it's time to sleep."

He chuckles and warm suction surrounds my right nipple. Damn, that feels good.

Sharp pain slices through me as his teeth dig into my flesh and pull. My eyes pop open and I hiss at the sting.

"Fucking Christ! I'm up!" I grab at his hair and he releases me with pop and quick lick. "What is with your nipple obsession?" I rub at the now red-and-purple teeth marks around my nipple.

He straightens up with a smirk and crosses his arms over his deliciously muscular chest. His pj pants are so low on his hips I can tell he has nothing on underneath them. "Yours are sensitive, I like that." Nick drags his eyes down my naked body and pauses at my dick that is chubbing up, then winks at me.

"Put some pants on, I don't want Neal to see what's mine."

He says it so casually, like it's obvious, that I smile. *I'm his. He's mine.*

I pull up my underwear and grab him, pulling him between my thighs while I sit on his bed.

"You want me to be yours?" My voice only wobbles a little at the question.

Nick's smile is happy this time and he brushes the hair from my face before he cups my cheeks and leans down to kiss my forehead, my nose, then my lips. "Mine," he whispers into our kiss. I wrap my arms around him, pulling as much of his body against mine as I can.

"Does that make you mine then?" I look into his eyes, more nervous than I should be considering what he just confirmed, but my lack of self-worth doesn't care. I need the reassurance.

"Yes. In every way you'll have me."

Excitement and terror war within me. I've never had someone that was mine. Never really dated, never had the time, but Nick knows my bullshit and is still here. Hell, he chased my ass. That has to mean something, right? That he won't resent me for taking calls from my family in the middle of sexy times or a date? That he won't get mad when the team needs something and I have to cut a call short on the road?

Nick runs his hand up the back of my head and forms a fist, not pulling but tight. "What's going through your head?"

"I'm scared."

He nods and releases my hair to sit next to me on the bed, threading our fingers together. "Of what specifically? I know your family takes a lot of your time and hockey is life right now. So, are you worried I'm going to get mad you don't give me enough attention?"

I sit back a little and think about it. Is that part of it? Maybe? I'm afraid to need him. I am terrified that I'll learn to lean on him and then he'll get tired of my family and bounce, leaving me to drown. I'm scared I won't be enough for him.

"Joey," Nick says my name in a quiet but stern tone. Patient but commanding. "I can see you spiraling, talk to me. Tell me what's worrying you."

I take a deep breath and close my eyes, then let the words tumble out. "I'm afraid you'll grow to resent me or my family because they interrupt all the time. I'm afraid you'll make me fall in love with you then decide that I'm too much work and walk away. I'm afraid that I won't give you enough attention and in doing so, I'll hurt you. I don't want to ever hurt you—"

"Joey—"

"—I'm afraid you'll get tired of my issues, tired of being patient with me, tired of waiting or finding workarounds because I'm fucked up and I don't know who I am. Not really. I never had a chance to figure it out because I was raising my siblings—"

"Stop—"

"I'm afraid—"

Nick's lips cut me off and I can't stop myself from clinging to him. I slide off the bed to kneel at his feet and wrap my arms around his waist with tears running down my cheeks. He cups my cheeks and holds my face while he leans his forehead against mine.

I open my mouth but my lip trembles and he shushes me softly.

"Okay, I get it." He wipes the tears from my cheeks with his thumbs. "Me telling you none of that will happen isn't going to prove anything, so I'll find a way to show you until you believe me."

He kisses my forehead again, then wraps his arms around my shoulders. My face is pressed against his chest, the rhythmic *thump, thump* of his heart calming my tattered nerves. I don't know what I did to deserve this man, but I know I'll die if he leaves.

The door opens and I tense. Shit. I don't have pants on.

The urge to run licks my spine but I force myself to stay put. Nick's body has tensed around me, like he's waiting for me to bolt like last time. I don't know what to do or where to go from here; this is awkward and there's no pretending it's not happening.

"That's Neal, he's cool, and to be fair, he saw us fuck already so..." Nick whispers against the top of my head.

Neal pauses, then goes into the bathroom and closes the door.

Nick lets me get up and I pull on my clothes quickly. I feel better, less vulnerable.

"Okay?" Nick asks, reaching for my hand. I let him take it and I thread our fingers together. The smile he gives me is...everything.

A cleared throat sound comes from the bathroom and I turn my head to look.

"I'm going to open the door. If anyone would like to disappear before that, do it now." Neal's voice is distorted by the wood but his words are clear.

Nick chuckles and looks at me. I was given an out, a way to pretend a little longer, but I don't want it.

"I'm not ready to make an announcement or anything but this feels like a good first step." I squeeze Nick's hand as the bathroom door opens.

"Okay," Neal says as he walks toward us and holds out his hand. "Nice to meet you, I'm Neal."

"Joey," I say as I shake his hand.

"Nice to officially meet you."

The man is huge. Easily wider than I am, though not as tall, and looks solid as fuck. He would be a good defenseman, actually. I can't tell what color his hair is since it's buzzed really short but it's not a pale color like blond. Not that it matters.

"I'm going to bed, so keep it down, though it already smells like cum in here, so I assume y'all are done." He walks past me and my eyes bug out of my head while my face is lit on fire.

"Really, dude?" Nick sighs. "I thought for once, you were gonna be nice."

Neal climbs into bed and smiles at Nick. "I don't know what gave you that impression but it sounds like a you problem. Good night."

Nick huffs and I lead us to the door, grabbing my bag and kissing him softly. "Good night."

"Good night, baby."

CHAPTER 26

nick

Since this is college and the frat houses need no reason to party, they're having a block party on a Wednesday for International Women's Day. Since women are badasses, it's a hero costume party.

So here I am in jeans and a hoodie with 'Hero' written on the front, looking for my favorite Anxious Andy. He's going to stress himself into a heart attack if he doesn't let go of some of the pressure he puts on himself.

The street has been blocked so no one can drive down here. All the houses seem to have their own theme, and there are people everywhere. The Barbie house looks like it's vomiting pink shit, and I am *so* glad I don't have to clean that up.

One house is clearly superheroes, there's one with what looks like Renaissance vibes, and another that looks like they sprayed the entire thing with glitter. They are going to be fucked if they can't get all that off, though the disco ball hanging from the porch is kinda cool.

As I wander around, getting a feel for everything, I notice every house has a drink station set up on the lawn and they are all different. Since Jell-O shots are the bomb, I grab two red ones.

"Oh nooo," Joey whines behind me. I turn with the little plastic cup to my lips and laugh—which turns into me inhaling Jell-O—when he looks distraught at the table I'm at. "Not Jell-O shots. These guys are going to be *wasted* and Coach is gonna be *pissed*."

I cough up the offending red gel then pat his shoulder. "Well, if you don't get drunk, it won't be your problem."

"I'm the captain, they are my problem."

I sling my arm over his shoulders and turn him in a circle to see the entire street. "They are grown-ass adults. You are not responsible for their lack of self-control."

A group of his guys—Brendon, Jeremy, and Paul—run past us, capes flapping behind them, laughing and shoving each other.

Brendon grabs Jell-O shots, completely oblivious to the fact that Joey is glaring at him, and wanders back to the group.

"At least Paul is here to keep Brendon from dying but where is Preston?" My poor boy is already stressed out and the night is just starting.

Leaning my mouth toward his, I lower my voice so only he can hear me. "You seem a little *tense*. I happen to have a great way to relieve that."

Joey glares at me next. "I can't take my eyes off these chaos gremlins long enough for that." He walks out from under my arm, his head constantly swiveling. I can't help but sigh and follow after him.

A couple of my teammates stop me to talk, wanting to know when spring training starts and how much time they'll have before summer camp. There's a pang of sadness in my gut that I won't be a part of it this year. I'm done. No more college football for me. Football has been such a big part of my life for so long that I almost feel lost without it. I should see if there are any peewee coaches that are needed. Teaching kids to play could be a lot of fun.

"What are you doing after graduation? You moving back home?" Allen, one of the freshmen, asks.

I shrug. "I dunno, man, maybe. That's future Nick's problem."

"Uh, it's almost current Nick's problem." His eyes get wide.

"Yeah, I'll figure it out. Enjoy the party." I pat him on the shoulder and walk away, only to realize I have no idea where Joey went. Shit.

Walking up the street, there's music blasting from the houses, laughter, and vomiting everywhere. It's amazing. So far, I haven't seen any fights but I'm sure there's been something. Cheering from a house across the road from where I am has me turning to see what is happening. On the grass is a big tub with water and something floating in it. A guy in a Superman costume is kneeling next to it, face drenched, and holding something up in the air.

Is that one of those stress balls shaped like a tit?

Obviously I have to know more, so I cut through the crowd to get a better look. Superman is none other that Jeremy Albrooke, one of the guys from the hockey team. He's flushed with alcohol but looking damn proud of himself as he shoves the boob in his costume before bounding away. Amazing.

"I hear," hot breath against my ear makes me jump, but a quick glance tells me it's Joey and I relax, "you have a cure for tension."

"I may know of something."

"Teach me your ways, magic man." Joey steps around me and without looking back, he takes off. With a smirk on my face, I follow him at a leisurely pace. Maybe there's hope for us, after all.

He disappears into the shadows between two houses. The second I'm in the dark, hands are on me, and his mouth is ravaging mine. I groan into his kiss, my body pressed against him while he drags his fingers across my skin. He's on edge and ready to snap.

Without breaking contact with his lips, I open his pants and slide my hand against his throbbing cock.

Joey thrusts against me and digs his fingers into my flesh, probably leaving bruises.

"Please make me come. I need to come," he begs through panting breaths.

With a sure grip, I stroke him hard and fast. Joey bends forward, mouth open in a silent moan, before he's able to gasp in air. I love the way he clings to me, the way he responds to me. "Are you going to come? Out here in the open where someone can walk by and see what a needy slut you are?"

He shudders and thrusts into my grip. It's so fucking hot when arousal has him in its grasp and he's unable to keep still. His back bows again and every breath that leaves his mouth has a moan accompanying it. Quickly dropping to my knees, I bring the head of his dick into my mouth and suck. The sound he lets out can only be described as a sob and he fills my mouth with warm, salty cum. The explosion of his taste on my tongue makes me moan, which makes him shiver.

I stroke and suck him through his orgasm, achingly hard myself, and lick him clean when he's done. He's weak against the wall, flushed even in the dim lighting of the dark, and breathing too hard.

"You're beautiful like this," I cup his face and brush my thumb over his cheek. Joey's smile is shy and I chuckle. "Men are beautiful too."

"I know that," he huffs but reaches for my jeans. "Let me? I want to taste you."

"When you ask so nicely..." I lean my palms on the wall on either side of his head and move my feet back to give him enough room to kneel. "Make it fast, we've been back here a minute."

Joey doesn't need any more instruction. In the next instant, his hand is wrapped around me and his mouth is working my head. He finds a rhythm quickly and I thrust into his mouth.

"Eyes on me." I can't see him perfectly, even with my eyes adjusted to the dark, but it's enough. He groans when I speed up my hips and I feel it through my whole body. Without much thought, I let my body take over, taking my pleasure from him and chasing the orgasm I desperately want.

"Oh fuck." I grip his hair with one hand as tingles break out along my skin and pressure builds in my groin. "I'm gonna come, baby, swallow it."

Joey whimpers and the first wave washes over me, damn near taking my knees out from under me and filling his mouth. Spurt after spurt shoots into his mouth until I shudder and lean heavily against the house. He gives me a final lick, then pulls off my dick with a self-satisfied smile, and stands.

"Kiss me," he breathes against my mouth. The taste of us mixes, like the air in our lungs, until we're one and the same.

High heels clacking on the sidewalk near us reminds us where we are and that we don't have all night.

"Thank you," Joey says as he watches me put myself away.

I wink at him. "The pleasure was all mine."

He leaves me with a quick kiss and wanders down to a table selling beers. I watch him from my spot in the shadows as Paul stops next to him in a Batman costume. They stand there, drinking beer for a few minutes, talking about something I can't hear and watching the people around them. I get the sense that Paul also has a high sense of responsibility that isn't his, so they get along well. Like kindred spirits.

Superman bounds up to them and Joey gets a confused look on his face before he points to Superman's crotch. That must be Jeremy. A discussion is had before Paul gets down on his knee and reaches his hand inside Jeremy's pant leg.

What the hell is happening right now?

Then, like a jack-in-a-box, Brendon pops up and jumps onto Superman's back. All three of them fall over into a tangled heap. I don't know if I should offer to help or laugh. Joey sighs, I swear I can hear it from here, but he puts his beer down and lifts Brendon off the pile. He's not at all perturbed by what has occurred, probably because he's drunk.

I guess I'm starting to understand why Joey freaks out at things like this. His guys are...intense. Paul is messing with his shoulder, Jeremy is holding his nuts, it looks like, and Joey has had enough and walks away.

Once I leave my hiding spot and catch up with Joey, we wander around for a while. We stumble across Riggs—Joey's freshman—passed out on a lawn. Joey has both hands on his hips and sighs.

"I swear to God."

"This time, you can't prove it was one of my guy's fault." I hold my hands up.

"What am I supposed to do with him? I can't leave him here."

Okay, he has a point since it's March in Denver. It's cold as fuck, we just don't care because...beer. But it's also why I'm not in some dumbass costume.

"We can either two-man carry him or one of us can toss him over our shoulder," I offer.

"Two-man carry would suck to get all the way back to the dorms."

"Correct."

"But what if he pukes? I don't want him to choke."

That's a fair point. "Okay, you carry him over your shoulder and if he starts to puke, I'll make sure he doesn't choke."

"So I'm getting puked on then?"

"Hey, you're his captain, not me."

Joey drops his head back and sighs. "Okay, fine, help me get him up."

It takes us a minute but we manage to get him up on Joey's shoulder. Dude doesn't even blink, it's kind of creepy, so I check his pulse just in case. It's there.

The walk back to the dorms is quiet once we leave the noise of frat row and I find myself wanting to just hold his hand, lay out on the grass under a blanket to watch the stars, and just exist. Maybe someday we can do that, but not today.

I open the door for Joey, and Riggs starts to grumble, so we freeze. If he's going to upchuck, it's better to do it outside than on the floor. He settles and we continue on, into the elevator, then to his room.

I try the handle but it's locked. Of course it is.

Joey growls and slides the unconscious man off his shoulder. He looks exhausted, poor guy.

"Go on up to bed, I'll wait for the roommate." I sit on the floor across from where Riggs is laying.

"No, it's not your job to wait for Willis."

"It's not your job either, man. That's what I'm trying to tell you." Joey sits down next to me anyway. "Since everyone is at the party and he's out cold, it's a good idea to stay with him in case something happens, but that's not the captain's job."

"Yeah, yeah, whatever." Joey yawns and lays his head on my shoulder. "Talk to me so I don't fall asleep."

"How about you tell me why Paul was shoving his hand up Jeremy's pants?"

Joey starts laughing so hard he snorts. "He's such a dumbass." He sits up but there's a smile on his face. "Jeremy got one of those squishy boobs and shoved it in his costume. Well, it kept falling to his crotch and he couldn't get it out because alcohol makes him dumber than usual, so Paul reached up to get it."

Joey laughs again. "Honestly, it looked like his nut was swollen to the size of, like, a baseball. It was terrifying for a second. But no, he's just an idiot."

We start talking about nothing in particular, just getting to know each other. Little stories from years of sports and travel, school, and siblings. Nothing heavy or painful. I don't know how long we sit in that hallway, waiting for people to come back—waiting for Willis. Joey texted him at one point but he didn't respond, not that it's surprising.

Eventually, Joey falls asleep on the floor with his head on my leg like a pillow and my hand in his hair. It's so damn perfect, I take a picture of it and set it as my phone's wallpaper.

CHAPTER 27

joey

The day after the heroes party was rough for almost everyone. Honestly, I was surprised to see Riggs outside of his room, but he made it to practice. Maybe there's hope for him, after all.

Since we're almost to our last two games of the season, we're all exhausted. Everyone but Preston anyway. He did nothing but yell at everyone today and I'm so tired of hearing his mouth. If it wasn't for Nick, I would probably be ready to beat him with my hockey stick.

The locker room is chaotic as always as we get changed. While we're exhausted from the season, we're excited for the game tomorrow too.

"Hey!" Brendon yells. "I'm bi or whatever. I like holes *and* poles. Anyone got a problem with that?"

Everyone stops talking and turns to look at him and Paul who's standing next to him, a little wide-eyed.

From the back of the room, Riggs yells, "Are we supposed to be surprised?"

Everyone laughs, me included. Riggs has a point. Brendon flirts with everyone. Even Jeremy and Preston, which is a death sentence if you ask me.

Paul says something to Brendon and backhands his stomach before getting changed. Conversations continue and once I'm clean, I hustle back to my room to wait for Nick and look for a hoodie. Now I'm cold and we need to go get dinner. I don't know what we're doing exactly since we don't have labels, but knowing I'm going to see him makes me stupid happy.

A knock on my door has me smiling like an idiot.

"Come in," I holler since I know it's Nick.

The cocky man strides in and leans against the door, watching me pull a hoodie on.

When I walk up to him, he doesn't straighten up, so I press myself against him. His dick thickens against my thigh and I bite his lip.

"You're a horndog."

"You're the one rubbing your cock against me. What do you expect?" He grabs my ass and thrusts against me.

I nip his lip again before sucking on it then finally kissing him. Nick groans low in his throat. That sound does tingly things to me. It's hot as fuck knowing I made him make that sound.

"Iwanttotellpeopleaboutyou." I rush the words but Nick smiles at me.

"I mean, I am pretty awesome. I can see why." He kisses the tip of my nose. "You should just rip the Band-Aid off. Get it over with so you can stop stressing over it."

He's probably right. Just drop it in passing, don't make a big deal out of it. Like, half the team is dating each other, so really, what's one more player who isn't straight?

"And if anyone is a dick, punch them." Nick shrugs.

I grab his hand and lead him to dinner. The entire way, I hold his hand. It's terrifying but amazing. I find myself relaxing after a few minutes when nothing happens. Did I really think something was going to? Not really but fear is rarely rational.

Nick and I sit at a table in the dining hall with Willis. Everyone is tense with finals next week but spring interterm is coming up and I'm hoping Nick is still planning to stay for it.

"You going home for break, Willis?" Nick asks, shoving a dinner roll in his mouth.

"Nah, I'm staying. You?"

"Same."

Paul and Brendon sit at our table. Brendon is digging through a grocery bag, shoving snacks into his mouth despite having a tray of food.

"You guys going to be ready for finals?" I ask the group, and everyone groans.

"Shhh, we don't use those types of words." Brendon throws a cherry tomato at me.

"What words?" Nick smirks.

"Finals, tests, midterms, lima beans, burpees, Brussels sprouts, surprise anal." Brendon ticks them off on his fingers.

Paul chokes on his water and ends up having a coughing fit. Nick and Willis laugh while I shake my head at him. Brendon is a strange dude but it's never boring with him around.

"The fuck, dude? What kind of list is that?" Paul wheezes.

"It's the naughty word list," he says, rolling his eyes.

"I swear, your brain is a weird place sometimes." Paul shakes his head.

I smirk and flick my gaze to Nick who is watching me back. Damn it. My foot starts bouncing. I want to blurt out that Nick and I are a thing or whatever, but I don't want it to be a big deal. It's driving me nuts.

"Surprise anal is never a good time," Nick agrees, shoving a fry in his mouth. "But I like Brussels sprouts and burpees."

"Excuse me?" Brendon sputters. "You can't sit with us if you like burpees. I can almost excuse the Brussels sprouts, but not burpees. Get out." He points away from the table, and Nick laughs but stands up.

No, no, no, don't leave yet.

"That's fine, I was done anyway. Gotta go *study.*" Nick says study but I'm pretty sure he means jack off. I force myself not to watch him leave but his hand appears on my throat and before I can think, his lips are on mine.

Oh fuck.

Well. That was one way to get it over with.

Someone shouts, "I fucking knew it!" and I can feel my face heat, all the way down my neck.

I duck my head for a second, waiting for the ribbing to start, and Nick kisses the top of my head before walking away. Bastard.

"Dude, this team has more than its fair share of queers." Brendon shoves another bite into his mouth. "We should start a queer league in the off-season."

"Do you have to be queer to join, or can we just be supportive?" Willis asks.

"I guess that would depend on how many people sign up." Brendon shrugs.

"If you need players, I'm in," Jeremy adds as he sits down next to his boyfriend. "And Preston will play too."

Preston sighs. "Good, you'll keep in shape during off-season."

Paul rolls his eyes and sighs.

"Paul, make notes. You're going to have to organize this." I point at him. Brendon is a cool dude but he's got the memory of a sieve.

"I will help if he asks for it, but he can do it himself if he wants to." Paul is clearly unhappy with me. I really didn't mean any offense.

Brendon smiles and hides his face from the table, almost like he's embarrassed.

I raise my hands, palms up, and dip my head. "I'm sorry, you're right."

The conversation flows again as we finish eating, then clean up. I have to go kick Nick's ass.

CHAPTER 28

joey

Standing in the hallway, waiting to take the ice for my last college game is...weird.

Nothing about this game series has been normal. Paul got appendicitis so he's out, and Brendon got targeted by some asshole at the game last night and got a broken nose. I was not mad about spending five minutes in the sin bin with Preston, Jeremy, and Willis for fighting. Dude had it coming for going after Brendon and I'm pretty proud of the fact that he needed to have his forehead glued shut. Asshole.

So, we're down a few players. This far in the season, that's not abnormal. Hockey is a physical sport, lots of injuries happen, but it's my last one.

We're announced, the crowd cheers since we're in our home stadium, and we take the ice. Jeremy looks back to slap sticks with Paul and Brendon but they aren't here, so I do it with him instead. I hope the good luck works. Riggs and Sinjen—a guy who's been trying to be on the active roster all season—fill in for Paul and Brendon with Jeremy.

They did some warmup stuff today, but honestly, Jeremy and Riggs haven't practiced much with Sinjen. It's either going to be awesome or a disaster.

Once teams are announced and the national anthem is played, the first lines from each team set for the puck drop, and my last game has begun.

Maybe it's because I'm too in my head tonight, but the game goes by in a blur. I'm out on the ice, protecting my goalie, with Matthews to keep these Minnesota assholes out of the crease. The one causing problems last night isn't out here from what I can tell and I get a sick sense of pride from it. I hope he's on concussion protocol. I'm going to have to ask Brendon about that dude.

The front lines switch before me and Matthews, which is fine because these guys are pissing me off and I'm about ready to hurt someone.

Jeremy gets the puck and races up the ice, Riggs on his ass, though he can't get ahead of him, so Jeremy is forced to pass it backward. Sinjen is off in la-la land and of no help, so Riggs passes to Jeremy who takes a shot on goal, but it bounces off the goalie's stick. Fuck.

A Minnesota player snatches it and comes for me. I don't know why but he's looking right at me. I think he's trying to psych me out but I swear he doesn't even blink.

Third line is switched out for first line so Louis puts on a burst of speed to catch up. When the Minnesota winger passes, Louis is there and shoots it toward the goal. By some miracle, it gets through and the lamp lights up.

Fuck yes!

The crowd cheers, the guys cheer, and me and Matthews are switched for Carmichael and Willis.

For the rest of the period, we're hustling. Minnesota beat us yesterday and think they'll take us out tonight, but we're hungry to show them we aren't easy. Despite being our last game after a brutal season full of injuries, we will not surrender.

During the fifteen-minute break, we recharge, hit the bathroom, and get pumped up.

"Listen here!" I yell across the locker room. "This is the last game of my college career, and I will *not* be defeated today! Not in our home stadium!" Cheers erupt. "They think we're too tired to defend our ice but they're going to learn tonight what happens when you fuck with Darby U!"

There are back slaps and war cries as we rush back to the ice, ready to show these fuckers just who we are. Yesterday they got the best of us, but they will not beat us again.

The next two periods are a mess but we hold the lead. They get angry and frustrated, making sloppy penalties and even worse shots. Austin barely has to try in order to keep their attempts out of the net.

When the final buzzer sounds, we've won. The team floods the ice, coaches too, and the stands are deafening. In a huge group, we hug each other. Sweaty, bloody, exhausted, but proud. We fucking did it.

Back in the locker room, we're all celebrating our win and taking longer than normal to get changed. Everyone comes by and pats me on the back, thanks me for being captain this year, and says they'll miss me next year.

"What the fuck?" Louis says, looking at his phone. He shows his screen to Willis in the cubby next to him who shrugs.

"Hold the fuck up!" Louis yells, getting everyone's attention. "Are you two fucking married?" He points between Paul and Brendon.

"I didn't think that sentence was going to end that way." Paul laughs. "Yeah, we got married in Vegas."

No shit? Well, that explains some things...

The locker room goes silent for a minute but Brendon can't stay quiet, so he opens his mouth. "Honestly, did you really think anyone else was going to put up with my shit? Good thing I've got a nice ass, huh?"

"New rule!" I announce. "No one talks about their sex lives. No details."

The entire room says "Agreed" in unison, and Brendon laughs.

"Oh, come on, you sure you don't want to hear about when Paul jack—" Paul puts his hand over Brendon's mouth, and everyone groans. Paul grimaces and pulls his hand away, so I assume Brendon bit him.

"Also," Brendon says as he picks up an adorable white puppy with a brown patch around one eye and ear. "This is Señor Butts."

"Seymour!" Paul shouts.

"That's what I said." Brendon shrugs.

Everyone laughs, a few people go over to meet the adorable puppy, and we go back to celebrating. Seriously, where did they get a dog?

It's a strange feeling to look around at these guys and know they won't need me next year. Some of them I've known for years, some only a few months, but this is the last time I'll share the ice with them again.

Hell, I don't even know what I'm doing after graduation. Maybe I will run into these guys down the road. I hope I do. I know I'll be watching the games and following their careers. They'll always be my teammates.

CHAPTER 29

joey

The finish line is right there, I can almost see it. I only have one more final and this semester is over. Leaving only one more semester until I graduate.

Since we didn't make it to post-season, I have more time on my hands and I'm looking forward to spending the next week with Nick. All day, every day. Neal is even going home for a few days, so I'll be able to stay in their room with Nick.

My knee bounces as I try to focus on the final in front of me.

My phone is vibrating in my pocket and I don't want to answer it.

Sitting in class, this early on a Thursday, it can only be bad news, and I have to focus on my finals. I wait for the vibration to end and try to read the question again, but the damn thing starts up again. Fuck.

That means it's probably Mom and she won't stop until she's had a chance to yell at me about Matt's shortcomings which are my fault.

I find the button on my phone and shut it off. I'll call her back when I'm done. She will just have to wait. If I fail this final, I won't graduate in June. Charlotte will not hang on any longer—I have to finish in June.

I get through the last few questions with my leg bouncing double time and nausea rising up my throat. What did he get into this time?

With my test finished, I bring it to the front of the class and give the teacher my Scantron. She checks that my name and class is on it and nods me good day. Thank fuck.

When I hit the hallway, my phone is powered back on, and I call Mom.

"Mom—"

"Finally! It's about time you answer your damn phone. Mathew fell off a fucking roof and broke his leg." She's pissed and that accusatory tone is a knife in my gut. She never talks to me any other way these days. Immediately, I'm fifteen and Matt has just broken a window while I was supposed to be watching him. Guilt and shame eat at me, beating me back into the little boy Mom has used as a verbal punching bag for a decade.

But my mind is running through check lists, moving schedules around, mentally tallying how much I have in my bank account and how much a Greyhound ticket costs, and how long it'll take for me to get there.

"How long will he be in the hospital for?" I interrupt her tirade. "I can get on a Greyhound tonight or tomorrow to come home, but classes start again in eight days so I have to be back before that."

"Probably until tomorrow," she snaps and I flinch. "Someone has to be here to take care of him since I have to work. If you have to miss classes, so be it. Your brother is more important."

More important than my entire life...

"I'll be home as soon as I can and stay as long as I can." The weight on my shoulders is heavy, dragging me down into the darkness that I've worked so hard to claw my way out of.

On autopilot, I get to my room, pull out my duffle bag, and start blindly throwing stuff into it. Clothes, toiletries, my phone charger. I found a ticket home that leaves in two hours. I hate taking the Greyhound, but I don't have a choice right now.

Zipping up my bag, I sling it over my shoulder and call Charlotte as I'm leaving my room.

"Hey," she answers, and it sounds like she's in the car. "Did Mom call you?"

"Yeah, I'm heading to the bus station right now, can you pick me up?"

We nail down details as I wait for the elevator. The doors open and Bryce stops, looking at my bag then at me with a raised eyebrow.

"Where ya going, man?"

"Home for the break." I step past him and hit the ground floor button. My phone buzzes with an alert from Uber, letting me know they've arrived. Perfect. I text the driver to let him know I'll be out in a second.

With a deep breath, I put my game face on and ready myself for a week under my mother's roof.

CHAPTER 30

nick

NICK:

Heading into my last final, dinner after?

The test is a lot fucking harder than I expected but when I exit the lecture hall an hour later, I'm almost confident I passed. Mostly. Kind of. Maybe.

I check my phone, expecting an answer from Joey, but it hasn't been opened. What the hell? He told me he had one final this morning and he was done. Didn't he?

Confused, I head toward the dorms and hope to find him asleep. I kept him up half the night, getting four orgasms out of him. His personal best. I smirk at the memory of his sweaty, exhausted, peaceful face. He didn't think he would get number two but with some encouragement, and a lot of dirty talking, he got there.

Joey is like a personal challenge. I know he hates when he struggles to stay hard or to get off, but I like finding new ways that get him turned on. And sometimes, that slowdown to touch and taste and explore is exactly what I needed anyway. After he's had a hard time, getting him to come is so fucking rewarding.

I stop at my room just in case he passed out in my bed waiting for me. Since Neal found out about us, he's gotten a lot more comfortable in his own skin. I love seeing him blossom. The confidence he's gained to tell me what he wants, what he needs, is sexy as fuck. Not only in bed but out of it too.

My bed is empty. Disappointing.

On the fifth floor, I knock on his door and Bryce yells to come in. I freeze in the door way when I see the mess that is Joey's bed and dresser. The drawers are all half open, there's clothes and a bottle of body wash on his bed. His backpack is on the floor and there's just stuff... everywhere.

"What the hell happened in here?" I close the door and head toward the dresser.

"I don't know, he said he was heading home for break." Bryce shrugs when I look at him. Heading home? What the fuck? Since when?

"What? When did you see him?" Yanking open the drawers, my heart sinks when they're mostly empty. What the fuck has happened? Is he running from me again? Has his family gotten their claws into him and forced him home? Why didn't he call me?

"Like three hours ago?" Bryce comes to stand next to me. "Why? What's up?"

"Does this look like normal Joey shit to you?" I wave my arm around and want to snap. It's not Bryce's fault.

"Now that you mention it, no, it doesn't. Pretty sure he took my shampoo too, actually." He scratches his jaw. "He didn't say anything, just that he was going home."

I pull up his name and hit call, but it goes unanswered. Fuck.

NICK:

> Hey baby, Bryce just told me you're going home for break? What happened? Are you okay?

"Where is home? Is it close?" I'm going to lose my mind if I don't find him. I can't lose another person like this. No reasoning, just taken from me. I can't do it.

"Pretty sure he's from Colorado somewhere, but I don't know where."

There's a rushing in my ears, making it hard to hear, and panic is threatening to choke me. Fuck! I can't do this. Not again.

With trembling fingers, I call Joey again.

I need to hear his voice.

I need to know he's coming back.

I need to know he's safe.

"Come on," I mumble under my breath, but once again it goes to voicemail. "Fuck!" I storm out of the room and into the stairwell. I don't know where to go or how to find him, and I'm losing it. Gripping the railing, I drop into a crouch and press my forehead against the cold metal. I close my eyes and force myself to take deep, slow breaths. My face is hot but my body is freezing as the anxiety of what I'll do if I lose him takes over my mind, spiraling faster and faster into the deep pools of despair.

It feels like my body is vibrating inside of my skin and I don't know how to make it stop. The urge to move, to pace, pushes me down the stairs to the ground floor. I need help. To calm myself.

Brent.

My hands are shaking so hard I have trouble getting my phone out of my pocket or to his name in my contacts, but I eventually manage it, cursing at myself on the urge of a breakdown.

"Hey, dumba—"

"I can't lose him."

"What? Who?" Instantly, my brother is in information gathering mode. His brain is firing on all cylinders to put together the pieces.

"Joey. He's gone." My voice cracks on the last word and my lip trembles. The pressure on my chest is so intense I can't breathe. "I-I can't. I can't lose him. Not again. I can't have someone else taken from me." I'm half hysterical. I can hear it in my voice but I can't stop the tidal wave of fear that's crashed into me and taken out my retaining walls. I'm flooded with every bad possibility, every way Joey can't be mine anymore.

"Nick."

Flashes of being sixteen and helpless as the girl I loved was taken away in the dark of night, never to be heard from again. I begged my parents to help her, to get her away from the abusive home she was with. Mom promised to help her, but she didn't. I never found out what happened to her. She could be dead for all I know.

"Nicholas!"

Tears roll down my face unchecked, dripping on my shirt. "I won't survive losing him."

"You have survived every bad day you've ever had. You will continue to survive because I won't let you do anything else." Brent's harsh tone wraps around me like a weighted blanket. Comforting and familiar. He won't let me suffocate. "Start at the beginning, what happened?"

"I don't know!" I rip at my hair and pace in front of the dorms. "Everything was fine this morning when we went to class. It's finals week, he had one before I did. I texted him before I went into my last one and he hasn't opened the message. His room is a mess, shit everywhere." Panic claws at my throat, stealing my ability to speak for a second. "His roommate says he was going home for break, but that was never his plan. He was going to stay with me! It's pretty obvious he packed in a hurry, and he's not answering his phone."

"Okay, take a deep breath. Fill your lungs then suck in more. Hold it, then slowly release it." His calm seeps through the phone and settles a part of me. I do what he says, closing my eyes and focusing all of my attention on breathing. "Good, again."

I do. Over and over until the urge to scream is a low rumble.

"Okay. Tell me about his family. He's close to them, right?"

Brent needs facts, to gather information to figure out what happened.

"Yes and no. He raised his brother and sister after their dad died. His mom blames him for his brother being a fuckup but she was working while they were growing up. Every time anything happens, they call him. It's bullshit. They've put the weight of the family on his shoulders and expect him to fix everything."

Why didn't I ask for Charlotte's number just in case of an emergency? I know having emergency contacts is important.

"Do you have any way to contact his family?"

I groan and wipe my face. "No. I'm a fucking idiot."

"You were a bit dick-stracted, it's understandable." His nonchalant tone makes me chuckle, breaking through the panic and anxiety to allow me to think clearly. "So he lets his family take advantage of him? Am I getting that right?"

"Yeah, that's pretty fucking accurate. And he's the scapegoat when anything goes wrong."

"So *logically* he probably got a call from his family and went home to deal with it since he's done with finals."

I sigh and hate that he's probably right.

Walking over to a bench, I drop down onto the cold metal and immediately regret my choice since my ass is now wet from the rain left on it.

"Probably," I huff and hate myself a little for immediately panicking. "But why isn't he answering his phone or texting me back?"

"I don't have the answers to those questions, but my best guess is either his phone is low on power and he needs to conserve it or his mind is so focused on what happened at home that he doesn't have the spoons for anything else."

"I hate you."

He chuckles. "I know. But you're kind of a drama queen and if whatever happened is bad, he needs to focus on it. Telling you what happened is energy he could be putting into surviving his family." His voice is softer when he continues. "You know that just as well as I do. Emotional abuse can be just as damaging. Just be there for him, be his safe space when he comes back."

The knot is back in my throat and my eyes burn. I don't want him to have to *survive* his goddamn family! I want to take him away from them and show him that love doesn't have to be a burden. That it shouldn't come with conditions and guilt and pain.

If I ever get a chance to tell his mother what I really think, I'm going to tell her all about herself.

"Why don't you come home for break? It'll give you something to think about besides how you aren't getting laid and worrying about the mess he's going to be when he gets back."

"Mom asked me to come home a while ago too." I pry my wet ass off the bench and head inside. Maybe Neal will keep me entertained tonight since he heads out in the morning. I don't want to go home. It's so much farther away from him. Would it be a good idea to get away from campus for a while? Probably, but what if Joey needs me and I'm in fucking Washington?

"You're thinking really loud, what is it?" Brent asks.

"What if…What if Joey needs me and I'm in Washington?" I've been working so fucking hard to get him to trust me, to lean on me, and if I wasn't here when he needed me, it would ruin everything. Not to mention the guilt that would eat me alive.

"You can hop on a plane and fly back. SeaTac to Denver is pretty cheap, especially if you fly red-eye. You know I'll help you pay for it, or Mom, if you need it."

I stab the elevator call button and drop my head back on my shoulders. "Yeah, thanks, man. I appreciate you."

"Of course. Anytime."

CHAPTER 31

joey

Ignoring Nick's calls and text is eating me alive. The guilt is an acid burning through my stomach, my heart, my bones, and straight into my soul. He's worried. He has to be. I left without a word and it wasn't what we had planned. My ass was on the bus for an hour before I realized I should have called him.

I'm not good at relationships. This is exactly the kind of shit I was worried about. He's going to be pissed and he has every right to be. I would be furious if he had done this to me.

By the time I get to the terminal, I'm an anxious mess. Between worrying about Nick's reaction to me running home with zero communication and the berating I know is coming from Mom, I want to puke.

I get off the bus, grab my bag from underneath, and quickly find my sister. Charlotte throws her arms around me and immediately starts sobbing. I have to drop my bag to hug her back. Fear wraps itself around my throat and squeezes my heart.

"What? What happened? Is Matt okay?" I want to shake her. What the fuck? I've been stuck on a fucking bus for hours and no one updated me of a major change?

"Matt's stupid ass is fine." She studders through the tears. "I'm just so glad you're here and I don't have to do this alone."

I sag with relief and my knees damn near give out. Fuck.

"I've got it now, you can breathe." I squeeze her for another minute before she pushes me away, frustration and anger on her face when she slaps at me.

"You shouldn't be here! Matt isn't your problem! I told you not to come back." Her emotions are going to give me whiplash. "What about school? You can't miss classes. You're almost done."

"It's spring interterm. No classes. I finished my last final this morning, I have, like, a week before classes start again." I grab my bag and usher her toward the parking lot. I can't drag this out any longer. Like ripping a Band-Aid off, I have to just go and deal with Mom and see what Matt's deal is. "How's Matt? Is he home?"

"Tomorrow. He broke his right leg and had to go in and do something, I don't know. He should be released tomorrow, but you know they're going to give him narcotics, so you'll have to lock up the pills." She's bitter about it all and I wish I had the mental space to be mad about it too. Anger gets me nowhere. I'm...resigned. It's the way my life is and I just have to deal with it.

"Seriously, why did you come?" Char asks once we're on the road heading toward our childhood house. It's not home. It hasn't been home since before Dad was diagnosed. Now it's a building that holds my worst memories. I wish it would burn down. Maybe then Mom could move on.

"I had to. You know I did."

I lean my head on the headrest and sigh. My soul is tired and all I want is Nick. I should have asked him to come with me. How fucked is it that I didn't even think about calling him until he called me?

"You didn't. Am I happy to see you? Yeah, I am. I missed you, but you shouldn't have come back." The dashboard lights illuminate her face enough to see a tear trail down her cheek. "We have to let him hit rock bottom." Her words are thick with emotion, and it breaks my heart to hear. My fearless, sassy sister is hurting and there's nothing I can do about it. I can't fix Matt, logically I know that, but I want to so fucking bad. Him being a mess feels like my fault. I was trying to navigate my father's death while trying to pass my classes and raise my siblings. Char was able to pull her shit together, but Matt wasn't. He lashed out and I was never able to get through to him. Not really. It's my biggest failure.

I failed my father.

Clearing the knot from my throat, I look out the window so I don't have to face her when I say my next words. "I can't give up on him."

Mom's car is in the cracked driveway when we get to the house. The porch light is off but it's probably because the bulb is burned out. The grass in the front is mostly brown dirt with some patches of weeds and the porch is starting to droop in the center. It's depressing. Grief soaked into every crack of the foundation, anger poisoned the air, and failure rusted the pipes, turning my home toxic. There's nothing good here. Not anymore.

"You can stay with me, if you want," Char offers. "Wait to face her until you have Matt has a buffer."

"No," I sigh, soul weary. "It's better to just get it over with." I open the car door and grab my duffle from the back seat. I wait on the uneven sidewalk until my sister has driven off and I can't see her taillights anymore before I walk across what used to be the lawn to the wood steps. I learned how to play street hockey out here with my dad. He taught me to play goalie, how to read people and anticipate their next moves before letting me play another position. It wasn't long before we had a whole team of kids out here being coached by him.

Raising my hand to knock on the door, I freeze. I don't think I've ever knocked on this door before and I don't know how to feel about it. Am I welcome? Probably not, but when was the last time I *was* in the last decade?

The TV is on but I can't tell what's playing. Mom is probably sitting on the left side of the couch with a folding table in front of her with her dinner, a beer, and the remote. That's where she settles after work. Always has. Dad used to joke that she would die in that spot, now I kind of hope she does.

Does that make me a bad person? I shouldn't wish that about my own mother. A grieving widow who lost herself when she buried him.

Since I've never been in her shoes, I shouldn't judge her, but what about us? What about her kids? She may have been physically here, paying for groceries and clothes and the mortgage, but mentally, she abandoned us. She left us in the ocean during a storm and told us to sink or swim.

I knock on the door and wait. Seeing if she'll open the door or just yell from the couch. Does she expect me to be here tonight? I texted her that Char was going to pick me up at the bus depot but she didn't respond.

The door opens and the yellow light from the lamp on the half-circle table in the entryway spills out. She looks older. Gray hair and wrinkles and gaunt. Like there's no life left in her. No joy.

"About time." She turns around and heads to her spot on the couch, dismissing me and my existence. I guess I should have expected it. The only time she remembers me is if she needs to yell at me for messing something up. If she had to deal with Matt or Char, she remembered me.

All I'm good for is keeping her responsibilities out of her face.

With a sigh, I come inside and close the door. The house hasn't changed in years. The couch is sagging on the side she sits on every day, the carpet is worn from the furniture being in the same spot for decades, and I no longer remember what the original color of the walls was but it's dingy and dusty now. The house isn't piled with trash but I doubt it's been deep cleaned since I moved out.

"Do you know what time Matt is supposed to be released tomorrow?" My voice is quiet and calm. A hope she won't snap and rip into me but at this point I'm not sure which is worse, being completely ignored or yelled at. At least if she's yelling at me, she sees me.

Mom huffs like me asking the question is the biggest inconvenience. It makes me drop my head toward the floor, looking at my feet instead of at her. I may be six-foot-two and a defender for a college hockey team but right now, I'm a gangly teenager who hasn't grown into his body yet.

"It depends on what the doctor says during rounds tomorrow. You'll have to answer your phone when someone calls you." The harsh tone of her voice tells me exactly how annoyed she is that sometimes I'm not able to answer when she calls.

I nod and step past her to head up the stairs to my room. At least, I think it's still my room. Since nothing else in this place has changed, I doubt she did anything with it.

I'm halfway up the stairs when she speaks again. "Get some rest, wouldn't want you to be too tired to go pick up your brother from the hospital after he fell off a roof and had surgery."

The condemnation she throws at me is another weight on my shoulders. I should do better, do more, try harder. Matt is like this because of me. It's my fault. I'm a failure.

In the dark, I pass Matt's and Char's rooms on the way to my own. There are no shoes, crumbled school papers, or jackets on the floor. There's no cologne and perfume scents fighting for dominance. The pictures on the walls show us as little kids, but nothing past it. Sometimes I think Mom has been frozen in that era all these years. Back before I became a teenager. When Matt still wanted to be the baby and coddled. When Charlotte would beg for girls' days with Mom and sleepovers.

Opening my door at the end of the hall, I'm surprised at how easily it opens. It's been over a year since I was here. Has someone come in here since then? The air is musty and when I flip the light on, dust dances in the space. It looks just like I left it. Hockey posters still up on the walls that I got from Dad right before he passed. The corners have been ripped a hundred times so pins are a good inch from the edges which are curling with age. The bed is stripped down to the old mattress but at this point, I don't care. I put my duffle down on the dresser that no longer holds clothes and is missing half of the knobs and sink down onto the floor.

I don't want to be here. Every breath is tinged with pent-up emotions I was never allowed to have, building up in my lungs. Soon I'll suffocate on them. Anger, guilt, shame, worthlessness, grief, sadness. Ugly emotions that no one ever wants to talk about or feel. No, just shove those into a little box and pretend to be happy. Fake it till you make it.

I didn't make it. I went numb. And I can feel myself sinking into it again.

CHAPTER 32

nick

I slept like shit last night and even Neal is avoiding me this morning. Usually he likes pushing my buttons but I guess one look at my grumpy mug was enough of a warning for him to fuck off.

I don't know how many times I've checked my phone but Joey hasn't texted me or called. He did open the messages from yesterday but hasn't said anything. Brent was probably right and he's dealing with some kind of family emergency but I just want to know that he's okay. That his family isn't fucking up his head. Since he's been radio silent, I assume they are and that's why he won't talk to me.

I open our thread and send him a message even though it's early and I don't expect him to be awake.

NICK:

Good morning, baby.

Dragging my ass out of bed, I take a piss and stand in the middle of the room. I should probably go eat breakfast. Or get drunk. It's five o'clock somewhere.

Food is probably a good idea and it gets me out of here for a while. Away from the memories of Joey and the plans we made for the week.

The dining hall is quiet enough that I have an entire table to myself. Not really what I wanted but probably for the best. I was hoping for some social interaction, something to distract me.

I'm shoving some French toast into my mouth when my phone lights up with a notification. An email from Expedia? What the hell? I'm about to delete it when the subject line catches my attention. *Your flight confirmation DEN – SEA.*

Clicking on the email, I sigh when I see my name and flight information. Brent bought me a fucking ticket home and it leaves in...seven hours.

I shove the rest of my food in my face hole and clear my tray. I should probably take a shower and shove some clothes in a bag. Do I have clean clothes? Who knows. I can do a load at home if I need to...

As I head into the dorm building, Bryce stops me.

"You hear from Carp?" he asks.

"No." I shake my head.

"I messaged his sister on the book of faces last night and she messaged me this morning saying he was home."

Why the fuck didn't I think of that? "Oh, thanks." I'm a fucking moron. Since I don't do social media—growing up with foster kids means no sharing of information online—it didn't even cross my mind to see if Joey had one. Now I have to go stalk it.

I shove some shit into a duffle bag, take a quick shower, then pull up the website on my phone browser, and search his name.

A few people come up but I recognize my Joey when I see him, even if the picture is old. His profile picture is a selfie from a few years ago with a group of hockey players in their kits. All smiles and cheering, so I assume it was a big game they won. He looks happy, despite the bags under his eyes.

Flipping through the pictures he has, I don't learn much. Hockey and his siblings are all he ever posted about and that was few and far between. His security is shit too. I can see places he's checked into, family members, friends list, pictures, schools he went to.

A text pops up in my phone and I switch over to look at it.

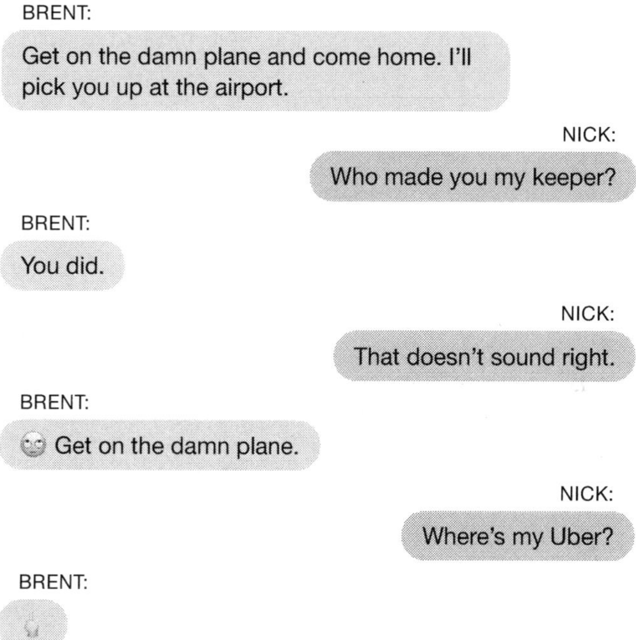

Since it's a Friday night and all of the universities around here are starting spring interterm, it takes a while to get through security, but the flight is short and Brent's stupid face is waiting for me when I land in SeaTac.

Brent gives me a half smile and a tight hug. Fuck, I needed that. Brent has been my person for years, even from several states away, and I miss him.

"Hey, man, welcome home."

"Thanks, I think."

We walk shoulder to shoulder toward baggage claim ten.

"How was the flight?"

I deadpan, "Flighty." He shoves me and I laugh. "How do you think it was? I made it here, so it wasn't terrible."

There are people bustling everywhere, some confused, some walking with purpose. It's an international airport, so multiple languages are being spoken around us, but it all blends together as background noise with the wheeled bags and crying children.

Of course, my bag is the last one to come out so everyone on my flight has walked off by the time we can leave.

"Do you want to come to my place tonight or head to Mom and Dad's?"

I drop my head back against the seat and stare at the freeway through the rain. Do I want to see my parents? Yes, but I also don't want to answer all of Mom's questions. I don't want to be alone but I don't want to be overloaded with people either.

"Your place."

Brent nods and on the way swings through a Carl's Jr. because Western Bacon Cheeseburgers are life and I'm starving.

"If you don't stop checking your phone, I'm going to take it," Brent says when we're sitting on his couch. He turns on *Doctor Who* but I'm not paying attention to it. I'm scrolling through my text thread with Joey. Again.

"Fuck off."

"That's it." Brent snatches my phone from my hand and jerks it as far away from me as he can get it while I launch myself at him. Crawling over him, I pull on his arm, trying to get my phone within reach. Unfortunately for me, he has long-ass arms.

"Goddammit, give it back!"

He rolls into me and we fall onto the floor with a loud thud that I'm sure his neighbors hate me for.

"You need to stop obsessing. Staring at your phone won't make him text you back!"

We're both starting to pant as the wrestling intensifies. Luckily, he doesn't have the athletic training I do, so I'm stronger and faster than he is. Not that it's doing me any fucking favors right now.

"This is the most reaction I've gotten from you since you got here!" Brent grabs my nipple and twists while I howl.

"Motherfucker! What are you, twelve?" I've got his arm in an armbar but it means I can't get his other one which has my damn phone.

"My bad, was that your favorite nipple?" Brent yells as I get my legs around one of his.

"Maybe it was, what of it?"

Brent laughs, relaxing just enough for me to get my hand into his armpit and tickle. He lets out a high-pitched screech that makes my ears ring, but he pulls his arm in to protect himself and I'm able to grab my phone. I shove Brent off me and roll away from him, shoving my phone down the front of my pants where I'm pretty sure it's safe for a minute.

"That was a cute scream," I pant. "You use that as a mating call so all the girls will come flocking to you?"

"Don't mock it till you try it," he laughs. "Fuck, my stomach hurts. I'm too full of bacon and cheese to be roughhousing like that."

"You'll be okay, drama queen." I pat his cheek and leave him on the floor while I go to the kitchen to get water. It's been a while since I was here but it's a typical, young person apartment. Dark brown shitty carpet, brown fake wood cabinets from the 80s, Formica countertops, linoleum that's probably older than me, and white walls. But it's clean and it's comfortable. Brent lived with a grandma who was a hoarder at one point and can't stand to live in messy or cluttered places. He's a clean freak to the extreme when he's stressed.

"If you leave the cap to that water bottle on the counter, I will put it in a very uncomfortable place for you to find later."

A shit-eating grin splits my face as I take another drink and toss the cap on the floor. It slides under the table and hits the wall.

"I'm going to murder you while you sleep."

I laugh and put the now empty water bottle in the sink, just to fuck with him.

He's still laying on the floor when I head to the bathroom. "You gotta get some stamina, bro. No wonder you're single."

He flips me off but manages to get off the floor while I go to take a piss. My phone slips down my pants and gets stuck at my knee. As I'm trying to reach for it, it starts to vibrate. Grabbing it in a hurry, my fingers hit the screen, and a voice comes from it.

"Uh, Nick?" *Joey!*

"Shit. Fuck! Joey, hold on!" The bunched-up fabric snags the corners, stopping me from lifting the damn thing free three times. "Hey! There you are."

My heart flutters in my chest, happy to see him but nervous about what he's going to say.

"Hey." There are dark purple circles under his eyes and his smile is small. He looks defeated but is trying to hide it.

"You okay?" I hop up to sit on the counter, ignoring my bladder for now, and lean against the mirror.

"Yes?"

"Are you asking me?"

Joey rubs his eyes, digging his fingers into them. "I'm sorry."

"For?" I don't want him to be sorry, I want him to trust me. *I want him to need me.*

"Disappearing on you and then ignoring your calls. It was shitty but I didn't know what to say." He's looking down, away from the camera, and I hate it. I want his eyes on me. Always on me. "I still don't."

"Yeah, that sucked. I'm not going to lie to you. I thought something bad had happened to you."

He flinches and I hate that too. After a minute of silence, he flicks his gaze up but doesn't really move to lift his head. "I'm not good at this."

"Me neither." I let out a breath, just looking at him. "But that doesn't mean I don't want to try."

His voice is so quiet I almost miss his next words. "I miss you." He wipes his hand under his eye and fuck if I don't feel that like a punch to the stomach.

"I miss you too." A small smile tilts one side of my mouth. "I was really looking forward to a record-breaking orgasm count during break."

Joey snorts a laugh but finally lifts his head. "For you or me?"

"Both, baby. Orgasms all around."

He smiles but something off camera catches his attention and it falls. Joey opens his mouth to speak but I talk first.

"What do you need right now?"

"You."

"You have me. I'm yours, remember?"

In the background, a feminine voice calls his name and he sighs.

"I have to go."

"Hey, look at me." He looks half irritated but I don't think it's with me. "Take a deep breath and don't believe the lies they tell you. Their fuckups are not your fault."

His next breath is shaky but he nods. "I'll talk to you later?"

"Yes, you will."

Joey gives me a small smile and the call ends. My body sags against the mirror as some of the anxiety drains from me. I'm still worried about him but I know he's physically okay. He didn't give me any answers but I didn't ask questions either. It was more important that he reached out to me. Even though he was nervous I would be angry, he called.

A text pops up as I slide off the brown Formica.

JOEY:

Was your phone INSIDE your pants?

I chuckle.

NICK:

Yes.

JOEY:

Why?

NICK:

How else am I supposed to send you pictures of the chocolate starfish?

JOEY:

The mental picture of how you would have to be contorted for that is not sexy.

I cackle as I take care of business and wash my hands.

"Should I be worried that you're laughing in the bathroom?" Brent is leaning against the hallway entrance when I open the door.

NICK:

How about my dick? It really misses you.

JOEY:

...that is acceptable.

I smirk and put my phone away, shoulder checking Brent on my way past him and ignoring his question.

"You look...happier. Did you jack off in there?"

"Just a little phone sex," I shrug and drop down onto the couch. "I'm ready for a nap."

"It's seven p.m. If you go to sleep now, you'll be up all night."

I roll my eyes. "Okay, Mom."

Brent's phone starts playing the *Star Wars* "Imperial March" and he laughs. "Speaking of her . . . Hey, Mom."

"Hey, B, do you have Nick? When are you guys heading out here?"

Brent comes around the front of the couch and turns so Mom can see me behind him.

"Hey, Mom." I wave to her.

"There he is!" She waves too with the biggest smile on her face. "I'm so glad you're home. When do I get to squeeze you?"

"Probably tomorrow," Brent informs us.

"Good, I'll make pot roast for dinner. Are you staying, Brent?"

They go back and forth while I close my eyes. The heaviness of the last thirty-six hours has lifted some and I can finally breathe. Before I know it, I'm asleep.

Emma's heart-shaped face is lifted toward me, tears in her big, tan eyes while her wild dark hair swirls around her in the wind. There's a large red mark on her jaw that's turning purple. I hate the family she was placed with.

No one cares or checks up on foster kids. They don't look into families to see if the kids are safe there, if they're happy. Since there are more kids than there are places for them, they don't care.

A tear falls down her cheek and I brush it away with my thumb, careful not to bump the forming bruise.

"I hate it here," she whispers. "I don't want to go back."

The roaring wind blasts us with rain, soaking the back of me as I try to protect her with my body.

"I have to tell my mom, she can do something. I'm sure of it." Before the words are out of my mouth, Emma is shaking her head.

"It'll just make things worse. An investigator will come in and I'll have to stay there while they look into it." She shivers in her too big black zip-up hoodie and ripped-up black jeans. Shrugging out of my jacket, I wrap it around her shoulders and zip it up before wrapping my arms around her.

My football hoodie isn't enough against this weather, especially since I'm now getting wet, but I'll be okay. She's so small compared to me, I have to protect her.

Emma curls into me, pressing her uninjured cheek against my chest. I cup the back of her head, offering her every ounce of comfort I can, but it's not enough. It's never enough. But Mom can help. She has to.

I kiss the top of Emma's trembling head, frustration and anger turning my face hot.

"Nick! Dinner!" Dad yells from the front door and dread cements my shoes to the ground. I don't want to walk her home. I don't want to leave her in that house and wonder what bruises she'll have tomorrow.

Sliding the sterling silver football helmet pendant over my head, I hang it around her neck. I kiss the helmet before tucking it into her sweater.

Emma lifts onto her toes and kisses me. It's soft but bitter with tears and fear and resignation.

"I love you," I whisper against her lips and they tilt up into a big smile. For just a second, her eyes are bright. "Don't ever forget that, okay?"

She kisses me again, a quick peck this time. "I love you too."

"Nicholas!" Mom yells this time, clearly agitated.

I growl and turn to wave, acknowledging that I heard her.

"Walk Emma home and come eat, let's go!"

Huffing, I grab Emma's hand and pull my jacket hood over her head before heading down the street.

"I don't want you to go in there," I say when we get close enough to see the house. Even though this is a nice neighborhood, the kind where kids run around unsupervised all summer, the cops are rarely called, there's evil here. Everyone knows to stay away from that *house. Yet somehow they keep getting foster kids. Kids that never talk about what goes on in there.*

"He's not home, so hopefully I can disappear into a bedroom and hide until school." Emma shrugs like it's normal to be afraid of the adults you

live with. I guess for her it is. Her birth mom wasn't physically abusive, just neglectful.

"If he comes after you, come to my house, okay?"

When she doesn't answer, I shake her hand a little and she nods, but I know she won't. She never does. She always stays to protect the smaller kids.

Wrapping her arms around my waist, she gives me a quick hug before running for the house and disappearing inside. I don't leave the sidewalk until I see her wave from the upstairs window. I give her a little wave then hustle back home before Mom gets really pissed.

I'm soaked when I get back, so I have to change my clothes. Mom huffs at me but I promise to be quick.

"Get Brent down here too!" she yells after me. My roommate, foster brother, and best friend typically spends most of his time in our room. He doesn't handle chaos well.

He's laying on his bed with headphones on and a book in his hand.

I point to my ears, telling him I need to talk to him, and he pauses whatever he's listening to and removes one earbud.

"Mom says go eat dinner with us." I change quickly and he grumbles but climbs off the high bunk bed and follows me out of the room. Mom made spaghetti and garlic bread, which is normally a meal I would inhale, but my stomach is in knots over Emma.

When everyone is sitting and plates have been filled, Mom flicks her gaze between me and my plate that I haven't touched.

"What's wrong with you? Are you sick?" She reaches for my forehead.

"Emma is being abused."

Everyone stops talking, even the little kids Jack and Ross who are sitting across from me. They're six and seven but they know what I just said. No one that comes into this house is unaware unless they're infants.

"Nick, this isn't really the place—"

"It's never the place or the time." I slam my hands on the table. "She's being hit. She's got a bruise on her face this time. That bastard hit her! You have to do something!"

Mom and Dad share a look, the little boys are curling in on themselves, and I want to scream. They don't handle raised voices well, I know that, and now I feel like a dick. Squeezing my hands into fists until my arms shake, I suck in a deep breath and force myself to speak calmer.

"You're a mandated reporter. You can't ignore this."

"I'm not ignoring it, Nick. I never have." Mom covers my hand with hers. "The first time you mentioned anything to me, I told our case worker." I scoff and pull my hand off the table, crossing my arms instead. "They said there was an investigation but nothing came of it."

"Because any kid that goes into that house is terrified to talk!" I swing my arm out like I'm pointing to the house. As if she doesn't know which one I'm talking about. "No one ever does and you don't think that's weird?"

"There's no proof, Nick. I'm sorry."

I shove back from the table, pulling at my hair, and let out a scream as I bend over my knees.

I hate this. I hate being helpless. I hate that someone I love is being hurt and all I can do is sit back and fucking watch.

Hands rest on my back and I don't have to look to know it's Brent.

"Breathe, man. Just breathe." He's crouched in front of me, talking quietly and calmly, giving me something to anchor myself to. Mom and Dad don't try anymore, they just let Brent deal with me while they take care of the mess I created.

Fuck. I have to apologize to the boys too. It's my fault they will be scared and probably jumpy for a while after this.

But all I want is for my mom to hug me and tell me we'll find a way to help Emma. I drop down onto my haunches and Brent wraps his arms around my shoulders.

I startle awake when something wraps around me. Without thought, I drop off the edge of the bed and roll to standing, panting and looking around for the threat. My heart is pounding and panic is riding me hard. Something tickles my cheek and I swipe it quickly, only to realize it's tears.

What the fuck is happening?

Rolling my shoulders, I force my body into a relaxed stance and look around again. I'm at Brent's apartment, not my childhood home. I'm no longer sixteen and helpless.

But you can't help Joey...

Scrubbing a hand over my face, I head to the bathroom to splash water on my face. I'm not sleeping any more tonight. If I close my eyes again, I'll be back on the sidewalk waiting for her but she'll never come out. One of the boys that lived in the house will bring me the necklace and say she left. No one ever said what happened, whether she ran away, was taken away, nothing. The girl I loved and would have died for was taken from me and I never found out what happened to her.

The cold water chases away the last of the fog from the dream, letting the pain of her wash over me and settle in my gut. I searched her name for years, looking for any tidbit of information, but I never found anything.

With my phone in my hand, I settle on the couch and scroll until the sun comes up.

CHAPTER 33

joey

Since Matt is an asshole and made everyone's life difficult, they kept him an extra day. Thankfully Mom worked a full twelve hours that day so I had the entire day to myself. I cleaned.

Now Matt has been home for all of twelve hours and I already want to murder him. He has crutches to get around but he refuses to use them, instead he just lies on the couch with his foot up on pillows and whines. He begs for more pain meds despite knowing I won't give them to him.

In the bathroom, I'm washing my hands when there's a crash from the kitchen. "What the fuck?"

Rushing out, I find Matt on the floor, holding the cast around his ankle, screaming in pain, and a dining chair on its side next to him.

"What are you doing?!" I grab the chair and slam it back where it belongs when what I want to do is wring my brother's neck.

"There's booze up there and since you won't give me more pain meds, I have to do something to make it stop hurting!" He glares at me, still holding his cast.

"Alcohol is the last thing you should be adding to pain meds, you dumb fuck!" Getting behind him, I grab him under the armpits and stand him up, then hand him the crutches. "I also found the stashes you left around the house and dumped them."

Matt's furious now and whirls around at me, swinging a crutch and yelling. "How dare you! You have no right to treat me like this! You're not my dad or my sponsor!"

Yanking the crutch from his hand, I throw it aside and get into his face. "If you don't want to be treated like a fucking child, stop acting like one."

His face is red and eyes glassy. The Percocet in his body is having an effect, just not enough of one for his liking.

"I hate you," he seethes in my face.

"I hate who you've become," I snap back. "You are better than this."

I brush past him, needing to get him out of my goddamn face before I hit him. Stomping through the house, I rip the front door open and almost run right into my childhood best friend, Josh.

He jumps and holds his hands up but smiles. "Hey, man, bad time?"

The anger burning my blood cools as I step out onto the sagging front porch. I sit on the step and Josh follows suit. How many nights had we sat out here growing up? More than I can count.

"I take it things haven't changed much?" he asks, knocking my shoulder with his.

"Nope."

It's cold but there are kids out on their bikes anyway, laughing and hollering.

"How long are you here for?"

"A few days. Classes start up next week." I grab a tall weed that's somehow hung around and wrap it around my finger. "How did you know I was here?"

"I saw Charlotte at the grocery store and she mentioned it."

I nod. Of course she did. Josh and I were inseparable for years but when I went away to college, we drifted apart. He stayed here and started working while I tried to move on. After a while, we didn't have anything in common anymore.

"It's good to see you," I tell him. "How have things been for you?"

He chuckles and leans into me. I take the simple comfort and lean into him too. Since Nick isn't here, I'll take what I can get.

"Shit, you know how it is. Everything changes but nothing really does."

I smile because he's right.

"Your mom still okay?" She had a lot of health issues for a while when we were in high school and I would feel like a real dick if she had passed and I didn't know.

He smiles. "Oh yeah, she's too stubborn to die."

It's quiet for a while but it's easy. We never did feel like we had to fill the silence with bullshit small talk.

I flick a quick look at his left hand but don't see a wedding band. When I left town, he was serious about the guy he was with...what was his name...

"You graduate soon, right?" Josh asks, interrupting my thoughts.

"Yeah, in June. Finally." Both excitement and dread hit my stomach. I want to be done with school but I don't know what I want to do afterward and I don't really want to come back here. I've been here, what, two days and I'm already itching to leave. And what about Nick? What's he planning to do after school? Is he staying in Colorado or going back to Washington?

Just the idea of him leaving without me makes me want to beg him to stay.

"Are you going to move back home afterward?" He sounds hopeful by the prospect.

"I honestly don't kn—"

The sound of breaking glass has me hurrying back inside, Josh on my heels. The living room is clear, Josh heads for the kitchen while I head down the hallway to the bathroom. I never should have left Matt unsupervised this long. Fuck. He probably went searching for the pills but I have them stashed in my room.

"Not in here," Josh calls as I am forcing my way into the bathroom. Something is blocking the door from opening more than a crack but the medicine cabinet mirror is shattered and there's blood sprinkled all over the counter.

"Matt! Open the fucking door!"

No response.

Fuck.

Adrenaline courses through me, shutting down everything that isn't needed for me to get into this bathroom and make sure Matt is okay.

"Josh!"

He's with me in an instant, helping me push on the door until I can force my way through. Matt is on the floor unconscious and shards of broken glass are everywhere. There's a cut somewhere on his head that's bleeding onto the white-and-blue linoleum and he's blocking the door.

Shards of glass pierce my bare feet and I hiss as I drop down to check his pulse. He has one; it feels like a heartbeat, but what the fuck do I know?

"Call an ambulance, I don't want to try to move him if something happened to his neck."

Josh doesn't question it, just does what I've asked. It's like I never left. We were a team when we were together. He helped me the best he could with Matt and Char when he wasn't taking care of his mom.

Matt groans and starts to move.

"Hold still," I snap at him. I don't know what happened in here but I have a pretty good idea it was his fault and not an accident.

"My head," Matt moans, lifting his hand to it.

"Yeah, I bet it hurts. You probably gave yourself a fucking concussion." Now that I'm pretty sure he'll live, I take a better look around the room. One of his crutches is in the shower upside down, the other one is bent and sticking out of the toilet. What the fuck was he trying to do?

"Ambulance is on its way," Josh says through the door.

"I don't need a damn ambulance," Matt mutters and tries to sit up but puts his hand in glass and hisses.

"What were you doing?" My feet are screaming now that the adrenaline is fading. "Josh, can you grab the broom?"

"Trying to take a piss, that okay with you?" Matt snaps. "Do I need permission for that too?"

"Really? You what, slipped and caused all this damage?" Mom is going to be furious over the broken mirror. I'll have to find a way to replace it and make sure the broken glass doesn't get tracked all over the house.

The broom handle is shoved through the crack in the door and I thank Josh before starting to clear the floor. Why am I always cleaning up Matt's messes? Everyone just shrugs and says 'that's Matt' and moves on but God forbid I fuck up. I would never hear the end of it.

Once enough of the glass is cleaned up, Matt sits up and Josh is able to get the door open. There's a decent pool of blood too since head wounds bleed like crazy. I grab a towel and press it to the cut in his hair, telling him to hold it.

The EMTs arrive a few minutes later and Josh brings them back here.

They take a quick look around the room, ask what happened, and get him on the gurney. Since he was knocked unconscious, they are adamant about him going in and getting checked out, so he does, but I don't go with him. Fuck that. I'll get enough of an earful from Mom when she gets home, I don't need to be at the hospital with him when she lays into me.

Josh gets the vacuum and together we get the rest of the mirror cleaned up and pull all the glass from my feet. How am I going to do this for another four days?

I drop down onto the couch and let my head fall back. I hate this place. Hate what it represents. Hate the memories that haunt every inch of it. Even the happy memories have been tainted.

Josh comes in from outside—when did he leave?—and hands me a beer from the six-pack he's carrying. I take it and lift it to my lips.

"I was planning to drink these on my own later but figured you would probably need one." He sits next to me, taking the middle seat. His thigh is against mine but I don't mind. It's quiet, the calm before the storm that I know is imminent, but, to be honest, I want to be gone before it gets here.

"Can we go somewhere?" I peel the label on the bottle.

Josh pats my knee and stands, offering me a hand up without a word.

Once I get shoes, a jacket, and my phone, I follow him out to his truck. It's big, shiny, and blue. I don't know how I missed it earlier, but oh well. The inside is tan leather and it still smells new.

"Damn, this is nice." I slide my hand along the door once I've buckled up.

"Yeah, she's pretty sexy." He pats the dash and winks at me. "One of the guys at the shop bought it but then realized the parking spots at his apartment are small so he couldn't get the doors open far enough to get out." Josh chuckles and shakes his head. "Dumbass. So I sold my old one and bought it from him."

He drives around for a while, pointing out things that have changed and sharing stories of shit we did when we were growing up.

"Hey, can we go to the cemetery? Do you mind?" I ask when we get toward the edge of town.

"Of course. How long has it been since you came out here?"

"Not since I moved."

My phone rings with Charlotte's picture on the screen.

"Hey."

"Where are you guys?" Wherever she is, it's windy.

"Well, Matt was being himself and ended up knocking himself unconscious in the bathroom so he's at the ER," I begin. "I'm out with Josh."

"Wait, what? Matt is back at the ER? Why didn't you call me?"

"Because you don't need to deal with his shit. I'm here, I handled it." It's quiet for a minute and I hear her sniffle. "You're not responsible for him." I soften my tone so she doesn't think I'm yelling at her.

"Neither are you," Josh mutters and I flip him off.

"While I'm here, you aren't taking him on. He's a menace right now." Despite not wanting to be here, I know I won't leave early. I'll find a way to stay here as long as I possibly can to help my sister and my brother, though he doesn't deserve it at this point.

"Where are you and Josh going?"

"To visit Dad."

By the time Charlotte gets out to the cemetery, I'm drunk. Josh pulled a bottle of Jack out of his truck and I've basically stolen it from him.

"Looks like you're having a party." Charlotte stands over me with her hands on her hips. "Are you drunk? Seriously?"

"Hey, shut up." I hold my finger up or maybe I hold them all up. I don't know. The world is spinning too fast and I can't stay upright. Why is my butt wet and cold?

"Are you sober?" She looks at Josh but I don't hear what he says.

I miss my dad. I hate that he missed so much of our lives. I hate how him dying made me grow up too fast. "I don't want to be an adult. It sucks."

Putting my hand on his gravestone that's laid in the grass, the cold of granite or whatever it is seeps into me. The black rock with gold flakes is pretty but cold. His name and dates carved into it break him down into nothing. It doesn't tell anyone about how he lived, how he struggled to live, or the life he left behind.

I wish Nick were here. He would know what to do with me. No one sees me as more than someone who can help them. I don't get help, though. Not really. Josh did when he could but he had his own shit, which is okay. But Nick wants to help me.

Checking my pockets for my phone, I fall over when I tip too far to the left.

Someone sighs and I look up to see Char.

"Charlie girl, did you push me?"

"I should have but no, I did not."

"Where's my phone? I want kisses."

She lifts an eyebrow at me. "What?"

"My phone, I need it."

Getting up off my back, I look around and find the bottle of whiskey. Lifting it to my lips, I drain the rest of the bottle and hand it to her.

"Can't litter. It's bad."

She looks at Josh. "Why don't you help me get him into my car? I don't want him to puke in your truck."

"Not a bad plan."

I'm lifted by my armpits, the world spinning around me, and my stomach makes a turn for the worse.

"Puke," I manage to get out before I bend over and vomit all over the grass while leaning on my knees.

"Have you eaten anything today? No wonder you got drunk so fast." Charlotte's disapproving tone pounds in my head.

Eventually I'm laid in the back of Char's car and when the engine starts, I fall asleep.

CHAPTER 34

nick

Not having access to Joey is going to land me in a padded room. Or jail.

Between memories of Emma haunting my dreams and lack of communication with Joey, I'm ready to snap.

Mom is busy in the kitchen getting lunch ready for the little ones, Sammy and Troy, while I watch *Bluey* with them in the living room, but I can't keep still. Between chewing on my fingers and my leg bouncing, I'm ready to slap myself to make it stop.

Picking up my phone, I text Joey again. I haven't heard from him today and last night he was drunk as fuck and wasn't making any sense. Pretty sure that's a bad sign. I've known him for a few months and have only seen him drunk, like, once. He's been home three days and he's already found the bottom of a bottle? No good can come of this.

The theme music for the show starts up and the kids start dancing. They're twins, a boy and a girl, and just turned three. Of course they're adorable and complete opposites. Sammy has straight brown hair and dark eyes with a little bit of a tan complexion while Troy is blond with big bouncy curls, bright green eyes, and I'm pretty sure he glows in the dark. If Mom hadn't told me they were related, I wouldn't have guessed it, but CPS swears they're twins.

"Time to eat!" Mom calls from the table where she's sets out plates and cups. Sammy takes off for the table but Troy watches me stoically. I don't know what their story is but I can tell Troy's trust in adults has been damaged badly, specifically by men. It breaks my heart but I don't take it personally.

"Come on, bud." I nod toward the table. "Mom, what's for lunch?"

"Mac and cheese, dino nuggies, and grapes for Troy. Everyone else gets strawberries."

Okay, that sounds amazing.

I stand from the couch and head to the table, hoping he'll follow me. On the table is two kid-sized plates and two adult plates.

"Thanks, Mom!" I text Brent to come eat lunch and take a seat across from the little ones. Sammy has cheese sauce all over her face and half a nugget in each hand. I love her.

Troy peers around the couch, watching me. I smile at him and scoop a bite into my mouth. Having grown up in a house with foster kids, I know a lot of them have trust issues but I'm not used to being put with the adults. I was a kid when I left, barely eighteen, and most kids didn't see me as intimidating. It hurts my heart to see him questioning if he can trust me.

"What's your favorite dino nuggie?" I ask him, lifting two different shapes to show him. "Mine is the pterodactyl."

Brent comes down the stairs and waits at the hallway entrance for the kid to see him. "Naw, stegosauruses is the best one," he says and Troy's gaze jumps to him.

"Raaawr!" Sammy yells, holding up a T-Rex missing a tail.

"Can I eat lunch with you?" Brent asks Troy. The little boy looks between us then nods, pointing at the table. Brent smiles a big, happy smile. "Thanks."

He walks slowly and sits down next to me then dips his long-neck dino into ketchup. Brent and I eat, laughing with Sammy when we make our nuggies fight. It takes a minute but Troy climbs up into his booster and starts eating. He's cautious and that's okay. I can be patient.

Maybe being raised the way I did prepared me for Joey. I know how to stay calm, take it slow, let him get used to me.

"Raawww," Troy says quietly, his T-Rex up by his face as he watches me.

I pick up one of mine and hold it the same way, rawring quietly back to him. The little boy smiles and it lights up his whole face. Behind him, Mom smiles and leans on the counter to watch. I'm guessing he doesn't warm up quickly to anyone, so it's good to see him interacting.

By the time we're done eating, Troy has decided I'm his new best friend, which is just fine with me. Since it stopped raining, we put on shoes and jackets and head outside to kick a ball around and run some energy out before nap time.

Troy takes my hand and walks with me out onto the patio then down the steps to the grass that's more moss. Perfect for little ones to fall on and not get hurt. The trees are all bare and the sky is gray, but I find the soccer ball and pass it to Sammy while Troy holds my hand.

"Come on, we gotta go get it," I say as I turn us around to go after the ball Sammy kicked. "You wanna kick it?"

"Yeah," he whispers and when we get to it, he runs and kicks it back toward his sister. She shrieks with delight and we continue on for a few minutes until they both get bored. Sammy decides it's a lot more fun to chase me anyway. I pretend to yell in terror and run, Troy giggles and runs with me. The sound is pure happiness and it sets my heart free.

I wish Joey was here to see it. I bet he would fall in love with Troy and Sammy instantly.

I wonder if he wants to have kids someday or if he's done since he raised his siblings...

"All right, guys, time to come in and calm down," Mom calls from the sliding back door. Sammy takes off for her, throwing herself into Mom's arms. She covers the little girl's face in kisses while she laughs and laughs.

"Up," Troy says, lifting his arms to me.

I pick him up and hold him on my hip but he pulls himself across my chest to lie on my shoulder. Holding him snuggly against me, I rub his back and before I get inside, he's asleep.

Since the kids are in toddler beds and Troy does *not* want me to put him down, I end up laying on my old bed with him snuggled up against me and Brent reading behind me. It only takes a few seconds for me to pass out too.

I'M shaken awake by Brent shoving my shoulder.

"Wh-what?" I try to blink my eyes open but they are *heavy.*

"Joey is on the phone." He shoves the phone in my face and I squint at the offending brightness.

"Oh hey." I scrub at my face and try to move but I'm squished between Brent and Troy. "I'm stuck."

Brent huffs but gets up so I can move, hopefully without waking the little man. Once I've tiptoed out of the room, I take a better look at Joey. My smile falling instantly at the look on his face. It's somewhere between betrayed, hurt, and pissed off.

"What? What's wrong?" My heart drops into my stomach, and I stop halfway down the stairs. What happened now?

"Are you fucking serious?"

My head blanks. What did I do? "What?"

"Your fuck buddy answered your phone!" The yell that comes from him makes me jump.

"Fuck buddy? No, no, no. That's Brent, my brother." Brent's cackle can be heard from the living room and I jog the last few steps to look into the living room to glare at him. "I would never cheat on you."

"Brother?" He's skeptical, some of the anger fading from his face, and the tension in his shoulders dropping. "You don't look alike."

"He was a foster kid in my house growing up, but he was family from the second he walked in the door."

"Aww punk'in." Brent looks over the back of the couch and cocks his head.

"I'm going to knock you out," I point at him as I head to the kitchen for some water. Sammy is already up, having a snack and playing with blocks.

"Where's Troy?" Mom asks when she sees me.

"Still asleep."

She's taken aback and her eyes widen. "Really? That's weird. I hope he's not getting sick."

"Who's Troy?" Joey asks, a little suspicious.

"He's a three-year-old my parents have right now."

Joey's cheeks pinken and it's so fucking adorable.

"I think you would really like them. Sammy and Troy are twins and opposites in every possible way."

Sammy turns when she hears her name and smiles at me. "Bock!"

She holds up a purple rubber block and I sit with her on the floor to stack them.

"You like kids?" I ask Joey as I build a tower that Sammy immediately knocks down.

"It's been a while since I was around ones that young but she's adorable." I set up my phone against some books so he can watch. She gets her face right up against the screen and screeches in laughter when he does the same.

"How's it going there? You want to talk about it?"

"No, I want you to distract me."

The tone of Joey's voice, almost stern, definitely needy, has my body responding. Fuck, I want to touch him, taste his cum, feel his skin heat against mine.

"Just a second, kid," I say in a rush and grab my phone to head out to the garage where I can hopefully have some privacy. "Are you somewhere private?"

I find a spot to sit in the garage and prop my phone up on the steel shelf where the boxes of Christmas shit lives. It's definitely been organized in here since I saw it last.

On the screen, I can see the rhythmic motion of Joey's shoulders as he jacks off.

"Oh fuck, baby, are you getting a head start?"

From the concentration lines on his face, and way he's squeezing his eyes shut, he's trying but failing.

"Joey." I put some command in my voice and he looks at me. "Did you ask to touch yourself? That dick is mine, hands off until I tell you otherwise."

His breathing deepens and his shoulders relax. There he is. Relaxing into the power exchange. It's sexy as fuck the way he does it without hesitation.

"Tell me what you would do if I were there with you right now." I pull my chubbed-up cock out and lazily stroke it. "Drop to your knees so you can worship my cock with your mouth? Stretch out your hole for me to use, over and over, until I'm satisfied?"

He shudders, the red blush of arousal starting to blossom at the bottom of his neck.

"Yes, both." He licks his bottom lip. "Fuck my mouth then my ass. Take me. Use me."

"Where? In your dorm room? The locker room where anyone can catch us? The stairs? The stands of the football stadium?" I've always wanted to fuck on the fifty-yard line, actually...

"Dorms." His face is red now, the blush having crawled up his thick neck. "So we can fuck more than once without interruption." Joey's breathing is getting faster and I can watch the muscles in his arms flex as he clenches his fists.

"Pinch your nipples." I love watching him comply. He bunches the T-shirt in his armpits, showing me the strong muscles of his chest and stomach as he pulls and pinches on the sensitive skin.

It's not long before his hips are rocking, unable to keep them still. Knowing that I've done this to him with just words has my hand speeding up.

"You're such a needy little slut, aren't you?"

Joey bites his lip and whimpers, "Yes."

"Show me how close you are. You gonna come for me?" The need to come is forcing my body to tense. I don't want to come before him and have him lose momentum but, my God, he's so fucking perfect.

"Daddy, I want to come." That quiet little voice is pure lust in my veins. "I need to touch myself, please?"

"You want to touch what's mine?"

His breathing hitches and he slides farther down whatever he's sitting on. "Yes, please," he begs.

"Show me. Show me what's mine while you come." The screen rotates and he's set the phone on something that appears to be at the end of a bed so I can see his entire body, thighs spread with his pants and underwear at his knees. Fuck, he looks half wrecked.

"Spit in your hand and jack yourself off like I would."

He complies immediately, stroking himself quickly with hard twists of his wrist. His tip is deliciously purple, the veins standing out as tempting ridges I want to lick, and his balls are full and heavy. The sound of flesh on flesh comes through the speaker and I speed up to match his pace.

"Good boy, knees wider. Show me your hole."

He pulls one foot from his clothes and spreads his legs wider. It's not a clear view but it's enough.

"Suck on your middle two fingers, choke on them." The words are a harsh demand but he loves it as much as I do. When he gags on his fingers, my orgasm threatens to overtake me. "Such a good little cock-sucker. You're going to come gagging on your fingers and pretending it's my dick."

His words are garbled when he says, "Yes, Daddy," but I understand them. My eyes are zeroed in on his fingers, how he pushes them as far into his mouth as he can, then slides them out some. He's fucking his mouth and it's got me fucked up. I *need* to fuck his throat, use his hair to hold him still, and make him take all of me until I fill his stomach with cum.

"Hng! Un! Fungk!" Cum splatters on his stomach and chest as saliva drips from his chin.

"Fuck, you're so goddamn good for me," I moan as I come onto my shirt. How I get this off without smearing cum all over everything is future Nick's problem. Right now, I'm coming with my boy and nothing else matters.

He's panting and relaxed against the wall, his face still a mess but his fingers no longer in his mouth. There's a tired smile on his lips that I want to kiss.

"That was hot as fuck," he mumbles.

I smile at him, taking in the dopey relaxation wafting off him. It's these little moments, when his head is quiet, and he can breathe, that I'm most proud of myself.

"Will you do that, for real?" He looks down, chewing on his lip a little.

"Do what? Fuck your throat?" My dick twitches at the very thought.

He doesn't raise his head but he glances at the phone and nods.

"Oh, baby boy, I would love nothing more than to feel you gag around me." I smirk at him as he pointedly doesn't look at me while cleaning himself up. "Dirty boy."

Once he's straightened his clothes, he grabs the phone and lies down, positioning the phone like I'm next to him.

"I wish you were here." There's something on his face, an emotion I'm not sure of.

"I wish you were here with me instead." I fold up my shirt and manage to get it off without smearing cum across myself. "I think you would like Brent and my mom would love you."

"You have a good relationship with your mom?"

I don't know how to answer that. Not really. I love her. I know she loves me. But...I wish I had been a higher priority sometimes. The kids who came into our home were broken more times than not, traumatized by the life they had lived, but I needed her too.

"Your silence tells me no."

"No, it's nothing crazy. I love her and I know she loves me," I sigh and try to find the right words. "I think she thought I didn't need her as much as the other kids, so I wasn't a top priority like they were."

Joey nods and starts to respond when there's a knocking, probably on his door.

"Yeah?" The telltale sound of a hinge squeaks before a female voice speaks. I can't hear what she says but he sighs and sits up. "Okay, I'm coming." He looks at me again. "I gotta go, Matt is being a dick and his surgeon wants an X-ray of his ankle since he keeps falling on it, so I have to go deal with him."

"Okay, I'll be here if you want to talk later." I wink at him. "And feel free to send me more fantasies."

He blushes but says goodbye and hangs up. I fucking hate this distance.

CHAPTER 35

joey

Talking to Nick is hard. I have to be strong here, take on everyone's shit, and never break. There's no space for it.

But I'm exhausted by it.

Nick lets me fall apart, lets me need him, encourages it even. The shell of who I am in this house doesn't fit anymore. It's too small, too tight, suffocating. I don't want to wear it anymore, but I don't know who I am here without it. I've worn this costume for so long, how do I change it? Sometimes it feels like it's become attached to me, like a growth, maybe tattooed into my skin, so I can't escape it. At school, with the team, the mask is similar, familiar. Until I'm alone with Nick. He sees past the front to the core of who I am and reaches out for the broken kid who never got a chance to grieve. The broken kid who's afraid of a hand up, afraid of comfort, but craves it just the same. I crave it. Crave him. Crave who I'm allowed to be when I'm with him.

My phone goes off with a text notification from Brendon Oiler.

OILER:

Theoretically, if rotting chicken was found in someone's dorm, and if the person who put it there was proven, would it get that person kicked off the team?

What the actual fuck.

CARPPY:

I swear to God, if you put raw chicken in someone's dorm, I'm not saving you from Coach.

OILER:

What???

I would never.

I can't believe you would think that of me.

CARPPY:

Where is Paul? Do I have to call Preston or is it his room you want to fuck with?

I love this guy but he's a mess.

OILER:

I mean, I've thought about messing with P Man BUT he's scary.

Leaning against the kitchen counter, I sigh and shake my head. While the season is over, some of the guys still come to me when they have issues. I was the captain this year and I've been here for four years, the guys know me, respect me, and trust me. Usually.

The oven starts beeping so I put my phone away and hope against hope that Brendon doesn't put chicken in someone's dorm room. I should probably text Paul...

"Damn, that smells amazing!" Charlotte comes in, sniffing the air. "Do I smell garlic bread too?"

I set the lasagna on the stove to cool, the cheese melted and bubbling, while I cook the bread.

"Of course."

Charlotte sets the table without having to be asked. It was always one of her tasks. I cooked, she set the table, and Matt was supposed to do dishes but more times than not, I did them. He couldn't be bothered to help. Hell, most of the time he would eat in his room anyway.

Matt hobbles his way to a chair and plops down in it. "Where's the boy toy? He still in nursing school?" The sarcastic tone grates on my nerves and I've had it with his shit.

"At least he's doing something with his life," she snaps. "You know, other than being a burden on everyone around him."

"He's a fucking lame ass," Matt scoffs.

"Shut up, Mathew." My tone is hard but not full of emotion. It's cold.

"Why? What do you care? You're just gonna leave in a few days anyway, right? Stop pretending to care about any of us."

"What the hell, Matt?" Charlotte crosses her arms on the other side of the table. "You and Mom seem to be the only ones who *don't* see how much Joey does for this family. Do you really think he would be here, taking care of you during spring break, if he didn't care?"

Matt shoves the chair back and awkwardly gets to his feet. "Sorry I'm such a *burden.*"

"You *are* a fucking burden! To literally everyone around you! How do you not see that?" Charlotte isn't holding back anymore and a part of me is struggling to let her go after him like this. Mom has always protected him and blamed anything he did wrong on me. He was the baby, he didn't know any better, he's just a kid.

I interrupt the two of them, talking over both as they yell at each other. "You know what, I'm done."

Heading upstairs, I grab all my stuff and shove it back into my bag, then stomp my way down the stairs. "Char, can I stay with you tonight? I'll get a bus back to school tomorrow."

She's looking at me in shock, but snaps out of it when I head to the front of the house. The front door opens and Mom stops in the doorway, eyeing my bag.

"Where do you think you're going?" She looks behind me, seeing Matt standing with his crutches at the table and Charlotte with her stuff behind me. "You're not done here, Matt's not ready to be left alone all day."

Steeling my spine, I square my shoulders and tell my mother what I should have years ago. "I am not my father and I am done raising your children."

I clench my jaw, forcing myself to hold back the tears that are threatening to choke me. How many times have I told Charlotte to ignore Mom's calls? To leave town? Time to put my money where my mouth is and take my own advice.

"How dare you talk to me that way!" Mom's face flushes with anger as she comes toward me. "You are an ungrateful, spoiled brat who never learned to put others above yourself! You didn't raise my kids, I did! Alone! With no help!"

"Bullshit. I've bent over backward for this family, raising my siblings while you worked to pay off medical bills. Me. Not you. Char has always understood that. You were the unreliable one and Matt decided I was the one to punish for all of it. I was the only one who didn't get to grieve the death of *my* father. I promised him I would step up, be the man of the house, watch over Matt and Char. I did all of that while you worked. You were *never* there. I will not allow you to take any more of my life."

She rears back and slaps me across the cheek. The sting is immediate, quickly followed by heat, and I'm left staring at the wall instead of my mother. Charlotte gasps behind me then moves around me to start screaming at her.

Slowly, I turn my head to look at her but I don't say a word, just let her stand there with what she's done hanging between us like a suffocating cloud.

Determination has me pushing past her and walking away. Away from my childhood. Away from the woman who took advantage of me for years. Away from the anchor of my past that kept me chained in the dark.

It's time for the light. For the future. For Nick.

The ride to Charlotte's is quiet. Both of us are in our own heads, processing what happened. When she parks in the driveway and turns off the car, we just sit there.

"The guest room is kind of a mess but the sheets are clean." Her voice is quiet.

"Thank you."

She nods and we get out, I grab my bag and follow her inside the little yellow bungalow with white porch railings. It's so perfectly her that it almost makes me smile. Maybe tomorrow I can smile again, but not tonight.

Tonight, I mourn the burial of my old life.

Without a word, I head to the room she indicated and close the door. There's boxes, college text books, and a sewing machine kind of thrown around in here but the bed is clear and I can get to it. That's all that matters.

Dropping my bag, I toe off my shoes and text Nick.

JOEY:

Are you busy?

NICK:

Never too busy for you.

JOEY:

Can I call?

My phone buzzes with an incoming video call. When the video starts, it's Nick's concerned face and a little boy snuggling into his chest. It's the most precious thing I've ever seen and I burst into tears.

Covering my eyes with my free hand, I let the sobs take me, the tears race down my cheeks, and I purge the built-up emotions. Nick doesn't say anything, he's just there. I don't know how long it takes but by the time the tears slow and I can breathe again, my throat is sore, my mouth is dry, and my eyes ache.

"There you are." Nick's voice is soft and reassuring when I glance at the screen, but I can't hold his gaze, not yet.

"Sad," a little voice says and I look at the phone to see the little boy in his lap pointing at the phone.

"Yeah, he is sad. It's okay to be sad sometimes." Nick rubs the little boy's back in a comforting rhythm.

"I left my mom's house, left Matt." The words sound like I've been gurgling gravel but Nick understands them.

"What happened?"

There's a giggle in the background from another little kid and the sound lifts the corners of my lips.

"I was making dinner, Matt started running his mouth. Char and Matt got into it and I don't know. I snapped, I guess, and decided I was done. Mom came in as I was leaving. I told her I was done raising her kids, she slapped me, and I left."

"What?! She hit you?" Nick's anger is like a physical touch. It flares in his eyes and tightens his body. The little boy in his lap flinches and Nick takes a minute to force himself to relax his body. "You're okay, buddy, you're safe."

"You mad?" he asks quietly, looking like he's expecting to be screamed at. The very idea makes me want to pummel whoever put that look on his face.

"I am mad, but not at you." Nick rubs his back again. When he settles again, Nick turns back to me. Seeing him take care of this little boy that he's never met is...everything. Nick was made to be a dad.

"You should have kids." The words blurt out of my mouth before I've thought about it. "You're amazing with him."

Nick smiles and hugs the little man. "It's definitely not outside the realm of possibility." He looks at me, dragging his eyes over every inch of my face. "Is there anything I can do? Are you okay?"

I shrug and sigh, lying back on the bed and holding the phone above me. "I'm going back to school tomorrow. I have to find a bus ticket." I'm exhausted and just want to sleep for a week.

"Where are you right now?"

"Charlotte's house."

"Good."

CHAPTER 36

nick

When the call with Joey ends, Brent looks at me for all of about ten seconds before he sighs. "You're flying out, aren't you?"

"I have to."

He nods and goes back to reading with Sammy on the floor. It's fun to see him with a toddler. I know he doesn't want kids but I think he would be a good dad. These two are special, though. There's something about them that makes my heart yell *mine.* I'll have to talk to Mom about what their situation is and if they'll have parental rights severed at some point. I can't stay in Colorado, I have to come back here for them.

It's a while later, after the kids are in bed, that Mom finds me packing my bag.

"Are you leaving already?"

"Yeah, I have to get back to school. Joey needs me." I don't take my focus off making sure I have everything.

"Oh, okay. Well, I'll see you for graduation then."

I turn and look at her. If Joey can stand up to his parents, maybe I can ask her about Emma.

"Do—" I take a deep breath before letting the words out. "Do you know what really happened to Emma? Did you know that night and just not want to tell me?"

She sighs heavily, leaning on the doorjamb. "I reported it again that night. You were so heartbroken over it that I knew there had to be something. Courtney, our case worker, told me that when they went in the next morning, she was gone and so was all her stuff." She shrugs, guilt weighing on her. "I searched her name for years, looking for any kind of information. Looked into Jane Does that were found around the area too. About two years ago, a skeleton was found in the woods about two miles from us that could be her but they've not confirmed DNA. I didn't want to say anything until I knew for sure."

Despite knowing in my heart that she was probably dead, it hurts to hear. It's not for sure until there's DNA but it's not likely she's alive. I nod, hating the answer, but knowing I don't have a choice but to accept it.

"Thank you."

"I'm sorry."

Getting up, I go to her, hugging her tightly. She cries into my chest, wrapping her arms around me and holding me just as tightly. Watching her purge the guilt she's carried for years has a knot forming in my throat and my chest tightening. It's a physical weight she's lugged around for six years. It wasn't her burden to carry.

"I'm sorry I couldn't fix it, Nicky," she cries. "I tried but there was nothing else I could do without putting the kids here at risk."

In the doorway of my childhood bedroom, we cling to each other and search for the comfort we needed all those years ago.

"Seeing you fall apart, it broke my heart. At that point, you leaned so heavily on Brent that when I tried to comfort you, you shrugged away. So I stopped trying."

"It's okay, Momma." I hate how the system has fucked over those who *actually* care and want to help. So many hands are tied. Now, as an adult, I know she couldn't have snagged Emma and kept her here without permission. She could have lost all the kids living here and had her foster license pulled. Hell, she could have been arrested for kidnapping if it got bad enough. "I'm sorry I put you in that position. That wasn't fair."

"Nothing about the situation was fair. To any of us." Lifting her head back to look at me, she cups my wet cheeks with tears trailing down her own face. "I love you, you know that, right? Always. Forever."

I can't breathe past the knot in my throat so I just nod. She pulls my head down to kiss my forehead then wraps her arms around my neck in a hug.

"I'm so proud of the man you've become."

"Thank you," I murmur.

"But you have to go, don't you?"

"Yeah."

She cups my cheeks again, this time smiling. "Okay. I want to meet him at some point, understand?"

"Joey. His name is Joey."

"You said that already. I don't care what his name is, I want to meet him." She steps back and I wipe at my face while chuckling.

"Yes, ma'am."

She wipes the tears from her face too and leans on the doorjamb. "Troy and Sammy are gonna miss you, so don't be a stranger, you hear me?"

While I finish packing, I ask about their situation and if they'll be available for adoption. If they are, I'm moving back here after graduation so I can be in their lives and start the process of getting custody of them. It can take a while but I'll wait as long as I need to. I need them just as much as I need Joey. Fuck, I hope he wants kids.

CHAPTER 37

joey

Sitting at the kitchen table in my sister's house is weird. She's such an adult. Her fiancé was up and gone before I got up but I can tell how much he loves her by the way she talks about him. The pictures all over the house show it too. She's happy here and it's all I've ever wanted for her.

She's making breakfast at the stove while I drink a cup of coffee. The bacon is sizzling away and making my mouth water. Charlotte is chatting away, talking about the flowers she wants to plant in the front yard and maybe some veggies in the backyard. I've never known her to want to garden but she's excited about it and I love that.

She's pulling bacon off the stove when the doorbell rings.

"Are you expecting someone?" I ask as I head toward it.

"Nope."

Matt is standing on the porch, leaning on his crutches, looking rumled and uneasy.

"Hey," he says, barely making eye contact.

I cross my arms and wait. If he thinks he's coming in here to sleep on Char's couch, he's got another think coming.

"Are you gonna let me in?"

"Depends on what you're here for."

He huffs and clenches his jaw. "I just want to talk to you for a minute."

I raise an eyebrow. "You aren't here to try to weasel your way onto Char's couch?"

"No. She's too damn peppy in the morning. It's unnatural."

That gets a chuckle because he's not wrong.

I step aside and give him room to enter.

"Who is it?" Char yells from the kitchen.

"It's Matt."

Her head pops into the hallway with a raised eyebrow. "Oh."

"For fuck's sake, I'm not that bad."

Char and I share a look that says otherwise but she tells him to come in and have a seat.

It's quiet, awkward, now with Matt sitting at the table with me while Char finishes cooking. I get him a cup of coffee but no one really says anything.

She gets the food plated and I bring it to the table for her while she grabs silverware.

"Okay, spill it, why are you here?" Char demands.

Matt looks between us and his shoulders droop as he sets his fork down on the table. He looks at his hands when he speaks. "You were right. Last night, when you said I took it out on you that Dad was gone and Mom had fucked off." He takes a shaky breath. "I know I'm a fuckup and if I don't get my shit together, I'm going to ruin my life or die. I'm sorry."

Char is obviously holding back tears while I fight with myself to let him off the hook and tell him it's okay. It's not, and fuck that hurts.

"We've relied on you for too long, demanded you sacrifice more than your fair share." He looks at me and I can feel how much he means it. It's not just words he's using to manipulate, he's thought about this and is actually trying.

"We all made sacrifices when Dad died."

"No," he shakes his head, "it was mostly you. Mom relied too much on you, Char tried to help but she relied on you too. I didn't do anything but cause you more problems. Hell, I'm still causing everyone problems."

Getting up from my chair, I reach for him and wrap my arms around his shoulders. He clings to me and for the first time in a long time, I have hope.

"I punished you for not being Dad, I'm sorry," he cries into my shirt.

"You were grieving, I understood," I say through my own tears.

"You never got that chance and the rest of us did."

Charlotte comes around the table and joins in our tear-filled hug. "We love you, even when you're a pain in the ass. Which is most of the time."

He chuckles and sniffs, wiping at his face as we break apart.

Char is dabbing at her eyes with a napkin, careful not to mess up her makeup or whatever, but she's got a big smile on her face.

"I think I should go to therapy and start taking AA seriously," Matt says once we've all taken a seat again. He's pushing the food around his plate and not looking at us.

"That's a good idea," I tell him. "It probably wouldn't hurt any of us to talk to someone."

Char nods. "I'll go too."

Matt smiles and shoves some bacon in his mouth.

For the next two hours, we share memories, spill some tea, laugh, and even cry some. By the time I have to get ready to head to the bus station, I feel lighter than I have in...ever? There's hope that things will get better, at least for the three of us. Matt will stumble, make mistakes, but if he really wants to change, he will. I know he will. As long as he's trying, Char and I will support him through the changes he needs to make to ensure his life is better.

Charlotte hugs me at the bus depot and I settle in for the drive. Luckily, I'm used to traveling by bus, though the ones I've been on with the team are full of my teammates and can get loud. This is dingy and quiet and not many people talk. It smells like dust and sweat in here, the air is somehow stale, and I wish I could cover my seat in plastic before I sit on it for the next four hours.

Pulling out my phone, I text Nick a picture of me with Char and Matt that we took right before I left.

JOEY:

So, I have news.

NICK:

That looks like good news…

JOEY:

Matt is going to go to therapy and AA. He wants to clean his shit up.

NICK:

Dude! That's fucking awesome! What brought that around?

JOEY:

Probably me ripping into Mom last night and her slapping me.

NICK:

I hate that that's what it took, but I'm glad he's realizing it.

The bus pulls away from the depot and we're off. It's just the beginning of a long afternoon and I'm already tired of being on this damn bus.

JOEY:

Me too. Anyway, I'm on the bus back to campus. When are you coming back?

NICK:

My ticket isn't until Sunday.

JOEY:

NICK:

The fuck? Did you just give me the 'fuck you' thumbs up?

I laugh so hard I snort. Tears fill my eyes and I can't catch my breath.

JOEY:

No?

NICK:

The fuck you didn't. You're gonna pay for that. 😈

JOEY:

Don't tempt me with a good time...

It takes a minute but a video pops up of Nick, so I grab some earbuds to listen to it.

"It's all fun and games until you're desperate to come but I'm not done with you yet." Nick's stern voice in my ears sends a shiver across my body and the look in his molten brown eyes promises pleasure. The video call we had the other day flashes in my mind and my dick perks up. I really can't wait for this. There's something so hot about being used by him and I desperately want to get back to it.

With a huff and burning cheeks, I turn toward the window and try to arrange myself so I can get a clear picture of my lap without looking like a creep. Pretty sure I fail. But I manage to get an image of my hand cupping my dick through my jeans.

NICK:

Fuck that's hot, baby.

JOEY:

Are you hard?

NICK:

For you? Always.

I stifle a groan and curse the length of this bus ride. Why can't it be faster?

JOEY:

I guess I'll have to jack off when I get back. There's no way I'm waiting until you get back.

NICK:

You better call me so I can watch.

A wicked smile curves my lips and I take a selfie to send him, biting my lip, cheeks pink, and looking ready for debauchery.

JOEY:

We'll see...

NICK:

Look at you, ready to be used. Fuuuuck. You're gonna make me jack off right here in the mall.

When I get there, you better be stretched and lubed up, ready to be fucked hard.

I squirm a little in my seat, not that there's much room in these small-ass chairs. Charter buses are not made for athletes. My knees are against the seat in front of me and my ass barely fits between the armrests.

JOEY:

I'm hard on a bus. I hate you.

NICK:

I'm hard in public. There're kids in here and I'm wearing sweatpants!

JOEY:

I crack up at the mental image of him trying to cover the tent in front of his pants. Man, I hope he's with his parents. That would be amazing.

JOEY:

Why are you at the mall? Reliving your high school days? Trying to pick up a high school chick?

NICK:

Fuck you. I did not pick up chicks at the mall in high school. I was getting blowies under the stadium bleachers like the other football players.

JOEY:

Classy. You're a real class act.

NICK:

Like you weren't doing the same thing in the ice rink!

Thinking back on those years, I can say that is one thing I never did. I never hooked up at the rink.

JOEY:

Nope, some of us didn't have time for shenanigans. I was busy trying to keep my brother out of juvie. And the ER.

NICK:

You never fooled around in the bleachers? Or the locker room?

JOEY:

Nope.

NICK:

Well, we're fixing that. Pronto.

I chuckle and shake my head.

JOEY:

The season is over.

NICK:

Look at all the fucks I don't give. You're not graduating without at least getting your dick sucked in that building. It can't happen.

JOEY:

WTF is wrong with you?

NICK:

IDK but you seem to like whatever it is so that says more about you than it does about me.

I sigh and lean my head back against the seat.

JOEY:

You aren't wrong.

A notification pops up in the chat.

Joey's nickname has been changed to Good Boy
Nick's nickname has been changed to Daddy

GOOD BOY:

Really?

DADDY:

Yup.

GOOD BOY:

You're a menace.

DADDY:

Yeah but I'm your menace.

His response has warmth blossoming in my chest. Makes butterflies dance in my stomach.

GOOD BOY:

Does that mean we're officially in a relationship? Like you're my boyfriend?

I chew on the inside of my lip as I wait for his response.

DADDY:

Baby, you were mine that first night in the bar. You just didn't know it yet. Label it however you want to. You're mine and I don't share.

GOOD BOY:

Good.

We chat for the rest of my trip and by the time I get to the dorms, I'm exhausted. Bryce stayed for break so he's probably in our room, which is not where I want to be anyway. I want Nick.

DADDY:

Did you make it back?

GOOD BOY:

Yeah but I don't want to be in my room, it doesn't smell like you.

DADDY:

I hid a key to my room in your desk.

I perk up at that, hustling up to the fifth floor and fumbling my way into my room.

GOOD BOY:

Seriously? When? Why?

DADDY:

A few weeks ago. IDK it felt important to have it there.

With a big smile on my face, I grab a change of clothes and take a quick shower.

Bryce is laid out on his bed when I come out.

"Hey, man, I didn't expect you to be back for a few more days." He pauses the show on his laptop and looks back at me. "Your brother okay?"

"Yeah, he's doing okay. I decided I had enough family time." I grab my phone, charger, and keys. "I'm gonna crash in Nick's room. Later."

He lifts a skeptical eyebrow at me but doesn't comment.

As soon as I get to Nick's room, the calming scent of him wafts over me and I fall face first into his bed.

CHAPTER 38

nick

It's late when I sneak into my own dorm room. I texted Neal earlier to make sure he wasn't coming back tonight or tomorrow before I left SeaTac so I know we won't be rudely interrupted.

The door closes with a soft click and I set my bag down carefully before stripping down to my boxers and sliding into bed with Joey. He's on his side, facing the wall, so I wrap myself around him and sigh. He jolts when I touch him but I *shhh* him back to sleep.

With my cheek pressed between his shoulders, I inhale his clean scent and my entire body relaxes. He's here with me. It's all I've needed for days. To know beyond a shadow of doubt that he's okay.

I fall asleep quickly with a smile on my face.

The next time I can think, there's a very insistent jock rubbing his hard cock against my hip. Sometime in the night, I ended up on my back with Joey half on top of me, his thigh currently dragging across my balls every time he thrusts his hips. His breath is hot against my neck, his whimpers filling my ears.

"Ung hunf fuck."

I'm awake now. My boy is about to come already? Fuck yes.

"Gimme your mouth," I croak. Joey shivers, latching onto the top of my shoulder and sucking on the skin hard enough I hiss. "That's not what I meant and you know it."

I grab his hair, pulling his head back, but he doesn't break the suction. My dick throbs at the dull pain mixing with the pleasure in my groin. Reaching for my dick, I jack myself, needing to get off with him. Him waking up needing me this much is hot as fuck.

Joey's hips pick up speed, which makes his thigh rub my balls faster. It feels so goddamn good.

"Dirty boy, are you gonna come in your underwear?"

He lets out a sound that's somewhere between a whimper and a sob but nods his head and finally releases my skin.

"Give me your fucking mouth. Those sounds are mine."

He shivers but adjusts so he can reach my mouth.

I don't care about the morning breath, it disappears in a minute anyway. I need his moans in my lungs. I need his pleasure to fill my soul.

Joey slides his hands under my back to grip my shoulders and uses the leverage to get better pressure on his aching dick. My boy grunts and whines into me, making me feel alive, breathe life into my heart, chase the darkness from my soul.

I love you.

The words whispered in my head have me wobbling on the precipice of orgasm. I fucking love him. It's as terrifying as it is exhilarating.

His face is red, glistening with sweat and lust. I love how he's using my body to get himself off.

"I. Fuck. Hung ah. Coming." Goosebumps erupt on his skin and he shivers as he comes. God damn, it's a beautiful sight, watching him lose himself to pleasure. It makes me want to cuddle him, fuck him harder, and paint him with my cum.

His thrusts slow down until he stops and he drops his forehead to mine, panting and flushed and glassy-eyed.

"You're so fucking hot when you're cum-drunk." I smirk at him, still pulling on my dick. Joey huffs a laugh and looks down at my hand and bites his lip.

"Want a hand with that?" He gives me a cheeky grin and I love that too.

"Put your mouth on me." I nip at his lip and he slides down my body to settle between my legs. With his eyes on mine, he cups my balls and rolls them in his hand before licking up the bottom of my cock.

"Choke me with it."

Fuck.

Gripping his hair, I pull his mouth onto me. The urge to be balls deep in his throat is strong and I really want to know if he can do it. I give him some test thrusts before I change my mind and want a different angle.

"Hang on," I say as I pull him off and he pouts. "On your back, head off the edge."

He hustles to obey and grimaces when he lays on his back.

"What's wrong?"

"Cum is making my underwear sticky and slimy. It's fine." He opens his mouth and sticks his tongue out. I don't even try to hold back my groan. Holding my cock, I feed it to him. Thrusting shallow at first before testing his limits. He's clearly getting irritated with me because he wraps his arms around my thighs and pulls me in deeper.

My eyes roll back and I let out a "Fuck" on a moan. Leaning on his chest, I watch my dick stretch his throat. In, out, in, out. Joey gags and when I try to pull back, he tightens his grip on my thighs. God damn, this boy is going to be the death of me.

If he wants me to fuck his throat, I will.

I pick up a little speed, a little more force, and he groans. Fucking groans.

"Such a good boy," I moan. His noises vibrate my cock and it takes me three more thrusts before I'm coming in his throat. He doesn't bat an eye, just swallows around me, making my toes curl. "Fuck, you're never leaving me."

My body is weak in the aftermath of having my soul sucked out through my dick but I want to taste him too. It's been too long since I had him on my lips.

I pull my cock from his mouth but don't move to let him up, instead I reach for his pants. He stiffens a little and I hesitate to give him a chance to tell me no, but when he doesn't, I continue. His trimmed pubes are a sticky mess and so is his soft cock. I want it in my mouth. Lifting onto my toes, I lean over him and manage to get the head of his dick to my lips. He gasps when my tongue swirls around the tip and under his foreskin. I groan at the salty tang of him.

He lets me play with him, licking and sucking on anything I can reach. I let him go when he starts to chub up.

He glares at me but sits up. "I need a shower."

"Yeah, you do."

I grab his neck and pull him to me for another kiss, sharing his taste with him and getting some of my own. He brings his body to mine, making as much of our skin touch as possible, and wrapping his arms around my back to keep me close. The kiss is slow but intimate. It's deep and calming and sensual. It's reconnecting. I don't know how long we stand there, just absorbing the comfort of being together, but when I release his mouth, my lips are chapped and his are swollen.

"Shower with me?" He's chewing on the inside of his lip again like he's not sure I'll say yes. Silly boy.

I wink at him and grab his hand, leading him to the bathroom.

ONCE WE'RE CLEANED UP, he goes to his room to get clothes. I see his teammates, Paul and Brendon, and have an idea.

"Hey, I have a favor," I tell them and they look suspicious. Okay, Paul does, whereas Brendon looks excited.

"What's up?" Paul asks.

"Can I borrow your car for an hour or so?"

He narrows his eyes at me. I get it, he doesn't know me well. "For what?"

"An errand. I'll bring you a cinnamon roll..."

Brendon immediately perks up. "Give him the keys, P Man."

Paul sighs and shakes his head but gives me the keys.

"If you don't come back with a cinnamon roll, I will be your worst nightmare." Brendon pokes me in the chest, and I believe him. He's so random that I believe he could actually fuck with me.

"I promise."

A smile breaks out on his face and he bounds away to the elevator with Paul muttering something about puppies behind him.

Joey comes out of his room and looks at me suspiciously. "Why are you standing out here alone, like a creeper?"

"I was talking to Paul and Brendon." I hold up the keys. "Come on, I have plans."

"That should make me nervous, shouldn't it?"

"Oh, absolutely."

But he follows me out of the building and while it takes us a minute to find the car, we do, and I head to the bakery. I need a hug from Debbi and some pastries.

"I don't want to hide you anymore," Joey says, forcing nonchalance. When I glance at him, he's picking at his fingers and chewing on that damn lip again. He's out to the team, since half of them saw me kiss him, and no one gossips like jocks, but I don't know about his family or anyone else.

"That's cool, I'm here for it." I'm really past the point of anyone giving a shit about my sex life. "Does that mean I can introduce you to someone important to me?"

He glances at me, a soft smile on his face, and nods. "Yeah, I would like that."

While the light is red, I give him a quick kiss and squeeze his thigh.

Since Joey wasn't with us when Brendon and Paul met Debbi, he doesn't know where we're headed until he sees the bakery name, Whisk Me Away.

"No."

I smile like the Cheshire cat. "Yes."

"I cannot face that woman after you ate her dessert off my dick!" He points toward the shop like I don't know who he's talking about.

"She doesn't know that unless you tell her." I pat his cheek. "If you're easily embarrassed, I suggest not telling her that."

I climb out of the car and turn to see Joey in the front seat with his arms crossed. Pulling open his door, I duck down to look at him.

"If you don't come in and meet her, she'll think you hate her, and her pastries." I shrug. "Up to you."

Joey growls but pushes me back so he can get out.

"Good boy."

"I hate you."

"No, you don't." I wink at him and open the door for him to enter. The little bell on the handle rings and Debbi pops her head out of the back.

"Nick!" She dusts her hand off on her apron and comes around the counter to give me a hug. I hug her right back, not giving a single fuck if I'm covered in flour afterward. "It's been too long. How are you?"

"I'm good, busy trying to finish my classes."

I watch Joey inspect the display cases like he's from the health department and stifle a snort. It's so painfully obvious that he's trying to avoid talking to her.

She glances over at him too and gives me a weird look. I smile and shake my head before loudly saying, "This is my boyfriend, Joey."

Joey spins around to stare at me, wide-eyed, but a little smile is tugging on his lips. I wink at him and Debbi gives him a big smile.

"It's so nice to meet you!" She reaches for him and he gives her a hug with red darkening his cheeks. It's cute as fuck.

"It's nice to meet you too," Joey stammers and when she steps back, I reach for his hand to bring him to me.

"I introduced him to your amazing cinnamon rolls, along with some of the other guys on his hockey team." I wink at him and the blush is now crawling down his neck. It's so fun to embarrass him. "Any chance you've got some today?"

She waves a hand at him. "Of course I do, they're my best seller."

Joey groans quietly and I cough into my hand to hide my laugh.

"I hate you so much right now," he whispers in my ear.

"Not as much as you're going to."

He groans out loud this time and I snort. Fuck, I love this.

"What else do you have today?" I step up the glass display and take in all the options while my mind goes crazy. "Donuts, we're going to need some of those too." I turn to look at a very red-faced Joey. "Do you think Brendon would like donuts? He seems to like... everything."

"I'm sure he would enjoy donuts."

"I already promised him a cinnamon roll." Debbi gets a box down and sets it up for my order. "Okay, I'm going to need three cinnamon rolls, six donuts—two frosted, two chocolate, two old-fashioned—two apple fritters, and... a croissant."

Joey sighs and steps up next to me. "You do realize that Brendon is going to attempt to eat half of this box?"

"I'll distract him, trust me."

"Oh God," Joey says under his breath.

Debbi gets it all packed up for me, and gives me a massive discount, which I add to her tip jar. She comes around the counter and gives me a kiss on the cheek.

"Don't be a stranger, you hear me? And take some business cards for the boys who need more pastries," she says with a wink. Joey takes the cards and puts them in his back pocket. "You too, don't be a stranger. It was good to meet you."

Joey smiles at her and gives her a hug. "It was nice to finally meet the infamous cinnamon roll baker."

She laughs and we say goodbye.

We're almost to the car when Joey says, "I'm not fucking another cinnamon roll."

"How do we feel about bagels? Donuts? Danish? Apple fritter?" I ask him seriously, because I have plans. Lots of delicious plans.

"What the hell is wrong with you?" He turns his back to the car and leans against it with his arms crossed.

"What? I like my pastries with a side of dick." Duh.

"You're broken."

"Don't yuck my yum." I lean into him, holding the box to the side so I can get close.

"I'm not yucking nothing."

"Good, then get in the car, open your pants, and let me suck your dick until we give this donut a new glaze." The fact that heat flares in Joey's eyes is a damn miracle. Fuck, I love this guy.

He reaches into my pocket, eyes locked on mine, and grabs the keys.

"I think you owe me road head for embarrassing the shit out of me in there." He quirks a brow and, yeah, fair is fair.

"Done, get that glorious dick out." I hustle to the passenger side, putting the bakery box in the back seat and grabbing a donut with icing on it. Joey adjusts the seat so I have room to suck his dick.

"Why is this so hot? You've ruined me for baked goods." Joey eyes the donut in my hand as he opens his pants and releases his beautiful cock. I really could worship this thing like it's a god.

I'm basically salivating for the taste of him.

I watch him stroke himself a few times before I can't take it anymore and slap his hand away. "Mine," I growl into his ear while I slide the donut down his shaft. He groans into my neck and my own dick aches. "I love how you take what I give you, let me play with you however I want. Such an obedient boy for me, aren't you?"

"Yes," he moans as I stroke him.

"Look at yourself, look at how hard you are for me."

He looks down at his lap, at the donut around the base of his dick that split in order to accommodate his girth.

"Your cock is fucking perfect." I nip at his earlobe then bend down to lick him. I slip my tongue between his foreskin and the head of his cock. The taste of his skin is more intense here, it's my favorite part. Humming, I surround his head with my mouth and he gasps, his hips jerking upward. "So needy."

Sliding my mouth down the underside of his shaft, I take a bite of the donut then lick back up to his tip.

"Please," he groans, his fingers flexing on my neck.

"Please what? Ask nicely." I cup his sack and stroke him with my hand, sitting up to put us eye to eye.

"Please, Daddy," he whimpers in that voice he knows gets me. "Suck me and make me come."

I drag my teeth over my lower lip and pulse my grip on him. He's trying so hard to keep eye contact but there's something that makes it hard for him, maybe he's embarrassed by having to ask? Or for liking it when I make him do it? That's a convo for another time.

Bending back down, I suck him as deep into my mouth as I can, using my hand to make up the difference. Joey shouts out his surprise and slams his hand on the steering wheel, gripping it so hard the plastic creaks.

He's a mess of noises, groans becoming whimpers that become moans. His hips keep moving like he can't keep them still, and fuck if I don't love the pride it gives me. I did this to him. Me. No one else. Hell, no one before me gave enough of a shit to try. This man was made for me and I am going to make damn sure he knows it.

Since we're sitting in a public parking lot, I work him up fast and sloppy. The last thing I want is to get arrested for indecent exposure or something out here. Saliva drips down his beautiful, throbbing dick as I work him over.

"Daddy..." he whines and I hum around him. He digs his hand in my hair and flexes his hips to meet my mouth. Filling my mouth a pump later with cum. Luckily, I emptied his tanks once already today so there isn't much and I don't miss a damn drop. After ripping the donut off, I lick him clean and thoroughly enjoy the combination of him and sweet icing.

When I sit back in my seat, a smug smile on my face, he snickers and puts his dick away. I get my seat belt buckled and start eating the donut.

"Seriously?" he asks while starting the car and backing out of the parking spot.

"I'm not wasting a perfectly good donut, especially because it was on your dick. These things must be savored and enjoyed." I shove another piece in my mouth and offer him one.

He glances at me skeptically but takes the piece and chews quickly. "It's weird to eat food that was basically a masturbatory aid."

I shrug and finish the piece in my mouth. "How is it different than putting olives or raspberries on your fingers and eating those?"

It's quiet for a minute before Joey bursts out laughing. Full-on belly laughing. It's a glorious sound, one I need to be able to play whenever I want. Grabbing my phone, I start recording him laughing while he drives. When he stops at a stop sign, he lays his forehead on the steering wheel for a second.

"It's completely different!"

"Only because an olive would not fit, you would destroy it if you tried." But the idea is kind of hot now that I think about it…

"Were you dropped on your head as a baby?" He gets the car parked at the dorm and turns to look at me.

"How is it different? You're sticking food on a body part and eating it."

"Because my fingers aren't part of my reproductive system? They aren't a sex organ?"

"Clearly you aren't using your fingers to their full potential." I open the door and get out, grabbing the box of deliciousness from the back seat. "Let's go give Brendon his treats, I have more plans for you."

"More? There's no way in *hell* I'm getting off again today." He holds the door open for me like a gentleman. Adorable.

"You got off twice, I did not." While we wait for the elevator, I motion to my crotch which is still half hard. "And I haven't had your ass in far too long. Time to rectify that."

CHAPTER 39

joey

A few hours later, Nick has a stomachache from all the sweets, my ass has been used spectacularly, and we're now watching a movie on the TV.

Nick is fidgeting, won't keep still, which is making me nervous. When he sighs for the twentieth time, I pause the movie.

"What is your problem?"

"I want you to move to Washington with me after graduation."

I blink at him as I process that since it's definitely not what I was expecting.

"You—" I sit up so I can look at him clearly. "You want to live with me?"

Nick sits up too, confusion obvious on his gorgeous face. "Uh. Yeah. Obviously."

"How is it obvious? What did I miss?"

He watches me for a minute, like he's looking for something or trying to figure out if I'm messing with him.

"I guess you missed that I love you." He shrugs. "You missed that you're it for me and I will make damn sure that I'm it for you."

Emotions build in my chest, excitement and fear battling for dominance until I'm choking on it. "How do you know?"

Nick holds my hand and laces our fingers together. "How do I know what?"

"That I'm it for you. How do you know you aren't going to get tired of my issues and start hating me for them?"

He thinks for a minute, taking my question seriously, which I appreciate.

"Sometimes, I might get frustrated but it would be weird if I didn't. Same for you. If you don't get tired of my shit sometimes, it would be weird. But that doesn't mean I won't want you. Or that I won't love you."

Tears fill my eyes and one falls down my cheek. Nick cups my face and brushes it away.

"One more thing, I hope you want kids, because I desperately want to adopt the twins my parents currently have. They were made to be mine, just like you were. I need all of you." Nick lifts onto his knees and pulls me against him, kissing me delicately. "What do you say?"

"Is it weird that I'm relieved I don't have to come up with a plan for after graduation?" I laugh through the emotions clogging my throat.

He smiles and kisses my lips again. "Don't worry, baby, I've got you."

I tackle him to the bed while he laughs. For the first time, I'm excited about the future, about what it holds. Matt seems to be taking this all seriously; he found a therapist and starts seeing her next week, and Char said he's gone to three AA meetings since I left. I'm proud of him but the real test will be when something goes wrong. I hope he's able to lean on us and stay strong.

"I love you too," I whisper into Nick's skin. I've never said those words to anyone but my family. They scare the shit out of me. He scares the shit out of me. "I want to move to Washington and meet these kids you're in love with. I want a future with you."

"I hear a but coming."

"But I'm scared."

Nick lifts my chin so I'm looking at him and drags his thumb across my lip. "Oh, I'm scared too. You're a flight risk, dude. But wanting you is stronger than the fear." He cups my cheek and I lean into the touch. "If you need me to be brave for you for a while, I will. Lean on me, I'll protect you. Even from yourself."

Sliding up his body, I kiss him with a smile on my lips. He wraps a leg around one of mine, anchoring me to him, and I've never felt safer.

"You can't die before me, okay?" I say against his mouth.

"I'll do the best I can but if I do, you can't turn into a workaholic and ignore our kids, okay?" Nick grips my chin, keeping me from kissing him.

"I guess, if you insist."

"Oh, I do insist."

The smile on his face fades as he looks at me. The light mood shifting to something thicker. I don't know what this look means.

"What is it?"

His eyebrows pull together, creasing his forehead. "I think I need to tell you about someone."

I sit up, giving him room to sit up too, and wait. My skin feels too tight as I prepare myself for a story he obviously has big emotions about. It doesn't feel like a happy story either.

"When I was sixteen, there was a girl who lived a street over from me. Her name was Emma and I was in love with her." Nick lifts his head to lock eyes with me. Dread fills me for him. I don't know what happened to this girl, but it clearly still haunts him.

As he tells me the story of this girl, he reaches for my hand. I don't hesitate to intertwine our fingers, giving him any comfort I'm able to. He tells me about the bruises, about the tears, and the fears. My heart hurts for him, for the pain he clearly still carries.

"The last time I saw her, I gave her my football necklace. It meant the world to me and I wanted her to have physical proof that she mattered to me." Nick gets off the bed and digs through his bag for a minute before coming back to sit next to me on the bed. He squeezes it in his hand for a minute before opening it to show me the tarnished chain with a football helmet charm hanging from it. "One of the other kids in the house brought it to me when I tried to pick her up for school. He told me she had left but wanted me to have that back." His glassy eyes meet mine. "She didn't leave. She's still there somewhere. Lost in the woods where that bastard hid her."

The vein in his jaw jumps when he clenches his jaw and a tear falls from his eye.

"I'm telling you this because I need you to know that you're not the only one scared. The last person I loved was taken from me. There one day and gone the next." He sucks in a shuddering breath. "And what I feel for you is so much bigger. I'm *terrified* of losing you but I'm taking the risk because having you is worth it."

June
Graduation

Nerves hum along my skin as I wait for my turn to get my diploma. The purple gown and cap feel weird. How are they not heavier? Graduating from college should feel heavier, shouldn't it? The necklace in my pocket is heavy. I got the football necklace cleaned and replated for Nick and I can't wait to give it to him.

At twenty-five, I should have my life figured out, right? I'm an adult, about to have a degree, was the captain of my hockey team, but I feel like a kid pretending to be an adult. Is that normal?

"Joey Carpenter." My name is announced but I don't hear anything past the rushing of my heartbeat in my ears. I walk up the stairs, shake hands with some people I couldn't care less about, take the diploma, move my tassel, and leave the stage.

The grin stretching my face almost hurts it's so big. I fucking did it. Somehow, against a fuck ton of odds, I did it. On my way back to my seat, I look around for Nick, but I don't know where he's at. I want him with me, though.

The rest of the names are called, there's a short speech, and we're introduced as the latest graduating class of Darby University. Everyone throws their caps, standing and cheering, and I'm right along with them. A weight has been lifted from my shoulders, a sense of pride for accomplishing this.

"Carppy!" I turn when I hear my teammates yelling my nickname after we've been released into the wild. Brendon tackles me, wrapping his arms around my waist, and forcing a grunt from me when the hit takes the air from my lungs. "Congrats, Cappy Cap!"

I laugh and give him a hug. "Thanks."

Jeremy and Paul both give me hugs too; Preston gives me a handshake and growls when I hug Jeremy.

"Not gonna be the same without you next year," Jeremy says.

"You were a great captain." Paul pats my shoulder.

"P Dawg can*not* be captain next year. He would kill all of us." Brendon shudders and we all laugh except Preston. He just rolls his eyes at Brendon's nickname.

The rest of the team surrounds us, giving me slaps on the back, words of encouragement, and wishes of good luck, until my sister's shrill scream cuts through the crowd.

"Joey!"

Charlotte and Matt are smiling at me, both give me hugs, and start dragging me away from the crowd. I quickly scan the crowd but I don't see Mom. Not that I really expected her to come, but a small part of me was hopeful. I haven't spoken to her since I walked out of her house during spring break. Char said she hasn't talked to Mom either besides to tell her off. It didn't go well for anyone, apparently. Matt was staying with her for a while but has moved out and gotten a job. I'm so proud of both of them.

"Beers at Rocky's tonight!" Brendon yells, and I give him a thumbs-up.

"When do you guys leave for Washington?" Matt asks as we head toward the prearranged meetup spot I have with Nick.

"Next week," I tell him but the second I lay eyes on my man, I run for him. He meets me halfway and we slam into each other. "We did it."

"We did. I'm so proud of you, baby." Nick cups the back of my neck and squeezes.

"Right back at you." I kiss his cheek. "I love you."

"I love you too."

I reach into my pocket for the velvet bag and take his hand to place it into.

He lifts a brow at me, flicking his gaze between me and the bag. "What's this?"

I open the bag and upend it on his palm.

The smirk on his face falls as he looks at it, weighs it in his hand, then closes his fingers around it.

"Our past can shape us, the good and the bad. She was a part of your past, but I think it might be time to start remembering the good parts of her, not just the sad ones." Opening his hand, I pick up the chain and slide it over his head to hang from his neck. "And I will help you hire a private investigator or whatever we have to, if you want to go looking for Emma. I want you to be able to find closure."

"It's perfect." He smiles, placing his hand over it. "You're perfect." I kiss his forehead and give him a hug.

"Uh, remember how you love me?" Nick says in my ear. "Keep that in mind..."

Pulling back, I cock my head, confused, until he turns me around and Debbi is standing there with a bakery box. My face immediately turns hot. Son of a bitch.

"Debbi!" Nick moves around me to give the older woman a hug. "You made it."

"I did," she says, but her tone is a little off. "Here you are, dear." She hands him a box and he turns a devilish smirk on me. "Yes, congratulations to you both." She pats him and gives me a very awkward hug.

"Thank you," I mumble. I don't know what is happening or why. "Is something wrong?"

Her cheeks turn a little pink and she fumbles over her words. "Well. Of course. No. It's not." She huffs a breath then shakes her head. "It's none of my business, dear." The tight-lipped smile makes me very uncomfortable.

Nick is watching her now too. "What's not? Miss Debbi, do you have gossip that you aren't sharing with me?"

She scoffs. "No, I certainly do not." Debbi slaps at his arm. "But," she lowers her voice, "you should be more careful about where you have *special* time. You know? Windows are pretty *see-through.*"

Nick looks dumbstruck for a minute while I swear all the blood drains out of my face. Oh. My. Fucking. God.

She saw us in the parking lot.

I can feel how wide my eyes are but I can't do anything about it. I'm going to vomit. It's a good thing we're moving because I can never look at this woman in the face again.

"I mean, really, a parking lot?"

Nick starts to cackle. It's not long before he's doubled over, leaning on his knees, wheezing from laughing so hard, while I'm having an existential crisis.

"I was worried you were having car trouble," she tells him earnestly. "But that wasn't it..."

I'm going to burst into flames. Right here on the grass. My tombstone will read 'graduated from college only to spontaneously combust via embarrassment' and it's entirely Nick's fault. The bastard.

He's dropped to the ground now, wiping tears from his eyes, as he shrieks with laughter. People are turning to stare at him, which only makes this all worse.

"Miss Debbi," I start, trying to find the words to apologize for her seeing me desecrate her pastry. "I am *so sorry.*"

Charlotte and Matt are standing back, watching the humiliation of their older brother, and I just don't know how I'm still alive. How has my heart not stopped? How is this my life?

"Nicholas, get off the ground, you animal." Mrs. Wyhe scorns Nick who still can't seem to catch his breath. He's holding his stomach and still laughing. Asshole. And I am just so glad this could be the exact moment I meet his family for the first time in person. Sure, why not?

I'm going to have a nervous breakdown, and it's noon.

"Joey." Mrs. Wyhe smiles at me and reaches for a hug. "Congratulations, love."

With mortification the only thing keeping color in my face, I give her a hug.

"Thank you. It's great to finally meet you in person."

Mr. Wyhe gives me a strong hug. "I'm proud of you boys." He cups the back of my head and the memory I get of my dad is so strong, it steals my breath. I cling to the big man for a second, fighting my memories. It's not often I meet someone bigger than me, at least not one who isn't a hockey player, but this man *feels* bigger. He *feels* like a dad. I barely remember what it felt like the last time I hugged my dad.

He must recognize that I need this because he doesn't try to let go. The strength of his hold doesn't waver. My eyes fill once again and I let them. This moment right here is healing something I didn't realize was still broken. A hidden scar I didn't know was still open.

A small hand touches my back and I sniff back the tears, turning to my sister. Her eyes are glassy with emotion too, a watery smile on her lips.

"You okay?"

I nod, wiping at my damp skin. "Yeah. He gives really good dad hugs." I point my thumb over my shoulder at him and try to laugh.

"Oh." Charlotte's voice wavers a little.

Mr. Wyhe opens his arms in invitation and Charlotte launches herself at him. He catches her with a smile and a small chuckle, wrapping his big arms around her as she cries into his chest.

I make room for them, and Mrs. Wyhe pulls me into her again. She kisses my cheek and Nick finally drags his ass off the lawn, brushing grass and dirt from his gown while holding a curly blond-haired boy. Troy.

"This is the best day ever," Nick says, smacking a kiss on my lips. Troy has wrapped himself around Nick, his head under Nick's chin so he's protected but can still watch.

"You're so making this up to me later," I mumble and duck down to look at the little boy. "Hey, Troy, I'm Joey." I give him a little wave. "Do you remember talking to me on the phone with Nick?"

He sinks into Nick a little farther but nods, and I give him a big smile.

"See these two?" I point to Charlotte and Matt. "That's my sister and brother. Do you have a brother or sister?" I know the answer but there's something about this little man that makes me want to get him to like me.

He picks his head up and looks around, then points toward Mrs. Wyhe. I exaggerate looking for the other child and gasp when I see the little girl with stick straight dark hair and warm brown eyes.

"Her?" I double-check with Troy and he nods at me. Dropping down to a crouch, I look at the little girl. "Hi, I'm Joey. You must be Troy's sister."

She giggles and jumps on me.

"Sammy." She smiles and points to herself. She starts talking and I only understand half of it, but I love it. She's so animated. The little girl glows.

Standing up with Sammy in my arms, I look at Nick, and everything clicks into place. This is all I need. Nick was right, there's something so damn special about these kids. They were made for us. I don't know what tragedy brought them to the Wyhes but I know I will die to protect them. We take pictures—a ton of pictures—and eat pastries, and I don't stop smiling the whole time.

Leaning into Nick, I press my forehead to his. "I don't know what the future holds, but I know there's no one else I would rather find out with than you."

He kisses the tip of my nose. "Doesn't matter what the future holds, we'll handle it. Together."

ACKNOWLEDGEMENTS

Honestly, this book is for the readers. For everyone who read Nick and Joey in the Worthy anthology and wanted more. This book is for you. I didn't plan to write them a full book. I thought they were done but you guys weren't done with them.

To my alpha readers, Kayla and Robin, thank you is not enough. I couldn't have done this without you. Kayla, you put in so much work and I honestly don't know how I got so lucky.

BSS you're unwavering support and encouragement held me together somedays. Vikki, Lisa, and Angela for proofing, and Colleen for beta reading, you guys are my rockstars.

For everyone else who kicked my ass into gear, refused to let me give up, refused to let me sink into anxiety and fear, and pushed me to finish, thank you.

Andi

ALSO BY ANDI JAXON

Darby U Boys

Hidden Scars

Blurred Lines

Bennet Family Novels

Rescue Me

Curves Ahead (MF)

Standalone

Broken

CoWritten Works with J.R. Gray

On Guard

ABOUT ANDI JAXON

Sarcastic and snarky, I love to laugh and read dark fucked up shit. I write about tortured pasts and hot sex, a happily ever after that has to be worked for. My stories tend to be a little dark but with some comic relief, typically in the form of sarcasm and usually include two men falling in love.

Made in the USA
Las Vegas, NV
30 November 2024

2f580f5e-6cfc-4b42-af27-5d59f1c440f6R01